"Come in, if you dare."

Ashley peeked around the edge of the door. "I can come back later if this is a bad time."

"Don't even think about it." Kyle walked out of the kitchen, a glass of water in one hand, Casey riding the opposite hip. He was barefoot, unshaven, dressed in a stained T-shirt and a pair of gym shorts adorned with fuzz from Casey's new baby blanket.

But Casey was smiling at him and clenching her fingers about his nose. He pried her fingers loose and tickled her tummy. She laughed out loud and then poked a thumb into her mouth and rested her head on Kyle's shoulder.

Something tightened in Ashley's chest and she found it difficult to breathe.

"I know I look like something Mikasa dragged in from beneath the stairwell," he said, "but you don't have to stare at me like that."

She kept staring, mesmerized. She'd never seen him look worse. She'd never wanted a man more. The feeling scared her to death. She took a step backward.

"Do I look that bad?"

"No, you look—fine."

"Now you're lying for sure. But lie all you want. Just don't leave, unless you want to hear a grown man cry."

Dear Reader,

I was thrilled when I was invited to be part of the TRUEBLOOD, TEXAS continuity project, and it turned out to be as much fun as I expected. Not only did I team up with some great writers, but I got to help create the wonderful Garrett family. They reminded me so much of some of the warm and close-knit Texas families I know. It was easy for me to understand how growing up as a Garrett would have a profound effect on forming my heroine's character. I loved watching Ashley Garrett unfold and change as she interacted not only with her family, but with her sexy but complex neighbor and the precious, abandoned baby girl. By the time the story concluded, they had all walked off the pages and into my heart. I hope the characters in *Surprise Package* touch you as they did me.

I love to hear from readers. You can write me at P.O. Box 2851, Harvey, LA, or e-mail me at JoannaWayne@msn.com.

Joanna Wayne

TRUEBLOOD, TEXAS

Joanna Wayne

Surprise Package

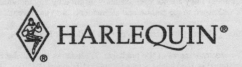

HARLEQUIN®

TORONTO • NEW YORK • LONDON
AMSTERDAM • PARIS • SYDNEY • HAMBURG
STOCKHOLM • ATHENS • TOKYO • MILAN • MADRID
PRAGUE • WARSAW • BUDAPEST • AUCKLAND

Joanna Wayne is acknowledged
as the author of this work.

I'd like to give special acknowledgment to Rick Redmann for his valuable input on the business of advertising. I'd also like to thank Emilie Richards, who taught the creative writing class that got me started writing romantic suspense and remains a wonderful friend. And to Wayne, always.

HARLEQUIN BOOKS
225 Duncan Mill Road, Don Mills,
Ontario, Canada M3B 3K9

ISBN 0-373-65086-8

SURPRISE PACKAGE

Visit us at www.eHarlequin.com

Printed in U.S.A.

TRUEBLOOD, TEXAS

THE TRUEBLOOD LEGACY

THE YEAR WAS 1918, and the Great War in Europe still raged, but Esau Porter was heading home to Texas.

The young sergeant arrived at his parents' ranch northwest of San Antonio on a Sunday night, only the celebration didn't go off as planned. Most of the townsfolk of Carmelita had come out to welcome Esau home, but when they saw the sorry condition of the boy, they gave their respects quickly and left.

The fever got so bad so fast that Mrs. Porter hardly knew what to do. By Monday night, before the doctor from San Antonio made it into town, Esau was dead.

The Porter family grieved. How could their son have survived the German peril, only to burn up and die in his own bed? It wasn't much of a surprise when Mrs. Porter took to her bed on Wednesday. But it was a hell of a shock when half the residents of Carmelita came down with the horrible illness. House after house was hit by death, and all the townspeople could do was pray for salvation.

None came. By the end of the year, over one hundred souls had perished. The influenza virus took those in the prime of life, leaving behind an unprecedented number of orphans. And the virus knew no boundaries. By the time the threat had passed, more than thirty-seven million people had succumbed worldwide.

But in one house, there was still hope.

Isabella Trueblood had come to Carmelita in the late 1800s with her father, blacksmith Saul Trueblood, and her mother, Teresa Collier Trueblood. The family had traveled from Indiana, leaving their Quaker roots behind.

Young Isabella grew up to be an intelligent woman who had a gift for healing and storytelling. Her dreams centered on the boy next door, Foster Carter, the son of Chester and Grace.

Just before the bad times came in 1918, Foster asked Isabella to be his wife, and the future of the Carter spread was secured. It was a happy union, and the future looked bright for the young couple.

Two years later, not one of their relatives was alive. How the young couple had survived was a miracle. And during the epidemic, Isabella and Foster had taken in more than twenty-two orphaned children from all over the county. They fed them, clothed them, taught them as if they were blood kin.

Then Isabella became pregnant, but there were complications. Love for her handsome son, Josiah, born in 1920, wasn't enough to stop her from growing weaker by the day. Knowing she couldn't leave her husband to tend to all the children if she died, she set out to find families for each one of her orphaned charges.

And so the Trueblood Foundation was born. Named in memory of Isabella's parents, it would become famous all over Texas. Some of the orphaned children went to strangers, but many were reunited with their families. After reading notices in newspapers and church bulletins, aunts, uncles, cousins and grandparents rushed to Carmelita to find the young ones they'd given up for dead.

Toward the end of Isabella's life, she'd brought together more than thirty families, and not just her orphans. Many others, old and young, made their way to her doorstep, and Isabella turned no one away.

At her death, the town's name was changed to Trueblood, in her honor. For years to come, her simple grave was adorned with flowers on the anniversary of her death, grateful tokens of appreciation from the families she had brought together.

Isabella's son, Josiah, grew into a fine rancher and married Rebecca Montgomery in 1938. They had a daughter, Elizabeth Trueblood Carter, in 1940. Elizabeth married her neighbor William Garrett in 1965, and gave birth to twins Lily and Dylan in 1971, and daughter Ashley a few years later. Home was the Double G ranch, about ten miles from Trueblood proper, and the Garrett children grew up listening to stories of their famous great-grandmother, Isabella. Because they were Truebloods, they knew that they, too, had a sacred duty to carry on the tradition passed down to them: finding lost souls and reuniting loved ones.

CHAPTER ONE

COWBOYS. Ranchers. Cattle. Beef.

Ashley Garrett typed in the words, Times New Roman font, eighteen point, and ran them across the page in the shape of a galloping horse.

Her mission was to put them all together and come up with an ad campaign and a slogan that was so terrific it would be on the lips and in the minds of every Texas citizen. In the process, she would put her name on the map—along with the Texas Ranchers Association, of course.

This was her biggest account to date, a chance to leap a few rungs up the advertising success ladder and put her one step closer to some swanky office on Manhattan's famed Madison Avenue. Let other women marry and cook pot roasts. She'd influence what their kids wore, the kind of car they drove and where they'd buy their groceries.

But for now, it was sell the Texas Ranchers Association. Sell beef. Sell an image. The task had seemed so easy when Mr. Clintock of Clintock, Mitchum and O'Connell had offered her the plum account. Four days later, she was drowning in insipid, languishing in schmaltz, when what she needed was a spark of genius. Of course, she'd let the Creative Department guys in on the fun eventually, but she wanted to be the mind behind the idea, not just a facilitator.

Stretching her fingers and placing them back on her trusty keyboard, she prepared herself for another go at releasing a rush of ingenious juices. When in doubt, start with a cowboy. They were sexy, virile, rugged, totally masculine. Except for the ones who were dirty, sweaty and smelled of cattle droppings.

"Wrong mind-set, Ashley Garrett."

Talking to herself again—a sure sign she'd been punching keys and staring at the screen on her computer too long. Fingering her favorite silver bracelet, she glanced at the chrome office clock on the wall over her file cabinet. Six-thirty. No wonder the office was so quiet.

Everyone else had gone back to their cozy suburban homes, where, according to someone's statistics, they could enjoy their four bedrooms, two baths, two and a half children, one dog, one cat and two goldfish. Or else they'd headed over to happy hour at the hotel bar across the street so they could fortify themselves to face their mate and two and a half kids. To each his own.

She had a session scheduled with her *personal* trainer at seven. She loved saying that. It sounded so impressive. Not that she could afford him on a regular basis, but after one session, she'd been so excited about the results that her brother Dylan had made exercise her Christmas present. He was springing for three months of sessions, two per week. She had six weeks to go, and she could already see progress. By summer, she'd be able to do great things for a bikini.

In a matter of minutes, she'd flicked off her monitor, turned her daily calendar to the next day's page and straightened her desk, readying it for the morning. Organization was a key factor in maintaining the level of professional excellence she demanded of herself.

Standing, she ran a hand down her skirt, ironing the pleats with her fingers so that they lay straight. The suit was teal, the fabric a silk blend, the workmanship exquisite. The price tag had blown her budget to heck and back, but she couldn't resist it. Work was her passion, but clothes ran a close second.

The phone rang just as she grabbed her briefcase and threw the leather strap over her shoulder. She considered ignoring it, but thought better of it. It might be her pregnant sister Lily, and who knew what a woman with a stomach the size of a bloated beach ball might need?

"Clintock, Mitchum and O'Connell, Ashley Garrett speaking."

"So this is where you spend your evenings. What a waste."

The voice was male and unfamiliar. "May I ask who's calling?"

"Guess I didn't make as much of an impression on you as you did on me this morning. I'd recognize that soft, feminine voice of yours anywhere. This is Jim Bob McAllister."

"Mr. McAllister?"

"Yes ma'am. It's me."

The Mr. McAllister from the Ranchers Association. She hadn't recognized his voice, but she'd make it a point to the next time he called. "What can I do for you?"

"I've been thinking about what we talked about in our meeting, you know, about how to help folks see beef in a new, much more acceptable light. Anyway, I made a few notes this afternoon and I'd like to toss them around with you."

"Great. You know what you want. I'm just here to put your desires into a total image package. I can see you tomorrow, any time that's convenient for you."

"I'd rather make it tonight."

Yuck. She'd spent an hour with him this morning, and enough was enough. "Are you still in town?"

"Afraid so. I had hoped to drive back to the ranch this afternoon, but my business took longer than I'd planned.

So, since I'm still stuck here, how about talking over dinner? My treat.''

"That's not necessary.''

"It is to me, little lady. I don't cotton to women taking out a wallet when they're out with Jim Bob McAllister.''

Little lady! Gag me with a spoon. But if he wanted to talk business, she couldn't very well turn him down. "Are you sure you wouldn't rather fax me your ideas? That way you could spend your evening in town with friends and not devote it to business.''

"No, once I get something galloping around in my mind, I just can't let it go till I've put the horse in the stall.''

Which meant there wasn't an easy way out of this. It could be worse. She'd met him on several occasions before today, mostly at Ranchers Association functions that she'd attended with her dad.

He was a respected rancher and around the same age as her father. Surely he wouldn't grope her thigh under the table like the last client had after he'd insisted she join him for dinner to discuss the *scope* of the campaign. She'd told him as nicely as the situation allowed just what he should do with his scope.

"Dinner would be fine, Mr. McAllister, if we can make it around eight-fifteen. Can I meet you somewhere?''

She wrote down the name and address of the restaurant. The office was quiet as she locked up and headed toward the elevator. The parking lot would be even quieter, almost deserted this time of night. It never used to bother her, but ever since her self-acclaimed secret admirer had started leaving cards and flowers attached to her windshield, she was a bit uneasy when leaving the office alone.

Not that she was afraid. It hadn't happened all that often and the cards were harmless enough, probably someone's idea of a joke. Besides, her brother Dylan was an ex-cop and he had made sure she was well-trained in the art of self-defense. Pity the poor mugger who mistook her for an easy target.

Still, she walked to her car quickly, anxious to get to the health club as soon as possible so she could finish her session before she met Mr. McAllister.

ASHLEY PUSHED the breath from her lungs as she pulled her body up in yet another stomach crunch.

"That's the way," Bernie encouraged. "Use the stomach muscles, no stress on the back and neck."

"How many more?" she gasped between breaths.

"Don't think of it in numbers. Just get in the rhythm of crunch-release. And think what a taut stomach you're going to have, not that your figure isn't already great."

"Then why am I paying for this torture?"

"You're not. Your brother is. One more. *Crrrunch* and down and stop."

She groaned and stayed flat on her back until Bernie took her hands and tugged her to a sitting position.

"We've worked on your abs, your stomach and your upper thighs," he said. "I guess that about does it for this session. Now you can go out and party the night away."

"Not me. I'm pretty much a dud."

"Really, I never heard that about you, but I did hear that you're a workaholic."

"Who would you hear that from?"

He glanced across the room to where her neighbor Kyle Blackstone was leaning against a weight machine, chatting with a couple of bosomy females in form-fitting tights and clingy tops.

"You surely don't believe everything Kyle says."

"I don't, but the women sure hang on his every word. You're about the only one in here who doesn't drool when he shows them a little attention."

Kyle caught her looking at him and waved. She hated that, but she waved back in what she hoped was a nonchalant, offhand manner. He started over, and her pulse shot up. No need for aerobics when he was around. But she had no intention of letting him know he had that effect on her. He was far too sure of himself as it was. She'd just as soon Bernie not know, either.

"The man spends a lot of time watching you," Bernie said. "Have you ever been out with him?"

"No."

"Good. You have a lot more class than those bimbos that follow him around like groupies chasing a rock star."

"He's not my type."

"I don't think you've convinced him of that yet."

"He's only interested because he thinks I'm a challenge." She groaned as she pulled her stressed muscles into a standing position. "Thanks for the session, though I feel like I've been run over by a truck."

"No pain, no gain. It's trite but true."

Kyle stepped up beside her. "That was quite a workout. If you need someone to massage those aching muscles tonight, I'm available."

"And just which muscles do you plan on massaging?"

"You name it. I'm very accommodating."

"I'll just bet you are."

"Well, if you don't want a massage, how about dinner? There's a new Italian restaurant just a block from our building. The pasta is *eccellente* and the vino is *squisito*." He used his hands, fingers and mouth to add emphasis to his claim.

"And I already have a dinner invitation. Just my luck," she teased.

He cocked his head to one side and flashed a devastating smile. "We can always do dessert at my place."

"Dream on."

"I already am." He closed his eyes. "Wow! You're good."

When he opened his eyes, she closed hers. "Yeah, I am, aren't I?" She gave him a playful right cuff to his upper arm. "I'm out of here. Thanks again, Bernie. And, Kyle, happy hunting. I'd hate for you to have to sleep alone tonight."

She turned and walked away, not stopping until she reached the door to the ladies' locker room. Bernie and Kyle were still standing together, immersed in conversation. Two very nice-looking men. Bernie had more of the macho build, huge shoulders, well-defined biceps, muscular arms and legs. Kyle was just lean and mean. Rock-hard body. Thick dark hair. Deep-blue eyes that a woman could drown in and never yell for help.

The man was drop-dead gorgeous—but he was not for her, and she needed to keep that thought firmly planted in her mind. The minute she became interested in a man, her life became complicated. The men either became possessive and jealous of the time she spent on her career, or else merely wanted to get her into the sack.

Without a doubt, Kyle fell in the latter category. Turning away from him, literally and figuratively, she pushed through the door of the locker room. She'd have to hurry to be at the restaurant by eight-fifteen, and it wouldn't be prudent to keep Mr. McAllister waiting.

ASHLEY STUDIED the menu. The restaurant was pricey for her expense account, but no reason to worry, since McAllister would be picking up the check. She'd offer again anyway. Mr. Clintock had informed her when he'd given her the account that he wanted the Ranchers Association to be extremely happy with both the treatment they received from all employees of the agency and the quality of the finished product.

The waiter stopped at her elbow and asked for their drink order. Jim Bob ordered a vodka martini. She ordered a glass of sparkling water with a twist of lime.

"Nonsense. You need a real drink," the rancher insisted. "Something to help you relax, so that we can get to know each other better."

"I never drink when I'm on the job."

"Then let's just call this a get-acquainted night. I always work better when I feel I'm in tune with the person I'm working with."

She cringed at the intimacy that had crept into his tone. It would never have been there if he was talking to Mr. Clintock or any of the other men connected with the firm. It was more of the "little lady" mentality that she hated. Or else Mr. McAllister was not as harmless as she'd assumed.

"What I'm most interested in are your ideas about the ad campaign," she said, making sure he realized she was here only for business purposes. "I know the Ranchers Association is eager to modernize their image."

"And Mr. Clintock assured me that you're the woman who can do that for us."

She centered her attention on the menu. By the time the waiter returned with their drinks, she'd decided on a green salad and a broiled trout filet. Jim Bob went for the steak, the largest and most expensive cut they offered, with a loaded baked potato and a side order of sautéed mushrooms. He ordered an appetizer of oysters Bienville for the two of them to share and a bottle of cabernet sauvignon with two glasses.

She waited until he'd gulped down half his martini, the time span of about four seconds, before she went back to the subject they had supposedly come to discuss. "Why don't we start with the ideas you've come up with since our meeting this morning? That will give me more insight as to how you see this working."

His mouth stretched into a smile. "I hate to talk business on an empty stomach. Why don't you tell me something about yourself? And, by the way, the color of that suit really brings out the green of your eyes."

"Thank you."

"You're welcome. Now tell me, what does an attractive little filly like you do for fun?"

"I work."

"That sounds much too boring, and I have a feeling you're not a boring lady."

"Actually, I am." She sipped her water. "But if you want to know about me, I can certainly give you the details that affect my ability to do my job. I have an undergraduate degree in graphic arts and a master's degree in commercial advertising. I've worked for Clintock, Mitchum and O'Connell for almost two years."

"And I'm sure you're very good at what you do. But you can't just work. As pretty as you are, I bet you have dozens of men on the string."

"Afraid not. I've never wanted the kind of man who would settle for dangling from a string."

"Then you must break a lot of hearts."

"None that I know of."

"I don't believe that for a second."

He scooted the candle from the center of the table. She met his gaze, hopefully achieving the look she was after. Business or nothing. "I'm sure that you're far more interested in what I can do for the Ranchers Association than you are in my personal life."

"Everything has a time and a place. Right now it sounds as if you could use more fun in your life. I know this great little club we could visit after dinner."

Another dirty old man. She'd have to nip in the bud any

ideas he had about including her in his extracurricular activities. But she couldn't nip so sharply that she drew blood, at least not if she could help it. She wanted to keep this account.

"I don't dance," she lied, "and I hate nightclubs. The smoke bothers my contact lenses. So let's talk about you. Let's see, you're *married* and have four children. Am I correct?"

His glowing ardor cooled as quickly as if she'd dumped her glass of water on his head. He downed the rest of his drink and motioned to the waiter to bring him another. After that, he sat quietly for a moment, his hand wrapped around the base of his empty glass while he stared at her from beneath his bushy, salt-and-pepper brows.

"You're correct," he said. "I have a lovely family, but that doesn't mean I can't enjoy the company of a beautiful woman. But if you're more comfortable talking strictly about business, I can do that, too."

"I appreciate that, and I want you to know that I'm committed to giving you and the association the type of modern, progressive image we discussed. I'll make sure you get what you're paying for." And that didn't include her. "So what are your ideas for the ad campaign?" she asked, determined to salvage something from the meeting besides irritation.

He rolled his fresh drink around in the glass, staring into it as if it were a crystal ball. Finally, he set it on the table and looked at her. "The association wants something bolder than we've ever had before, something that says we're happening and on the technological edge of beef production. But we don't want to lose our image as ranchers. You know, kind of John Wayne and Bill Gates rolled into one. Does that make sense to you?"

Perfectly. He wanted a miracle. And she darn well planned to give it to him, just as long as she didn't have to get any closer to him than she was right now in order to deliver.

The rest of the meal passed without incident, though she was certain from some of the looks he gave her that he was still eager to inject her *boring* life with just about anything she wanted, as long as the facts never got back to his wife.

What she wanted was to go back to her apartment and sink into her nice, comfortable bed. Alone.

IT WAS NEARLY half-past ten when the elevator stopped at the eighth floor of the Prentiss Apartment Building. The door slid open, but before Ashley stepped out, she noticed a woman rushing toward her, head down, her raven-colored hair pulled back from her face. She looked up for a second as they passed, and Ashley could see that her eyes were swollen as if she'd been crying.

"Is something wrong?" Ashley asked. "Can I help you?"

"No." Her voice wavered, and her hands were shaking as she put them up to stop the door from closing.

Ashley hesitated, then walked toward her own apartment. If the woman didn't want her help, she couldn't force it on her.

Besides, she was exhausted. Of course, she could always knock on Kyle Blackstone's door and tell him she'd come for the massage.

Or she could jump off the balcony onto the street below. It would be about the same kind of suicide. She had will-power, but not the kind that could survive Kyle Blackstone's hands roaming over her. Even the thought of it sent tingles to parts of her body that didn't need to tingle.

She walked past his door on the way to her own. A huge wicker laundry basket sat in front of his door. Probably a gift from one of his many admirers. She was

tempted to go back and peek inside but changed her mind.
It was probably better not knowing what kind of gifts
women sent that man.

Once inside her apartment, she twisted the dial of her
dimmer switch until the living area was bathed in a wel-
coming glow. Neither her brother Dylan nor her sister Lily
could ever understand how a person raised on a ranch
could consider an apartment in a high-rise in downtown
San Antonio home, but it fitted her lifestyle just fine, provided everything she needed.

She walked to the bedroom and kicked out of her black
pumps, shedding her panty hose before she took off her
suit. She draped the skirt and jacket over the hanger but
didn't bother to change into her pajamas. Her black slip
would do just fine for the activities she had planned. A
nice settling glass of wine while she worked.

Ranchers. Cattle. Beef. The words came back to ramble
through her mind as she poured a glass of chardonnay and
curled into her overstuffed chair. Ranchers. Cows. Worse
than counting sheep, she decided as her eyes grew heavy.
Her weary mind lost the power to concentrate, and instead
pictured Kyle dressed in a cowboy hat and boots.

She closed her eyes. She didn't want the man, but she
might as well enjoy the image.

ASHLEY JERKED AWAKE, spilling half a glass of wine onto
her living room carpet as she did. She'd obviously been a
lot more tired than she'd realized. Only half-awake, she
stumbled to the bathroom, wet a cloth, then hurried back
to get the stain out before it had time to set.

Down on all fours, she had pain in places she didn't
even know she had places—proof that with Bernie's help
she was working muscles she'd never worked before. And
now either she was hearing things, or there was a kitten
trying to tell her something.

She looked around the room, half expecting her neighbor's cat to poke its head from beneath the couch. Mikasa liked nothing better than to sneak in while the door was open, hide out and then pounce on Ashley when she least expected it.

The cries stopped, then started again, several decibels louder this time. But the sound was coming from the hall and not inside the apartment. Ashley stepped to the door and put her eye to the peephole. There was no sign of a cat. No sign of anything or anyone, except that basket in front of Kyle's closed door. For a second she thought it had moved, but when she blinked and looked back, it was still. Nonetheless, the noise persisted.

If it was Mikasa, she was in trouble, likely caught behind or under something and couldn't free herself. Ashley slid the dead bolt until she could open the door a crack. She peered up and down the hall, searching for some sign of the cat.

She was nowhere around. The noise had stopped as well, but the basket in front of Kyle's door was most assuredly shimmying now. She crossed to the basket and leaned over.

Ohmigosh! It definitely wasn't a cat but it was alive. An absolutely adorable baby girl—at least it looked like a girl—with chubby cheeks and the most beautiful dark brown eyes Ashley had ever seen. She fell to her knees and tugged the blanket to the side so that she could see all of the surprise package. The infant kicked her tiny feet and threw a few punches into the air.

"Don't cry, baby. Whatever's wrong, we'll find someone who can fix it."

The baby stopped whimpering and stared at Ashley, her tiny lips quivering. Poor thing. Ashley fumbled with the fastener on the safety belt that held her in the car seat. Once it was loosened, she picked up the baby and cuddled her awkwardly. If she had any maternal instincts, they'd never surfaced before, and they didn't seem to be kicking in now.

There was no telling how long the baby had been out here, but it had been at least two hours since Ashley had first noticed the basket. She was probably hungry. Or maybe she was wet or worse. Ashley reached into the basket, feeling behind the seat for some kind of instructions. Surely babies came with instructions. If they didn't, they should.

She pulled out a bag of baby supplies. Tucked beneath it was a piece of folded notebook paper. There was something written on it, but one glance and she knew it didn't contain nearly enough instructions to help out a novice like herself.

Still, she scanned the note until the crisp ring of the elevator bell alerted her she was not alone. She turned as Kyle Blackstone and a shapely brunette with half a dress stepped into the hall. As they got closer, she could see that he was with Alicia, one of his groupies from the health club.

"Oh, look. It's my neighbor, and doesn't she look maternal, especially in that little black thingy she's wearing."

Ashley glared at him. He was only a few steps away now, and the leggy brunette had draped herself over his left arm so that they looked like one body with two heads and four legs.

Kyle took his arm from around Alicia and dug in his front pocket until he pulled out his key ring. The baby started crying again. He stared first at the baby and then at Ashley. "I hope you're not at my door looking for a baby-sitter. I'm all tied up tonight. You know how it is."

She stepped between him and the door. "I know exactly how it is. I'm pretty tied up myself, so as much as I'd like to help out, *Daddy,* this baby is all yours."

For once the man was speechless.

CHAPTER TWO

KYLE STARED at Ashley. As much as he loved playing mind games with his sexy neighbor, this was carrying things too far. "Cute trick, Ashley, but I'm not even biting on this one."

"I don't call deserting an innocent baby a trick, Kyle Blackstone. I'd call it a crime."

Her usually lyrical, seductive voice struck with hard-hitting bitterness.

"I think this is a little more than I bargained for."

Alicia. For a minute he'd forgotten she was with him. Now he wished she wasn't, but he had to keep up some kind of front. "I'm sure this is a mistake."

She let go of his arm and backed away. "Why don't you call me when this *mistake* is back with its mother?"

"You don't have to leave."

"No, by all means stay," Ashley insisted. "I imagine Kyle will need some help tonight. That is unless he plans to invite the baby's mother over. Then it might get a little crowded. Of course, what's a crowd for some people is a ménage à trois for others."

"Call me later, Kyle, like when the baby starts college." Alicia turned and headed toward the elevator.

"Oops. Looks like you lost that one. She'd have to be wearing skates to escape any faster."

"Thank you, neighbor. I didn't really want to enjoy myself tonight anyway. Now, take your borrowed baby and go home." He leaned against the door. "Unless you'd like to take Alicia's place. Actually, it's the least you can do, now that I think about it.''

''You're such a romantic. No wonder the women flock to your door.''

''No, that's the result of my other talents. So, what do you say? Do you want to take that baby back to wherever you got her and join me for a nightcap?''

''You just don't get it, do you? This baby is *yours*.''

''No way. I—''

The baby started to cry, interrupting his protests. Ashley rocked the infant in her arms until it quieted, then poked the note in his face. ''This was in the basket. The message is extremely clear.''

Kyle took the note and read it slowly, panic whipping through him as the words jumped from the pages in alarming clarity.

Dear Daddy,

　　Mommy can't take care of me right now, so I'm coming to live with you. All you have to do is make sure I'm fed regularly and have a warm, safe place to sleep. Mommy put an empty bottle and a plastic pouch of my formula in the back corner of the basket. Just mix it according to the directions. There's a few diapers there, too, to get you started. You'll need to change me when I'm soiled or wet. But most of all, Daddy, I need you to love me as much as Mommy does, and to take care of me until she comes back to get me.

Your daughter

Holy smokin' gun. This was too crazy for words. It had to be some kind of sick joke. No one in their right mind would leave a baby in his care.

Ashley pushed the baby into his arms, leaving him no

recourse but to hold it. The infant wiggled and squirmed so that he was afraid he might drop it.

"Looks like you have things under control," Ashley said, but her voice had lost its acidic edge. "I'll leave you two alone."

Panic struck again, this time with the force of a huge fist to the gut. Ashley was about to walk away and leave him with this—this little person. He'd never begged before, but this seemed like a real good time to start. "Please, Ashley. You can't be heartless enough to leave me all alone with this baby. If you're not worried about me, think of the baby. I don't have a clue what to do."

"Then I guess you better call 911."

"What? And have the cops come out and arrest her?"

"They don't arrest babies."

"Well, she's a little young for the cops to give her an ice-cream cone and have her wait at the station house until her mother shows up to claim her."

"They won't do that, either. They'll call the authorities."

"What authorities?"

"How would I know."

"You're the one who said to call 911. You shouldn't give advice if you don't know what you're talking about." This was ridiculous. He was standing in the hall arguing about what to do with a baby someone had abandoned at his door. Still, the mother had asked him to take care of this baby until she came back to get her. With luck that would be in the next minute, but he sure couldn't count on it. And now she was starting to cry again.

"What do you think's wrong with her?"

"She's probably hungry, for one thing."

"Then don't you think we should feed her?"

"*We?*" She spread her hands palms up and her gorgeous green eyes flashed fire. "There is no we, Kyle. Never has been. Never will be."

The baby's cries became a loud wail. His muscles tightened and his insides bucked as if someone had force-fed him a jar of jalapeños dipped in chili powder. "Please, Ashley. I'll owe you one, anything. Just help me feed her and get her quiet."

"Anything?"

"You name it."

"Clean the grout on my kitchen floor?"

"You'll have the cleanest grout in the building," he promised. "I'll scrub it with my own toothbrush if necessary."

"Deal." Ashley took the baby from him. She didn't look much more adept at holding her than he'd felt, but she settled the baby on her shoulder, and after a few pats on the back, the baby stopped crying.

"That's right, sweetie. Ashley has you now, and she's going to help your daddy fix your formula."

"I'm not her daddy," he said, but he opened the door, grabbed the basket and followed Ashley inside his apartment. Amazing. He'd been trying to get Ashley inside his place for months. One crying baby had accomplished the task in mere minutes. A crying baby and a promise to clean her grout.

Ashley Garrett was definitely not easy.

ASHLEY COULDN'T imagine that she was going to be much help. She knew less than nothing about taking care of infants. Even when she was little, she hadn't been much of a doll person. Books, computer games and puzzles had been more to her liking. But a bargain was a bargain, and her grout could use a good cleaning. Besides, she couldn't trust Kyle with the care of this poor baby. He'd probably feed her cold pizza and beer.

"I'll prepare the formula," Ashley said, walking straight to the kitchen. "You change her."

"Change her into what?"

"Change her diaper. She's probably wet, maybe worse."

"Oh, no. I don't do dirty diapers. I draw the line there."

"Then you're going to have a very smelly apartment."

"If I'm doing the grout, the least you can do is change diapers."

"I don't think so, *Daddy.* The deal is just that I help you get her fed and quieted down until you hand her over to someone who'll know how to take care of her properly." She passed the baby to Kyle. The darling wailed in protest, not that Ashley blamed her. He held her like a sack of potatoes. Still, he did look a little different with a baby in his arms. Less suave. More vulnerable. Sexier than ever. Not that she'd admit that to him.

"Give your daddy a break, sweetie. He'll probably get your diaper on backward, but at least you'll be dry."

"Backward, huh. How hard can it be to change a diaper?"

"I guess you'll soon find out."

"And don't call me her daddy in front of her. She may start to believe it."

"Why shouldn't she? I do."

He made a face as he turned to carry the baby and one of the diapers to the bedroom. Ashley went back to the task at hand. What a night this had been and it wasn't over yet. Well, technically it was, because it was half-past midnight according to the clock on Kyle's microwave, but she had the feeling it might be a long time before she got to crawl into her own bed and get some sleep.

KYLE LAID THE BABY on the bed, then sat down beside her. She kicked and boxed her little hands in the air, though she was no longer crying. In fact, she appeared to be enjoying the opportunity to stretch and kick, unhindered by her baby seat or someone's arms.

He eased his face closer to her bottom and was grateful that no unpleasant odors assaulted his nostrils. Actually she smelled…like a baby. Not that he knew a lot about how babies were supposed to smell.

She made a cooing noise and kicked all the harder. She'd be a heartbreaker when she grew up. Thick, dark hair that curled around her heart-shaped face. Big choco-latey eyes accented with thick lashes. And the cutest little mouth he'd ever seen. He touched a finger to one of her chubby little hands, and she grasped it, holding on to him as if she wanted to shake hands.

"At least you're not as unfriendly as Miss Ashley," he said, talking to her as if she were a peer. He wasn't about to try that baby-talk stuff Ashley spewed when she talked to her.

When she let go of his finger, he sat back and dealt with the shock of a baby in his bed. "Your mother must have been desperate to desert a little charmer like you. But don't worry, she said she loves you. She'll be back soon."

Only if she really loved her little daughter, why had she dumped her at his door? What if he hadn't come home tonight at all?

Easy question. If he hadn't come home, Ashley would have been stuck taking care of the baby by herself instead of the two of them doing it together. But here they were, all nice and cozy, with Ashley in his kitchen wearing noth-ing but a silky black slip that showed off her body to perfection. Admittedly the slip and garments she had on under it covered far more than Alicia's dress had, but still, a slip was one of those unmentionables, and that was sexier than any dress.

He chucked the baby under the chin. "Ah, now I know

who you are, sweetheart. My own little Cupid who dropped by to get Ashley and me together. You just keep working your magic, and I'll turn on the charm. With us teamed up together, she'll never be able to resist me.''

Now for the diaper. He held it up. It looked fairly simple, but the last thing he wanted was to get it on backward and prove Ashley right. A row of pink and blue bunnies danced along the top border. He was sure that was a clue, but the thing had obviously been designed by a woman. A man would have just printed the word *front* on one side and *back* on the other.

He lifted the hem of the pink dress and pulled off the ruffled bloomers, a task far more difficult than it looked. Evidently babies didn't know they were supposed to co-operate during the procedure.

''Is that as far as you've gotten?''

He looked up as Ashley stepped to the door, bottle in hand. ''I could have been finished, but Cupie and I were bonding.''

''Cupie?''

''It's a private joke.''

''Well, drop it. A nickname like that could scar her for life.''

Ashley stepped to the bed and took over the chore of changing the diaper while he stood back and watched carefully so he'd be sure to do it right next time. If there was a next time. With any luck, he'd be able to keep Ashley on duty until the real mom came to her senses. Or until he was forced to call the authorities Ashley talked about and have them take her away.

Take her away. Even the words were cold—heartless. He forced them from his mind as he watched Ashley tug and smooth the diaper before finally snapping it into place.

''All done,'' she said, smiling as if she'd accomplished some major feat.

He realized then that she was a big fake. She didn't know any more about tending babies than he did, yet she was giving this her best shot. He'd lusted after her for months. Found her wit and sexy looks a killer combination. But this was the first time he'd realized that he actually liked her.

Her hips swayed seductively as she marched into the bathroom, disposed of the wet diaper and washed her hands before rejoining him at the bed.

She picked up the bottle and held it out to him. "Do you want to feed her?"

"Me?"

"Well, if it turns out that she is your daughter, you'll have to learn. You might as well start now."

"It's not going to turn out that way. I'm telling you this is all a mistake."

"How can you be so sure? Every time I see you, you're with a different woman. You don't expect me to believe that you've never had sex with any of them."

"Not as many as you seem to think. I'm rather choosy about who I go to bed with. Besides, when I do have sex, I use protection."

"Protection is not a hundred percent. You won't have to worry about it for long, though. I'm sure that once the authorities read the note the mother wrote, they'll demand that you have DNA testing to determine whether or not you're the father."

A new blow to his system. He hadn't even considered that possibility. Not that he was afraid of the outcome. No one was more careful than he was to make sure he avoided this kind of surprise. He had his life all planned out and it didn't include kids until he was at least forty. He had fourteen years to go before that date approached.

"Guess your daddy is scared to try." Ashley crawled

onto his bed, picked up the baby and poked the nipple into the tiny mouth.

The baby latched on to it as if she'd been starving for days, though the rolls of fat on her thighs indicated otherwise. He could hear the sucking sounds from where he was standing and the soft mewing purrs of contentment as warm milk filled her stomach.

His own problems slipped to the back of his mind as the image seared its way into his consciousness. Ashley Garrett on his bed, bottle-feeding a tiny, helpless baby. The sight of it made him feel funny, like watching a sad movie and pretending not to be affected.

He wasn't sure what it was all about, but he had the sneaking suspicion that it couldn't be good.

"SHE'S ASLEEP," Ashley whispered. "Throw back the spread so that I can lay her on the sheet."

He did as he was told, and Ashley put the infant down slowly, right in the middle of his king-size bed. She wiggled a little but didn't open her eyes. So far, so good.

Ashley eased from the bed and started toward the door.

"Where do you think you're going?"

"To get the baby's blanket from the basket. It's softer than yours."

"Just so you don't think you're sneaking out of here."

"No way."

"Good."

"I don't sneak."

He flashed her a less than authentic smile as she sashayed out of the room. By the time she returned, he'd kicked off his shoes, settled back on the pillow and closed his eyes.

"Kyle, wake up and look at this."

He opened his eyes a slit. Ashley was standing over him

holding a doll. "Uh-huh. That's good, Ashley. You can bring your dolly to bed with us if that makes you happy."

"It's not my doll. I found it in the basket when I pulled out the blanket. Apparently it had fallen beneath the covers." Her voice rose excitedly.

"So, what's the big deal? The kid's mom probably wanted her to have a toy from home to play with."

"This isn't a baby's toy. It's porcelain, very delicate and easily broken."

"What do you expect from a mom who leaves her daughter in my care? She probably never heard of toy safety."

"Try to pay attention and follow me. This could be important. Since the doll is obviously not for the baby, it must represent something, be some kind of message to you. Why else would it be in the basket?"

"There are no messages in that basket for me. I am not the father." But he reluctantly rose to his elbows. "Maybe it's some kind of family heirloom and the mother wants the child to have it."

"Possibly. Or maybe it's something you gave the mother and she put it in the basket so you'd know who gave birth to your child. Are you sure you've never seen it before?"

"No. That's my final answer. And to set the record straight *again,* this is *not* my baby."

"Your baby or not, I think the doll represents something. It could be the woman's way of crying out to be found. She could even be in danger."

"And you could be suffering from lack of sleep or plain old delirium."

"When I got off the elevator tonight, I ran into a young woman who looked frightened and nervous. I'll bet anything she's the one who dropped off this baby. I think she was Hispanic. She even had the same dark hair and eyes as the baby, and I know I've never seen her around here before.''

"Why didn't you mention that before?"

"I didn't think of it until I saw the doll. Something in the doll's expression reminded me of the woman. Kyle, the baby was left at your door. That makes you morally responsible. You have to help that woman.''

"Hold on, Ashley. Your reasoning is faulty." But the fear in her voice caught him off guard. Tending a baby for one night was one thing. Getting involved in the mystery of who she was and how she'd come to be left by his door was a different ball game altogether.

"Just give this a little time," he said. "If it's a joke, someone will show up any minute. If it's a mistake, the mother will surely realize it soon and come back for the baby.''

"Can't you at least consider the fact that this may be your child?''

"No.''

"Think about it. She's not very old. She can't sit up by herself, but she's not a newborn, either.''

"Should this have some significance to me?''

She nodded. "If I had to make a guess, I'd say the baby's three, maybe four months old. Who were you dating twelve or thirteen months ago?''

"Thirteen months ago, I was—'' Damn. He blew out a slow stream of air, suddenly feeling as if he'd boarded a runaway train and they were approaching a cliff. His gaze went from Ashley to the sleeping baby in the center of the bed. Dark hair. Big, expressive eyes. Hispanic mother.

Ashley stepped closer, staring at him as if she could read his mind. "You look as if you've seen a ghost.''

"Worse.'' The room closed in around him, making the air so stifling it seemed to cut off his breath. He rose and planted his feet squarely on the floor. "I need a breath of fresh air. If you need me, I'll be on the balcony."

"Don't jump," she said, her voice softer, gentler than it had been all evening. "It could be a lot worse."

"Yeah. She could have been twins."

ASHLEY EYED Kyle's stooped shoulders as he walked from the room. Anxiety looked strange on him, destroyed the air of cocky self-confidence that before tonight she'd accepted as the sum total of who he was. Seeing this different side of him made her uncomfortable, made her fear that they would never go back to the impersonal level of playful sparring that had characterized their relationship.

They'd been neighbors for nearly a year, but she seldom ran into him in the apartment building. Most of their encounters had been at the health club. Something about sweating together two or three nights a week worked wonders at breaking down the barriers empty apartment halls raised.

She flirted, he teased. He tried to talk her into going out with him; she came back with witty put-downs. It was harmless fun for both of them, especially when she'd had no intention of ever letting the devastatingly handsome man into her life. Now she was in his apartment. In his bed. Fretting over a baby that might or might not be his, though the look on his face a few minutes ago made her think it was.

The baby squirmed in her sleep, lifting her hand to her mouth and inserting a chubby thumb. Poor darling, deserted by her mother—though Ashley had the distinct feeling the mother must have had a very good reason for what she'd done. Now everything was up to Kyle.

Like it or not, if he was the father, he'd have to take care of her and he definitely couldn't depend on Ashley to play nursemaid. She had the biggest opportunity of her career staring her in the face. Tomorrow she'd be facing it with bags under her eyes from lack of sleep. She tugged a fallen slip strap into place and eased from the bed so as not to wake the baby. She'd fulfilled her part of the bargain and it was past time she went back to her own bed.

A few seconds later she stepped out the French doors and onto the balcony. Kyle was standing near the railing, staring into the moonless night. "The baby's asleep, and I'm going now. You should be able to handle her the rest of the night on your own."

He turned toward her, and even in the dim glow from the streetlights below them, she could see the strain that had settled into the muscles of his face. "I wish you wouldn't go."

"I don't know what else I can do to help."

"Suppose she wakes up crying."

"Then you feed her. There's enough formula left for a couple more bottles."

"I can't feed her. I can't change her diapers." He threw up his hands. "I have no idea how to care for her."

"But you're no longer insisting that she's not yours."

He shrugged his shoulders and ran his hands deep into his pockets. "I still don't think I'm the father, but I could be. I was dating a woman named Tessa Ortiz about the time the baby would have been conceived."

"You're always dating a woman, Kyle. One after the other. You had to know something like this would happen sooner or later."

"If she's mine, I'll take care of her—somehow."

She was on solid ground with her accusations, but still the desperation in his voice weakened her resolve. At least he wasn't screaming that it was the woman's fault, or blindly denying his responsibility in the matter.

"You'll need to have DNA testing done."

"I will—when the time comes."

"Why not now? It's quick, simple and the only way you can be sure."

"If I do, I'd be undergoing the tests to prove that she isn't my daughter, not that she is. It just doesn't seem right."

"Right or not, the authorities will insist upon it."

"Not if I don't call them."

"You said yourself you have no idea how to take care of a baby. Besides, it's illegal to keep a baby that's not yours."

"Let's not get into this tonight. If I don't hear from the baby's mother by morning, I'll locate Tessa and find out what's going on. If I can't find her, I'll take the baby and go in for DNA testing."

She stared at him, amazed by his decision. Her expectations were that he would either call the authorities at once or have paternity testing done as soon as possible. But it seemed as if he really cared about what happened to this baby. He got to her, weakened her resolve.

"I can't believe I'm saying this, but if you're going to take care of the baby tonight, I'll stay and help. I just need to go home and change into a sweatsuit."

"Oh, no!" He grabbed her hand. "If you walk out that door, you'll never come back."

He had a point. "Then I'll need to borrow a pair of pajamas.

His face finally split into a grin. "You're on."

He took her hand and led her back to the bedroom, and she had the strange feeling that she might have just been had. Still, a promise was a promise. "Remember, this is only for tonight, Kyle. After that, you're on your own with this project."

"One night at a time. That's all I'm asking. There is one slight problem, though."

"I'll bite."

"I don't own any pajamas and I only have one bed."

"Then I hope you have a very comfortable couch. Otherwise you may wake up with a stiff back."

"If you want stiff, I can give you stiff. All you have to do is ask."

"While you're waiting, why don't you hold your breath and count to infinity."

He nodded. "I'll take the couch."

CHAPTER THREE

"No, I'M NOT sick, Ellen. I just have a personal emergency
that I have to tend to." Ashley stared at the phone and
wondered how she'd gotten herself into this mess. All the
work she had waiting for her at the office, and here she
was trying to explain to her secretary why she wouldn't
be in today. But there was no telling what would happen
to that poor baby if she just walked off and left her in
Kyle's care.

"I hope there's not anything wrong with your sister
Lily's pregnancy," Ellen said.

"Lily's fine. Just look at my calendar and see if there's
anything that can't be postponed."

"You have that shoot of the TV ad scheduled for ten.
Do you want me to cancel it?"

"No, I called Mark Beall over in Media about that. He's
agreed to handle it for me." And if he screwed it up, she'd
kill him. "Remind him that if he has any concerns, no
matter how small, he should page me. That's one of my
most persnickety clients."

"I'll tell him, Ashley. And what about Mr. McAllister?"

"What about him?"

"Should I give him your pager number if he calls here
for you?"

"Give it to him if, and only if, he says it's important
that he talk to me today or if he pushes for it." Yesterday
she wouldn't have hesitated to say yes. What a difference

a day made—or in this case, a dinner for two. But the RA account was too important to risk getting him all worked up over minor technicalities.

"I'll take care of everything, Ashley. I just hope there's nothing seriously wrong."

"Nothing that won't be handled in one day. That, I can promise you. If you need me for anything, page me or call me on my cell phone. If I don't hear from you, I'll call you this afternoon to see how things are going."

Once she'd hung up the phone, Ashley crossed her sunlit kitchen, walked to her coffeepot and poured another cup of the strong brew. She usually used cream and a sprinkling of sugar substitute, but this morning she needed a full-strength blast of caffeine. She'd slept very little, stirring with every movement of the baby sleeping beside her. Then she'd gotten up at five to give her another bottle.

In all fairness, Kyle had untangled himself from the sheets on the sofa and padded to the kitchen after her. She'd turned down his offer of help. Not so much that she didn't need it, but it was incredibly awkward sharing early morning with him, especially with him in his boxers and her in an oversize cotton shirt that she'd confiscated from his closet.

Now she was missing a day of work. This wasn't her problem, but how could she ignore the needs of a helpless baby? Tessa had to be desperate to leave her daughter with Kyle. Maybe she was dying of some horrible illness or perhaps she was in imminent danger.

Ashley took a long sip of the coffee and tried to remember the face of the woman she'd glimpsed at the elevator last night. She had looked upset. And she had the same dark hair and eyes as the baby. But if she was Tessa Ortiz, and if the baby was Kyle's daughter, why had the woman waited until now to tell him?

Jumping at the sound of battering knuckles on her door,

she set her coffee mug on the table with such force that the hot liquid sloshed from the cup. She grabbed a napkin and wiped the spill from the counter and from her fingers as the pounding started again, this time louder than before. No surprise that when she unlatched the door and swung it open, Kyle was standing outside with the baby in his arms.

"I told you I needed an hour to shower and dress. I have ten more minutes," she announced.

He gave her a quick once-over. "You look dressed to me."

"I haven't put on my makeup."

"Forget it. You look fine. Besides, we have a problem."

"There you go with the 'we' again."

"I think the baby is sick," he said, ignoring her comment.

Ashley studied the baby, a sense of panic stewing inside her. "What makes you think so?"

"This." Kyle pointed at a disgusting spot on the shoulder of his T-shirt. "She started crying, so I picked her up. I held her on my shoulder the way you did this morning, and she spit milk all over me. Stinky milk!"

"Good going, sweetie!"

"This isn't funny, Ashley. I think we should take her to a doctor."

Ashley doubted it, though in all honesty, she couldn't be sure. What she knew about babies would make a book about as thick as one on *Women Who Long to Be Poor and Ugly.* "I'll call my sister Lily. She's pregnant. She'll know if spitting up is normal or if it's serious."

"How much do you plan on telling her?"

"Just the basics. I won't even mention that the baby in question came by special delivery. But you might want to tell her more."

"Why would I?

"When she's not about to have a baby, she and my brother Dylan operate Finders Keepers, a private detective agency that specializes in locating missing persons. They could help you find Tessa."

"I'd prefer to handle the search myself." He paced the floor, still holding the baby, his hair mussed and his chin darkened by whiskers. She couldn't help but notice how appealing he looked, but then any man with a baby would effuse a certain amount of charm.

She turned away and dialed Lily's number. Thankfully it was her sister and not her husband, Cole, who answered the phone. The fewer people Ashley had to talk to, the better it would be.

"Lily, how are you?"

"Big and beautiful. At least that's what Cole said this morning when I needed help tying my shoes. It's no wonder I love that man. What's up with you?"

"I have a question."

"You, miss career woman, have a question for me. Can you wait while I circle the date on the calendar?"

"What are you talking about? I ask you questions all the time? Anyway, this question is way out of my area of expertise. It's about babies, or about one in particular."

"Whose baby?"

"It belongs to one of my neighbors."

"The woman with the cat is too old to have a baby. You're not talking about that hunk across the hall, are you?"

"Actually, it does belong to Kyle Blackstone. It's a long story. I'll explain it to you one day when you have absolutely nothing to do."

"So, what's the question?"

She could hear the suspicion in her sister's voice, but a little suspicion was better than telling the whole story and providing her family with entertainment at her expense.

"The baby in question spit up some milk after she took her morning bottle. Is that normal?"

"Absolutely, especially if it's just a small amount."

A direct answer without questions. So far, so good. "What do babies eat besides formula?"

"How old is this mystery baby?"

"I'm guessing three or four months."

"That's pretty vague. Can't you just ask Kyle how old she is?"

"He's not sure."

"And I have the distinct feeling that wool is being pulled over my eyes. Spill it, sister. I'm not getting off the phone until you tell me the true story."

She sighed and stared at Kyle. He probably wouldn't like it, but if he was going to keep this baby while he searched for the mother, he had to know how to take care of her. "Okay, Lily. The truth is that someone left a baby in a basket in front of Kyle's door last night." Lily listened, interrupting occasionally to ask questions while Ashley gave her the briefest of details.

"I think I better have a look at this baby. I'll get dressed and be there as soon as I can. In the meantime, try to talk some sense into your neighbor. He needs DNA testing— pronto. Deserting a baby is a crime, and if the child isn't his, he should turn it over to the Department of Social Services and the police immediately so they can search for the mother."

"I've already suggested he call the authorities. He's a very hardheaded man."

"Too bad that isn't the only thing he has that's hard. If it were, he wouldn't be wondering if this baby were his."

"I've already pointed that out to him, too."

By the time she hung up the phone, Kyle had quit pacing and moved to stand at her elbow. "You squealed on an innocent baby. How could you do that?"

"I didn't squeal."

"Tell her that to her face." He held the infant so she was practically nose to nose with Ashley. "Tell her that you want me to call the cops and have her picked up on vagrancy charges for loitering in our hall."

She patted the baby's cheek. "Your father is a little unbalanced, sweetie. But don't worry. His kind of weirdness only affects males. You're immune."

"So what's the verdict? Is she sick or not?"

"Spitting up is perfectly normal. And my sister isn't going to alert the authorities or anyone else about your predicament. In fact, she offered to come over. I'm not sure why, but I know she'll give you some advice on tending the baby. And she thinks you should call immediately and get an appointment to go in for DNA testing."

"I'm thinking about it."

"What is there to think about? You have to find out if she's your daughter. You can't just keep her if she isn't. A baby's not like a stray puppy that followed you home."

"You make it sound like I kidnapped her. I doubt very seriously that she's my daughter, but someone reached out to me for help, and I'm trying to oblige."

"You're serious about this, aren't you?"

"Does that surprise you?"

"Yeah. Frankly, it does. I never pictured you as having a heart, much less a bleeding one."

"It's not like I'm planning to raise her to adulthood. I'll track down Tessa and find out what's going on. If I can't find her, I'll take the next step. If that makes me a bleeding heart, so be it."

"In that case you better make a long list of questions for Lily, because after today you'll be on your own unless you get one of your lady friends to come help you. This is it for me."

He studied her floor. "I don't know. As dirty as that grout is, you may want to keep me on retainer."

"Today only, Kyle. I'm not kidding."

"Fine. Now how about watching her while I grab a shower." He handed her the baby, then put his mouth close to the baby's ear. "Be a good girl for Miss Ashley, and feel free to do any pooping you think is necessary or any further spitting up while I'm gone."

The darling snuggled against Ashley, resting her head over Ashley's heart. It felt strange to hold her, kind of warm and satisfying. And once again, all Ashley could think of was what terrible thing could have driven a woman to desert this child.

"Tell me about Tessa, Kyle."

He had already started toward the door but he turned back at her request. "Why?"

"Because I need to understand how she could walk away from her own flesh and blood."

KYLE FELT HIS muscles tense as old memories surfaced. What caused any woman to put her own needs above the needs of her child? It was a question as old as time, or at least one as old as he was. But it wouldn't do to fall back into the shadows of his past. He'd worked too hard to put them away.

"I don't know that much about Tessa," he answered, realizing how little he really did know about a woman who had shared two years of his life. "She was a very private person."

"Were you in love with her?"

"I liked making love with her. Does that qualify?"

"Not even close."

"Then I probably wasn't in love with her, but I liked her a lot. We had fun together. She laughed at my jokes.

I brought her coffee in bed. It worked for us—for a while.''

"And she never called you to tell you she was pregnant?"

"Not a word."

"It doesn't make sense. Even if she didn't tell you when she had the baby, why wouldn't she have come to you when she was in trouble instead of just dropping the baby at your door?''

"Your guess is as good as mine. I like women. I never claimed to understand them.'' He didn't wait for more questions. Tessa Ortiz was the one with the answers. More to the point, she had the answers if this baby was his. He still didn't believe that she was.

But then he'd been wrong before.

LILY GARRETT BISHOP moved to the back of the elevator as two men stepped inside after her. They turned and let their gaze settle on her bulging stomach. Both of them nodded and smiled. It was always interesting to watch strange men's reactions to her condition.

Some looked away, as if anything associated with the birds and bees embarrassed them. Others smiled or started talking about their own kids, treating the fact that she was pregnant like the miracle of life it was. She felt much more comfortable around the latter.

The younger man was at least six feet tall and close to two hundred pounds, most of it muscle, judging from the way he filled out his jeans and the arms that protruded from the rolled sleeves of his plaid shirt. Dark hair, piercing blue eyes, probably in his mid to late thirties. Slight limp. Handsome but not a pretty boy. More of a man's man. Could be a construction worker, a truck driver, maybe a cop.

She smiled as the elevator stopped on the fourth floor

and the two men stepped off. Before starting Finders Keepers with her brother Dylan, she'd worked in forensics for the FBI, and she prided herself on her observation skills. Very little ever got by her. Another floor or two and she'd have had the guy's facial features down, maybe even some of his expressions. Little things were all important when you were searching for missing persons. That and the ability to get leads from thin air.

When the elevator jiggled to a stop on the eighth floor, she stepped out and headed to Ashley's apartment. She'd planned to spend the day writing thank-you notes for the baby gifts she'd already received, but nothing short of labor pains would have kept her from coming into San Antonio today.

The reality of her career-minded little sister tending to and fretting over a baby that belonged to her amorous neighbor was too good to miss. She'd always suspected Ashley had the hots for the man. Once she saw them together, she'd know for sure.

She knocked on the door and waited. Ashley opened it with a finger to her lips. "Shhh. The baby just fell asleep."

Lily stepped inside and gave Ashley a quick hug. "So where is this mystery baby?"

"I made a pallet for her in my bedroom. That way she won't roll onto the floor if I don't hear her the minute she wakes up. You can take a peek, but don't wake her. I'm already exhausted and it's not even 9:00 a.m. But then I was up past midnight with her and back up before daybreak this morning."

Lily patted her stomach. "And this is the life I can't wait to start. Do you think I'm crazy?"

"No. You're very lucky. You have a wonderful husband who loves you. I, on the other hand, am playing nursemaid to the baby of a man who drives me to distraction."

"So why are you doing it?"

"Go ahead and peek into the bedroom. You'll see."

Lily did as she was instructed. The baby was lying on her side, sucking her right thumb for all she was worth. Cute as a bug—what baby wasn't—but still she couldn't imagine that Ashley had actually missed a day of work to baby-sit.

"Would you like some coffee?" Ashley asked when she joined her in the kitchen.

"No, I've already had my one cup limit. Too much caffeine isn't good for the baby. I'll take a glass of milk if you have one."

Ashley opened the refrigerator door and stared at the meager contents while Lily peered over her shoulder. "No milk. I have Diet Coke."

Lily walked to the cabinet and pulled out a glass. "Water's good for me." She filled the glass with cool bottled water and took a seat at the breakfast nook. "I think your assessment of the baby's age is probably accurate." She sipped her water. "Did you tell Kyle that I recommended immediate testing to determine if he's the father?"

"I did." Ashley took the seat opposite Lily. "He wants to try to locate Tessa Ortiz first. He seems sure that if he's the father, Tessa is the mother."

"Are you sure he's not just putting off the inevitable, trying to delay finding out the truth about whether or not he's the father?"

"I'm not sure of anything."

"But you're getting involved all the same."

"No way. I offered to help out this one day, watch the baby while he tries to track down Tessa. Tomorrow I'm back on the job. The world needs beef, and it's my job to convince them of the fact."

"Well, if your hunky neighbor is going to keep this baby, he'll have to find someone to watch her. Four-month-old babies require constant care."

"Do me a favor. Never mention the word *hunk* in front of him. He takes it to heart."

"I'll watch my tongue." Only she wasn't going to watch it about everything. She'd driven all the way into town. She might as well say her piece. "Even if he only keeps the baby a few days, she'll need clothes, toys, food, a crib. Babies don't just camp out."

"He plans to buy those things today."

"He's also taking a risk. If something happens to the baby while she's in his care, and she's not his baby, he could face a lawsuit or worse."

"He'll be over here in a minute. You can tell him all of that to his face, and I hope you get further than I did." The phone rang and Ashley jumped from her chair. "That's probably him now."

Lily watched as Ashley spoke a series of hellos into the phone, then slammed the receiver down. She stood staring into space, her lips pulled tight.

"What was that about?"

"I'm not sure. I thought it was a crank call at first, but just before I hung up, a man with a deep-set voice warned me to stay away from Kyle Blackstone. He said the man couldn't be trusted. Before I could ask what he meant, he hung up."

Lily stood, walked over and put a reassuring arm about Ashley's shoulders, though she didn't feel particularly calm herself. "Did you check the caller ID?"

"It said unable to identify."

"Has this happened before?"

"Never."

Lily grew uneasy. She didn't want to frighten Ashley, but this whole situation was sounding fishier by the minute. Ashley was proficient, intelligent and ambitious, but she was still a bit naive when it came to the ways of the world. Lily was probably partly responsible for that. She

nd her brother Dylan had both been overly protective
vhere their little sister was concerned.

"What do you really know about Kyle Blackstone?"
;he asked, other than the fact that he frequents the same
health club you do and lives across the hall?"

"Not all that much. He's an attorney with Bragg, Cotton
and Lerner. He works out two or three evenings a week
and he has women out the kazoo." Ashley dropped to a
chair. "You think that call might be on the up and up,
don't you? That someone actually thinks I need to be
warned about Kyle."

"I just think you need to be careful. Don't rush into any
kind of relationship with him. I know how easy that would
be if the two of you start tending to this baby together."

"I'm not getting involved with him at all. I've made
that clear to him."

"Then you have nothing to worry about."

She'd probably said too much, made Ashley uneasy
when it was unlikely there was anything dangerous going
on. It was just that searching for missing persons had exposed her to some pretty ugly situations, taught her that a
lot of people were not what they seemed.

"I wouldn't worry, Ashley. Just be careful and keep
your eyes and ears—" Before she could finish, the front
door burst open and a man stepped inside. Though Lily
had never met Kyle Blackstone before, she immediately
recognized him from her sister's descriptions. The only
difference was that the man was even better looking than
Ashley had admitted, even in his present state. Right now
he looked like a little boy who'd just lost his ice-cream
money.

Lily watched Ashley's reaction to the man, saw her
tense the second she picked up on his agitated state. Ob-
served the look that passed between them. It appeared a
lot more than neighborly to her.

Ashley crossed the floor and stopped just in front of Kyle. "What happened? Did you get in touch with Tessa?"

He shook his head and exhaled sharply. "But I finally got in touch with Tessa's sister. The news was not good."

CHAPTER FOUR

A FATHER. Kyle had always expected to be one—one day. He'd imagined himself tossing a baseball, taking a son to football games, putting together a train set on Christmas Eve. He'd never been opposed to having a daughter, either, though he'd never given that possibility much thought.

The whole concept of fatherhood had loomed somewhere in the distant future. A contingency for much later—when his career was firmly established. When he'd sown his wild oats, driven his share of fast cars and grown bored with skiing in the mountains of Colorado and scuba diving off some exotic island in the Bahamas. When he was ready for a life of bottle-feeding and diaper changing.

That was indubitably not now.

Ashley stepped closer. "Did Tessa's sister say that she'd given birth? Is Tessa in some kind of trouble now?"

"No, nothing that specific. Actually, nothing that offers any real solutions. She hasn't seen or heard from her sister since a year ago. She's pretty sure she's moved out of town. Evidently they had a major argument and parted company." He dropped to the couch and that's when he noticed the other person in the room. She was taller than Ashley, her hair long where Ashley's was short, but she had the same expressive green eyes and dark, shiny hair. And the evidence was jury-proof. She was most definitely pregnant.

"I'm Lily," the woman said, walking over to shake his

hand. "If this is personal, I'll be glad to step into the bedroom while you and Ashley talk."

He stood and extended his hand. "No, you already know about as much as I do anyway."

Ashley sat down on the couch beside him, but not too close. Lily took the chair across from them, lowering herself slowly and holding her back as she did. He tried to picture Tessa in the same condition. Awaiting the birth of a daughter that for some reason she had decided to keep from him. He had trouble with the image. Tessa wasn't the type who liked to suffer alone. That much he did know about her.

Ashley turned to face him. "A year ago... Tessa would have had to be pregnant even then, but maybe not far enough along to realize it. When did the two of you break up?"

"Right after Christmas. We'd been living together. She moved out."

"Did you talk to her after that?" Lily asked.

"She came by to pick up her mail a few times. I asked how she was doing. She asked how I was doing. That was about it."

"So why are you suddenly so upset?" Ashley asked. "An hour ago you were vehement that you weren't the father. Now you seem worried that you are."

He crossed an ankle over his knee, an effort to hide just how flustered he really was. "I expected this to be a done deal by now. I'd get Tessa's number from information, which I tried to do. No listing. Or I'd talk to her sister Margaret and find out for certain that Tessa had not given birth. Now I find out Tessa likely moved out of town months ago and her sister doesn't know how to contact her."

Lily pulled her hair off her neck, then let it settle about

her shoulders, all the while keeping her gaze pinned on him. "Then it's possible that you're the father?"

"I'm not denying that it's possible, it's just that it's not likely. We used protection. But even more than that, I can't see Tessa deciding she'd go through a pregnancy and birth without telling me about it. And even if she had, she'd have no reason to stick the baby in a basket and leave her at my door. She's the type who'd just come by and say she needed help."

"Maybe she's afraid of how you'd react."

He threw up his hands. "Do I look like some deranged brute to you? I'm a sensible man, an attorney for God's sake. People come to me to get them out of a jam. It's what I do."

"As an attorney, you must know what options are available to you."

One thing about Lily, she didn't back down. "The way I see it, I can try to find Tessa, though I doubt she's the mother of this baby, or I can sit around and hope the woman who left the baby at my door will come back for her."

"You can make certain the baby's not yours, and if that's the case, you can notify the authorities," Lily offered.

"That would be the easiest thing for me to do, but that seems like the worst thing I can do for the baby."

Ashley laid a hand on his arm. The touch surprised him, made him even more aware that the woman he'd tried to get close to for weeks was seeing him at his most vulnerable. Not confident and self-assured, but reeling from a situation he seemed to have little control over.

Last night he'd felt certain this would all be settled by morning. Now all he felt was the crushing weight of responsibility bearing down on his shoulders. "I'm not ready

to give up," he said, "not yet. But I could sure use a cras[
course in baby care."

Lily nodded. "I can do that, but you can't put off learn
ing the truth indefinitely."

"I know. I'm thinking a few days, a week at most. [
have some vacation time coming, and I can do a lot of th[
prep work for the cases I'm working on now via the com
puter. If I don't turn up anything in that time, I'll go wit[
the DNA testing."

"You'll have to buy baby clothes and supplies. An[
you'll need to borrow or rent a crib."

"Just give me a list and tell me where to go to find th[
items. I'll do the best I can. Right now I'm all the bab[
has. Well, me and Ashley."

Ashley shook her head. "Don't let that thought land a[
it flies through your mind. I have a career and an assign
ment that can't be put on hold, and I will—"

"I'll tell you what," Lily said, warding off Ashley'[
tirade. "Since Ashley's already taken the day off, I'll mak[
a list and the two of you can shop for the needed supplies
I'll baby-sit while you're doing that and try to make note[
of things Kyle needs to know, like making sure the bottle[
and nipples are sterile and how to bathe the baby."

"Beef," Ashley asserted. "I'm supposed to be concen
trating on a way to sell more beef to the citizens of Texas
Not on buying diapers."

But the resignation in her voice was obvious. Kyle wa[
certain he'd won this bout, thanks to Lily. He would neve[
have deliberately used the baby to get to Ashley, but h[
might as well play the cards he'd been dealt. A man wit[
a baby. No woman could resist them.

Unless the baby was his for life.

LILY WATCHED Ashley and Kyle walk out the door. Kyle
Blackstone was not what she'd expected from Ashley'[

previous descriptions of him. He did have the great body he'd mentioned, the dark, wavy hair and the easy smile, but he had an aura of genuineness that had caught her off guard.

Still, the morning's phone call warning Ashley to beware of him made her nervous. Add to that the fact that Ashley knew nothing concrete about him except that he was an attorney with a prominent firm and attracted women the way her black slacks grabbed lint. And he was awfully hesitant to go to the authorities or have DNA testing conducted.

But a few phone calls, a few record checks, and she'd likely find out all she needed to know about Kyle Blackstone. She wouldn't even mention this to Cole and Dylan unless she found out something they needed to know. Cole would be upset that she was conducting any kind of investigation when she was supposed to be taking it easy until the baby was born. And Dylan had a tendency to blow everything out of proportion if it even remotely involved the safety of their little sister.

Walking to the bedroom door, she peeked in on the baby. The darling was still sleeping soundly, likely as exhausted as Ashley and Kyle had been from the change in her schedule. Lily spread her hands across the bulge of her stomach as her own baby kicked hard against the lining of the womb.

It wouldn't be long now, and she'd be able to stare at her own baby as she slept. The anticipation filled her with an eagerness like none she'd ever known before. A sweet yearning that made her arms ache to hold her own child in her arms. Yet the mother of this baby had put her child in a basket and walked away.

The situation wasn't unheard of. In fact, she'd run into problems caused by child desertion more than once since she'd gone into the business of finding missing persons—

some firsthand, others in her research. Young mothers wh
didn't know where to turn. Emotionally unstable mother
who went over the edge and knew no other way to cry ou
for help. Uncaring mothers or those addicted to drugs o
alcohol. Desperate mothers.

She hated to even imagine which category Tessa Orti
fell into. Hated worse to think that Kyle might know thing
he wasn't admitting. He seemed honest, deeply concerned
yet he was hesitant to do the thing most men would hav
considered first.

Find out if the baby was his.

Turning away, Lily walked to the phone, picked it u
and punched in the number of a friend at police head
quarters. Arrest records were always a good way to begi
a search into a person's past. She'd follow the paper tra
and see if Kyle was merely a nice guy with a body lik
Adonis and the looks to rival Brad Pitt, or if Ashley'
caller had been right and he was a man to be avoided.

For the baby's sake and for Ashley's, she hoped he wa
the man he seemed. Unless her instincts were way off base
Ashley was already falling hard for the guy. Of course
Ashley would be the last to admit it.

"WE HAVE TO GIVE the baby a name," Ashley said as the
walked toward the baby section of the department store
"I can't keep calling her sweetie."

"We can call her Cupie."

"Not me! How about Annie or Lucy? Or Janie?"

"I'm not good at this. You pick one."

She thought for a minute, picturing the cherub face, th
dark eyes. Deserted by her mother. "What about Casey?"
she asked, turning down an aisle bordered by baby clothe
"It's short for Casilda. The name means 'unknown,' an
almost everything about her is unknown."

"Casey?" He rolled the name off his tongue, the

smiled. "I like it. Not that she'll keep the name long. I'm still counting on her mother coming back for her—soon."

"But until she does, she's Casey. It fits." She stopped and pulled an adorable pink frock from the rack and held it at arm's length. "Look at this one. Lace and ruffles and tiny rows of smocking. We absolutely have to buy this for her."

He fumbled for a price tag. When he found it, his mouth flew open. "Do you know how much this costs?"

"You get what you pay for."

"Yeah, but I'm the one doing the paying."

"But it's so cute."

"Cute? For that price, it should be a national treasure."

"Wait until your daughter finds out you're a cheapskate."

"Don't say *daughter*. It makes me nervous." He held up the list Lily had made for him. "Nowhere on here does it say lace, ruffles and smocking at ridiculous prices."

"It says clothes."

"It says soft, sensible, *unfettered* clothes. Lace, ruffles and smocks are legally considered fetters."

"We're not in court, counselor. Just think how adorable Casey's going to look when you show her off to all your friends."

"She looks adorable in diapers. I have no intention of introducing her to my friends and you are having entirely too much fun spending my money."

"I'm hanging out with *you*, Kyle. By no stretch of the imagination can that be called fun." Except that it was. And not only because shopping was her second favorite pastime—right after work—but because, as much as she hated to admit it, Kyle was fun to be with, as long as they were only friends.

He pulled a pair of pajamas emblazoned with the Dallas Cowboys logo off the rack. "Now this is more like it."

She stuck up her nose. "No self-respecting little angel would be caught sleeping in those."

"Hey, watch your mouth. This is the Cowboys you're talking about. Sacrilegious comments like that can get you thrown out of Texas."

"I'll take my chances. Let's go for something a little more feminine."

"Then how about these?" He exhibited his next choice.

She rested her hands on her hips. "What's feminine about cowboys and horses?"

"Shucks, ma'am. I thought all women liked cowboys."

"Hmm." Cowboys and romance. Her mind jumped from babies to the Ranchers Association. "You might have hit on something, counselor."

"Does that mean I should invest in a Stetson and a pair of boots?"

"Why would you?"

"To impress you, of course."

"It really bothers you, doesn't it, that I don't chomp on your bait and fall at your feet like the other women in your life."

"I'm a man. We have fragile egos and we hate rejection. Fortunately, I know you go to bed every night wishing I was there with you. You're just too stubborn to admit it."

"Yeah, hold on to that thought, take it to the bank with a hundred dollar bill and see if you can get five twenties for it."

He smiled seductively. "Methinks the lady doth protest too much." He picked up a stuffed bear and tossed it to her. "If you like, I'll buy this for you, give you something cuddly to sleep with on cold winter nights. Or leave the bear, and I'll come over."

"No, thanks. I have a blanket, and it doesn't snore."

"I don't snore."

"Then you must have had a wild animal sleeping with you on the couch last night."

"I could have. You and Casey ran her off."

"You poor dear." She played a fake violin with her hands. "Could I give you music with that whine?" Turning away from him, she picked up a pair of pajamas in a buttery soft fabric patterned with sleeping kittens. "Entirely unfettered," she said. "What do you think?"

He fingered the row of snaps that ran up and down the inside of both legs and across the crotch. "Am I supposed to do something with these when I dress her for bed?"

"That would be my guess."

"You don't suppose she can dress herself, do you?"

"In a few years."

Kyle grimaced but took the pajamas from her and dropped them into the basket. Ashley kept shopping until they easily had enough outfits for him to change the baby's clothes a half dozen times a day. "I say we move on to the next department."

"What else is on the list?"

"Toys," Kyle answered. "She likes to pull hair. Maybe we could get her a wig."

Ashley led the way to a display of cuddly baby toys. "How about a doll?"

"Good idea, especially since you said the one her mother left with her wasn't meant to be played with."

"A doll? Hmm." She put a finger to her chin as if she were giving the matter serious deliberation. "Like the blow-up ones you usually sleep with?"

He wrapped an arm around her shoulder. "You could change all that, neighbor. One night and I could melt you down to nothing more than liquid gold."

"And then what would you do for a challenge?"

"Bathe a baby." They spoke in unison as they passed a counter of plastic baby bathtubs.

They both dissolved in laughter before their gazes met in one heated instant. The mood changed from easy to awkward as quickly as if a cold wind had blown through the department store.

"Did I say something wrong?" Kyle asked, knowing full well what had just passed between them.

But she could play the game as well as he could. "No. Everything's cool. Let's just work our way down the list and get out of here."

"So cool, your face is still red. You really need to loosen up, Ashley. All we did was laugh together. That's not like having sex."

"You just never give up, do you?"

He smiled a devastating smile. "Only when I have to."

But the easy teasing mood was lost. Playing games with Kyle was playing with fire. Step over the line and she'd be involved with him. Get involved with him and she'd be sleeping with him. Sleep with him, and her life would become a complicated, convoluted, giant headache that aspirin wouldn't touch.

They finished their shopping and Kyle paid for the purchases, handing her two of the lighter shopping bags as they hurried back to his sleek black sports car. They still needed to make a stop at the grocery store and one at the rent-all business to arrange for a crib to be delivered.

She settled into the car beside him, then let out a groan as her cell phone rang. "I hope this doesn't mean trouble at the office." She punched the Talk button and stuck the phone to her ear. "Hello."

"Ashley?"

She recognized the voice at once. Delia was not only her best friend but the most talented art director in the city. Fortunately, she worked for Clintock, Mitchum and O'Connell. "What's up?"

"Hey, that's my question. You're the one playing hooky

today. Tell me it's cause you're off having a wild affair with some hunk.''

"I could, but it would be a lie.''

"Then tell me you can drag yourself into the office.''

"Is something wrong?''

"Trouble in paradise.''

"Keep talking.''

"I just walked in on a conversation between Mr. McAllister and Mr. Clintock, and I distinctly heard the bigshot rancher say in his exaggerated Texas drawl that he would like to have you replaced as head honcho, his word choice, of the Ranchers Association account.''

"Don't tell me Mr. McAllister is back in the office today. When does the man run his ranch?''

"Don't ask me. Anyway, I thought you'd like to know what's going on.''

"Thanks. Did you happen to hear Mr. Clintock's response.''

"No, they quit talking when they realized I was at the door. But you know Mr. Clintock. He never argues with the man with the checkbook.''

"Okay, if Mr. McAllister starts to leave, stall him.'' She pushed up her sleeve and checked her watch. "I'll be there in ten minutes.''

"Any idea what trick I should use to stall him?''

"Use your feminine wiles. It's guaranteed to work with him.''

"I'll give it my best shot.'' Delia promised.

"I'm counting on you.''

Kyle was staring at her as she finished the conversation. "You'll be where in ten minutes?''

"At my office. It's an emergency.''

"An emergency at an advertising firm? What would that be, a broken slogan?''

"Just drive.'' She gave him the directions and then

started to punch in her home number so she could tell Lily they'd be a few minutes longer than they'd intended.

He revved the engine. "I can't get to your office in ten minutes."

"You have to."

"You make it sound as if your job is at stake."

"Not my job. My career. My first installment on a ticket to Madison Avenue."

Kyle swerved in front of a blue car and put the pedal to the metal, or as much as he could in downtown San Antonio traffic at midday. "Never let it be said that I couldn't deliver in a crunch."

"If you really want to help, tell me how to work with an arrogant, *married* Romeo who expects me not only to perform miracles for his association but to stroke his ego and anything else he wants stroked while I'm at it. And if I don't, he apparently wants me replaced."

"The dirty bastard. Tell me his name. I'll kill him."

"That isn't exactly the kind of solution I had in mind."

ASHLEY'S HEELS clicked on the hard tiles as she marched down the wide halls to the offices of Clintock, Mitchum and O'Connell. It would have been nice if she'd worn her power suit today instead of her brown slacks and green sweater, but what she lacked in professional garb, she made up for in determination.

She was the best man—uh, woman—for the job, and she would not let that oversexed tomcat yank it out from under her just because she'd rebuffed his advances. This would require diplomacy and firmness. But she would handle it.

"You want me to do the talking for you? I'll flex my muscles a bit, tell the old buzzard we're engaged and that I'm a very jealous fiancé who would become extremely volatile if he caused trouble for you."

She spun to face him as they came to the double glass doors. "Please, Kyle. Don't do anything to embarrass me. This is exceedingly important."

He put a hand up in surrender. "It was only an offer. I'll just find the water cooler and stand quietly with the office slackers."

"Promise?"

"Scout's honor."

Only she had the feeling he'd never been a scout. A minute later, she burst into Delia's office. "Where is he?"

"He's in your office, waiting on you. I told him you wanted to see him and that you'd be here any minute."

"Wish me luck." Gulping in a deep, steadying breath, Ashley struggled for her best professional demeanor and walked the few steps to her office.

CHAPTER FIVE

MR. MCALLISTER STOOD, leaning against the back of Ashley's most comfortable office chair. He was dressed in jeans and a western shirt, more casual than the day before, but still he emitted a sense of power and control. He removed his hat as she stepped inside. She tried to read his mood, but his face showed no expression. She faked a smile.

She stepped behind her desk, trusting it gave her an aura of authority and professionalism her age and position didn't invite. And there, taking up space on the polished surface was an extravagant bouquet of flowers and an unopened card. It wasn't her birthday, which made it extremely likely that this was a peace offering from the man standing in front of her. If he thought this was enough to make up for having her dumped, he was wrong.

Keep your cool, Ashley. Handle this with finesse.

"I didn't know you were coming in today," she said, striving for a level tone that belied her anger. "We didn't have an appointment."

"I hadn't expected to be in town, but my wife had a doctor's appointment and I offered to drive her in."

"Nothing serious, I hope."

"Not physically. She is upset, however." He lowered his voice and moved from behind the chair, stepping closer. "It seems that someone told her about us."

His tone and insinuation rolled in her stomach. "There's nothing to tell about *us*."

He grimaced and shook his head. "You and I may know that. She doesn't. Apparently one of her friends saw us together last night and called her."

"Surely you explained that it was all business."

"I tried to. I told her who you were and why I was with you, but she was in one of her sod-pawing moods where the more I try to explain, the more upset she gets. I suggested she call you, but she claims that's my way of humiliating her. I swear the woman doesn't believe a word I say."

Wonder why? But Ashley didn't point out to him that if he'd never played the cheating game, he probably wouldn't have the name. "Is that why you came in today and asked that I be removed from your project?"

"So you heard."

"But not from you."

"I came in to talk to you about it. You weren't here, so I went to Mr. Clintock. It's not personal, Ashley. And it's not because things didn't go so smoothly between us last night."

Like hell it wasn't. For all she knew the story about his wife was sliced baloney, but she'd bet her last tube of lipstick that if she'd been willing to dance to his tune last night, he wouldn't be standing here today asking that she be removed from the project.

He stepped from behind the chair. "I just feel that under the circumstances, I could work better with someone else and that you would probably prefer that as well."

"I'm sorry to hear you think that, and I definitely don't prefer it that way. I've given this campaign a lot of thought and time, and I feel I can give you and the Ranchers Association exactly what you're looking for. Did you give Mr. Clintock a reason for having me replaced?"

He dropped to the same leather chair he'd been guarding. "No. It's not easy telling people that your wife is a green-eyed monster."

"You told me."

"I guess I just felt like you'd understand. And now that we're on the subject, I owe you an apology for my behavior last night. I'd had a few too many martinis before I met you, and I just stepped over the line. I'm sorry."

"I accept your apology, but I'd like more. I'd like the chance to head up this campaign for your association. If it means your bringing your wife to our meetings, that's fine by me. I'm sure that once your wife sees me, she'll realize that my interest in you is purely professional."

"You're hard on a man's ego, Ashley. But you're determined, I'll say that for you. I guess I didn't realize this account was so important to you. I figured after last night you'd be glad to dump me."

And she would have been, if he hadn't represented her biggest project to date. This was just the kind of campaign that would spice up her portfolio, impress any prospective employer.

"I'd like the chance to work with you, Mr. McAllister, and I feel I have a lot to offer the campaign."

"That's what Josh Clintock said. I guess I better go in there and tell him that we're on again."

Her muscles began to unknot. "I promise that by the time we have this thing finalized, we'll have painted a new, dynamic image for the association and for beef cattle."

McAllister stood and slapped his hat against his thighs. "Well, little lady, I don't know how a man could ask for more than that. The campaign is yours, but I hope you're not going to let me down."

"You can count on it."

"So, what do you say we meet next Monday to take a look at what you've got to that point?"

Monday, and it was already Wednesday. That meant

she'd have to put in lots of overtime hours this weekend, especially since she had no idea how she was going to keep the standard of excellence she'd just promised. It also meant that Kyle Blackstone would have to find someone else to help with baby-sitting chores. Not that the task should present a problem. He could stop by the health club on the way home and pick up a few of his adoring body watchers. She was sure they'd be glad to accommodate him.

"Next Monday it is," she announced, standing, hopefully to usher the tall, imposing rancher out the door. "At 10:00 a.m.?"

"Perfect." He held her hand a tad too long as they shook and sealed the new alliance, but she could handle that. An older version of Kyle Blackstone, she decided. But even if the comparison gave her a smidgen of pleasure, she knew it was neither fair nor accurate.

Kyle was a flirt, but he wasn't nearly as arrogant as the rancher she'd just dealt with. And he had a soft spot for babies. That definitely went in his favor.

Perhaps good old Jim Bob was more than he seemed, too. The content of a book should never be judged by its cover. She of all people should know that. Shadings and colors and sometimes even optical illusions made advertising the creative venture it was. You did what you had to do in order to get people's attention. Make them receptive, then hit them with the message.

She watched McAllister stroll down the hall, to Mr. Clintock's office stopping to talk to the sexiest of the receptionists, leaning over so that he could see a little further down her blouse. No, she decided. Past the facade, he was still a jerk. Pity the poor woman who'd married him.

Pushing the rancher from her mind for the moment, she went back to her desk and punched in her home number to give Lily an updated estimated time of arrival—and to see how the baby was faring without them. Strange as it seemed, she couldn't wait to get home and try the cute clothes on her. Couldn't wait to feed her again and hold her close.

"Beef," she chided herself out loud. "Think beef, not babies."

Her home phone number was busy. She thumbed through her messages for the day and decided they could wait. With luck, she'd find Kyle and get out of here before Mr. Clintock or anyone else saw her and hit her with a new complication.

Kyle saved her the trouble of going to look for him. By the time she'd told Ellen she was leaving again, he stepped through her door. "How'd it go?"

"Better than I expected. The job's still mine, at least for now."

"And someone sent you flowers. Is it a special occasion?"

"Not that I'm aware of."

He fingered the big yellow bow that was tied around the glass vase. "Aren't you going to read the card and see who they're from?"

"I'm not sure I want to know."

"What? Some poor slob spent his hard-earned cash trying to impress you and you won't even read his name. I'm never sending flowers to a woman again."

"Oh, all right." She took the envelope and slit it open with the silver tip of her letter opener. The message was printed in black ink. It read, "Your beauty is greater than a golden sunset. Your love is more desired than riches and gold. I will think of you constantly until I see you again. From one who admires you from afar."

There was no name. She handed the card to Kyle. "They're someone's idea of a joke. Now are you satisfied?"

He read the note, turned it over in his hand, then picked up the envelope and examined it. "No name of sender or florist. Do you get these often?"

"No. Why?"

"It just looks a little suspicious to me. I thought secret admirers went out with the Middle Ages."

"I told you, it's someone's idea of sick humor. I'm tough. I don't have admirers."

"Not true." He pulled off one of the blooms and stuck it behind her ear. "You have me. You have the rancher. And you have some guy in the media department named Mark Beetle."

"His name is Mark Beall, and he is not an admirer. Where did you get that idea?"

"I met him at the water fountain. He's one of the slackers, and when I told him I was here with you, the man's face turned a nice shade of irritated red."

"You're imagining things."

"No. I'm a man." He stepped closer and gave her a look that turned her insides to mush and sent her awareness level spiraling off the charts. "If another man is after my woman, I pick up on it real fast." He leaned in close.

Too close. For a minute she thought he was going to kiss her. She stepped backward, more shaken than she cared to admit.

"We better get out of here," he said, "before I forget that this is your office and that you'd probably frown on making love on your desk."

For once she had no comeback. So she just grabbed her handbag and followed him out the door.

THE REST OF THE DAY passed in a flurry of activity, and Ashley felt as if each leg were tied to a different runaway horse, galloping in opposite directions. The ad campaign claimed her mind one minute, the baby's antics took control the next.

The little sweetheart was on a folded blanket in the middle of Ashley's living room floor now, kicking at the plastic Tigger and Pooh that dangled from the baby gym Kyle had picked out that morning. She cooed and gurgled and Ashley was literally mesmerized by her.

Her briefcase was on the kitchen table, work spread out as if it were a tablecloth, covering almost every spare inch of the glass top. But as important as the Ranchers Association's project was, she couldn't bear to ignore her enthralling charge.

It made no sense at all. She didn't even like babies. They were squirmy little creatures that cried and required constant care. When her college friends had jumped into marriage and motherhood, she'd felt sorry for them, believed they were throwing away the best years of their life. Yet here she sat, absorbed in the kicking and punching of an infant while the project she'd fought to keep gathered dust on the kitchen table.

A couple of female voices from a balcony somewhere below Ashley's apartment drifted through the open French doors. Casey turned toward the sound expectantly. A second later, her lips trembled and she started to whimper and fuss.

"You miss your mommy, don't you, sweetie? I'll bet she misses you, too." She put a finger to the tiny dimpled chin and Casey smiled, throwing her hands in the air and catching a wisp of Ashley's hair. She had to pry the chubby fingers loose.

"What a grip! Your dad will have you pitching baseballs before you can walk. Whoever your dad might be. Whoever your mother might be, for that matter."

Perhaps the pretty but nervous lady she'd encountered in the hall. But if that was Casey's mother, why hadn't she come back for her daughter? If it was Tessa, why hadn't she just come to Kyle and asked for help instead of abandoning her child? Was she afraid he wouldn't help? Or were her fears grounded in something far more sinister?

Casey started to fuss. Ashley picked her up and sat her on her lap, bouncing her gently until the fussing dissolved into baby chuckles. But the disquieting questions that filled her mind didn't vanish.

Kyle Blackstone was the variable in all of this, the piece of the puzzle that didn't fit. He liked women and having a good time. She'd seen him in action enough to know that. So if he thought there was a chance he might not be the father of this baby, why hadn't his first priority been to arrange for DNA testing? That way he could have just turned the baby over to the authorities and gone on with his life. Instead, he was taking his vacation so that he could look for Tessa and take care of Casey.

Her thoughts were broken by a rhythmic knock at the door. Standing, she balanced the baby on one hip and crossed the room, stopping to look through the peephole before she swung the door open.

Kyle smiled and stepped inside. "Honey, I'm home. You can fetch my slippers now and bring me a drink. Scotch with a splash of water over ice. Go easy on the ice." He kissed Ashley's cheek as he brushed past them.

"If you're thinking of becoming a comic, I suggest you not quit your day job."

"The baby's smiling."

"Give her another month. She'll develop more discriminating taste."

"No. The better women know me, the more they like me."

"It hasn't worked that way for me."

"You're a little slow, but don't worry. Another night in my bed and you'll catch the full effect of my charisma."

"Another night in your bed and I'd probably catch something it would take penicillin to cure."

"My, you have a cruel streak." He went to the kitchen and set the groceries on the counter. "Hopefully a little food will sweeten your disposition," he announced as he began to unload items from the bags. "Steaks, salad—" he pulled a bottle from one of the bags "—and an excellent cabernet sauvignon, Napa Valley, 1992."

Before Ashley could stop him, he was already opening a package wrapped in butcher paper. "Did you forget our agreement, Kyle?"

"What agreement was that?"

"That if I watched Casey this afternoon while you played detective, you'd pick her up when you finished and remove the both of you from my life so that I can get some work done."

"Of course I remember that. Cut me some slack here, would you? You've helped me, now I want to repay you. I'll cook. You work. It's the least I can do."

"And who's going to tend Casey while you cook?"

"The sandman. The steaks can marinate while I get her to bed. Then we'll grill the steaks at my place. You won't have to do a thing but work on your project and eat."

"You've planned my whole evening."

"Absolutely. I don't know why you're wasting all this time arguing about it." He held out his arms. "Here. Hand me the baby. You go right to work. Time's a wastin'."

"I thought you were going to marinate the steaks."

"I can do both at once. I'm a miracle man with my hands."

"I'll take your word for it."

"I accept that—for now."

She shook her head in exasperation. Arguing with him was a waste of time and she had none to spare.

Doing her best to ignore him, she dropped to the kitchen

chair and picked up her sketch pad. The top page contained mostly simple drawings and key words. Appetite—a steak sizzling on a grill. Tradition—a kid eating a hamburger. Scenic—a cookout with the backdrop of Big Bend country behind it.

Positive images. Beef. But nothing that made them cutting edge. No magic. What she needed was—a ringing phone. Tension swelled inside her. Yet another interruption.

"I'll get it," Kyle offered. "You just keep working." He put Casey back on her pallet and grabbed the receiver.

She tried to immerse herself in her work, but found herself listening to Kyle's end of the conversation instead. It was her phone he'd answered, but he was chatting away as if he knew the caller.

"Yeah, buddy, we're neighbors." A brief pause. "I can't imagine where you got that idea. We're very close. I'm over here now helping her out with a project."

She tossed her pen across the table and glared at him. He smiled condescendingly and motioned for her to go back to work. "I'm sure she just forgot, but I'll tell her to call you for a new appointment. Meanwhile, you take it easy. There's more to life than muscle building." He hung up the phone and rejoined her in the kitchen.

"We're very close? Compared to what—Pluto and Venus?"

"We spent last night together and most of today."

"Not by choice."

"I didn't hold you against your will."

She gave up the argument, mainly because he was right. "Who were you talking to?" she asked in a reasonably civil tone.

"Your friend Bernie."

"Ohmigosh." She threw her hands in the air and pushed

back from the table. "I had an exercise session scheduled with him this afternoon. I forgot all about it."

"That's what he said."

"And he's such a stickler for scheduling. He's probably furious with me."

"He was, but don't worry. I smoothed his ruffled edges for you."

"I heard how you're here to help me with a project. I didn't hear you mention that the biggest problem I have is getting rid of you."

"There you go with that sharp tongue again. You need to try to be more like your sister Lily. I didn't hear her talking like that."

"That's only because she doesn't know you. Give her time."

"I plan to." He walked up behind her and laid his hands on her shoulders, digging his fingers into the fabric of her sweater and massaging. "Your muscles are tight as a drum."

"They wouldn't be if I'd gotten to keep my appointment with Bernie."

"Forget Bernie. Anything Mr. Muscles can do, I can do better." He made circular paths with his fingers, kneading away the tenseness as if he were smoothing a tight wad of dough. "And you'd feel a lot better if you quit fighting me. We're neighbors. And you know you like me. From neighbors to friends to lovers. It's a perfect arrangement. Look at Chandler and Monica."

"Who?"

"Chandler and Monica, on *Friends*."

"Those are fictional characters in a TV series. In real life she's married to someone else."

"That cheater." He moved his mouth close to her ear. "You and I together. Does that scare you so much?"

"Yeah, Kyle. It does."

"Why? You like me. I like you. If we decide we don't later, we break up. So what do we have to lose?"

"My nice, uncomplicated life." She turned to face him. "I've tried having guys for friends, tried casual dating. It doesn't work for me."

He gave her shoulders a few quick strokes, then ran his thumbs up her neck to her earlobes and back down again. The movement was sensual, heated, and she ached to just lean back and go with the flow.

The man was not only a hunk, he was dangerously sexy. For months she'd managed to fight off his advances, play a titillating verbal game of thrust and retreat without letting him get the upper hand. She couldn't let her resolve fall apart just because an innocent baby had dropped into his life—no matter how tempting it was.

"I'm not interested in a relationship with you, Kyle, friendly or any other kind. I helped you out in a crunch. Now I'm through helping. The baby is your problem, and I have work to do." The words came out gruffer than she'd intended.

"If that's the way you want it."

"It is." The words were a lie. She wanted to step into his arms and ask him to stay, wanted to sleep in his bed, with him in it. Wanted it all, but she just couldn't. Not now.

He dropped his hands to his side and backed away. "If you change your mind about the steaks, you know the way to my apartment." He went to the living room and picked up Casey. "Looks like it's you and me, pumpkin. Auntie Ashley has more important fish to fry—or is it cattle to brand?" A few minutes later, he was gone.

There were no distractions now except the lingering odor of Kyle's aftershave and the sight of the pallet where Casey had played. Ashley tried to work, tried to think of cowboys and ranches and beef. But her mind merged the images, put Kyle's face on the cowboy. Replaced ranch expressions with words like *diaper* and *bottle* and *adorable*.

Damn. It had happened already. Twenty-four hours with Kyle and her life was sinking into the relationship trap. Thinking of him when she should be working on a project that might set her career in orbit. Worrying over a baby girl left in his care.

The mother had to be nuts to leave her child with him. He didn't know a thing about feeding or bathing babies. What if he let her slip in the plastic tub? Or let her choke? Or let her get hold of a plastic bag and smother?

Think beef.

Only she couldn't—not until she knew that Casey was cared for and safe and settled in for the night. One more night. Not for her or for Kyle, but for the poor baby who'd been left in a basket.

She poked her feet back into her shoes and grabbed the bottle of wine Kyle had left on the table. Might as well take the steaks and the salad fixings as well. They were his groceries.

Her heart beat a little faster as she knocked on his door. But the sudden rise in her pulse rate had nothing to do with the fact that she was about to see Kyle again.

And if she could convince herself of that, she should probably set up an office at the Algonquin Hotel and start selling the Alamo to tourists.

CHAPTER SIX

KYLE ROLLED UP a sleeve and stuck his elbow in the plastic tub of water he'd positioned on the kitchen counter. Warm, but not hot, exactly as Lily's instructions specified. What she hadn't explained was how he was supposed to hold the squirming baby so she didn't slip through his soapy hands and into the water while he was in the process of washing her.

Man drowns deserted baby believed to be his daughter.

He could see the headlines now. Frankly, he didn't see why she needed a bath anyway. It wasn't as if she'd been outside making mud pies. But Lily said babies needed baths. If Ashley had half a heart, she'd be over here helping him right now.

But she had her own life and priorities and a tiny, defenseless baby wasn't one of them. Apparently neither was he. Of all the women he'd met since moving to San Antonio, she would be the one he'd fall for the hardest. Or maybe it was just that getting close to her had offered the biggest challenge.

He'd lost another round tonight. Still, he wasn't a man to give up on a challenge. He'd have never made the steep climb from where he'd started out to where he was today if he'd let a few setbacks defeat him.

He walked back to Casey and loosed the strap that held her securely in her baby seat. Lifting her, he started stripping the soft pink jumpsuit from her body. She helped by kicking her feet as hard and as fast as she could and swinging her arms like a punch-crazed boxer.

"You could make this easier, sweetheart. Remember that you're dealing with an amateur when it comes to undressing women who don't walk and talk yet."

She smiled and reached for his nose, getting a good grip before she decided the fun and games were over. Her face turned red as she produced a blood-curdling yell. When she stopped to catch her breath, he heard the tentative knock at his door.

"Be Tessa," he pleaded as he rested Casey against his shoulder and headed toward the door. "Please be Tessa or whoever in tarnation left this baby in my care."

He swung the door open. It was Ashley, as gorgeous as ever, with his groceries in her hand.

"You left these at my place."

The ungrateful wench, and after he'd bought the most expensive steaks he could find. "Whatever you're selling, I don't want any."

"I'm not selling. I'm delivering." She stared at his chin. "You're drooling."

"Not at all." He used one leg of the jumpsuit to wipe a smear of formula from his chin. "Casey and I just mixed tonight's nourishment, if you can call powered milk nourishment."

"It's all babies need. Lily said it and Lily knows best." She stepped inside and he kicked the door closed behind her. Not that he was in the habit of kicking the door, but when you were holding a squirming baby in check, the foot was the only available appendage. "What happened to the beef crusade? I thought you couldn't possibly spend a minute away from your glorious calling."

"I shouldn't, and if you're going to get all huffy, I'll go back to it. Otherwise I came to help you get Casey ready for bed."

Relief surged through him, but he wasn't about to let her see it. Instead he relied on the seductive teasing that had always characterized their relationship, the kind of interchange that didn't leave him vulnerable. "Come on. Admit it. You missed us."

"You're half right." She smiled and sashayed by him, heading straight for the kitchen with his groceries. "Besides I was worried that you couldn't handle the baby without me." She stepped around a puddle of water he'd splashed out of the tub while getting it to just the right temperature. "Apparently my assumption was correct."

"So did you come to gloat or to work? The bath water is waiting. Why don't you show me how it's done, oh wise advertising guru?"

"No way, counselor *daddy*. I came to help, not to substitute." She looked around. "I see the tub and the water, but where are the rest of the bath supplies we bought today?"

He moved Casey to the other hip. "Is that a trick question?"

"They have to be around here somewhere, Kyle. They were in one of the bags you carried in from the car."

"See, it was a trick question. If you'd said that in the beginning I could have gotten the answer right away. I threw everything in the hall closet for safekeeping."

She started down the hall. "Put Casey in the water very carefully, and make sure the water isn't too cold or too hot. I'll find the towels and baby soap."

"Okay, but be careful when you open that door. Sometimes objects shift during flight."

"This isn't an airplane."

"Then your guess is as good as mine as to why things tend to fall on my head whenever I open that door."

She made a face and stuck out her tongue. Damn cute she was when she did that. Spunky, smart, a great body and cute. Too bad she didn't realize yet that she was crazy about him.

While Ashley rummaged, he managed to get the baby out of her diaper, which fortunately was not filled with any disgusting mass. "Do you see that water, young lady?" He dipped his hand under the surface and initiated a few ripples. "That's your new bathtub. Guys don't care much for the things. We shower. But women like to soak in tubs for hours."

He eased her into the tub. She squirmed and kicked, but her lips split into a big smile and she started hitting the water with the palms of her hands, apparently used to the ritual. He held on to her with both hands as she splashed. The majority of the spray hit him chest-high, drenching the front of his shirt.

"You can save those antics for Miss Ashley, little lady. She'll look much better in a wet shirt than I do."

"I look better in any shirt than you do," Ashley said, rejoining them in the kitchen.

Casey kicked her feet, making waves that spilled water over the edge of the tub and onto the counter. Ashley grabbed a dish towel and wiped it dry. "You didn't have to fill it to the rim, but she likes water. That's a good sign."

"Why?"

"It just is. You can take her to the beach and go boating, even teach her to water-ski when she's old enough."

"Do you water-ski?"

"Not so much anymore, but when I was in high school, I was terrific at it. I was slalom champion in the senior field events."

"You probably just got the votes because of the way you looked in your bikini."

"Well, that, too."

She tossed her head tauntingly, then dipped the soft

washcloth into the tub before squeezing on a dab of liquid baby soap. She rolled the cloth across Casey's tummy, then washed her short stubby arms and legs. Casey squirmed and he had to adjust his grip to keep her from sliding out of his hands.

"Hold her up so I can get her bottom," Ashley instructed.

He did and Ashley leaned in close. Their hands collided, hers soapy, his wet. Their thighs were touching now as well, separated only by the thin fabric of their slacks. The scent of her attacked his senses, like flowers on a sultry, summer night.

Ashley's hand stopped moving, as if she could sense the fact that his body had come alive, growing rock hard and cruelly traitorous. She glanced up, but there was no mocking laughter in her eyes. Only something dark and smoky that looked a lot like desire. He swallowed hard, wanting to kiss her so badly he could taste it.

With any other woman, he would have done it without thinking. But Ashley wasn't any other woman, and he wasn't about to risk offending her again or causing her to bolt out of his apartment. But he couldn't turn away and it seemed to him that her lips were almost inviting his to touch them.

Finally, Casey broke the trance, picking that moment to let out one of her trademark wails, jerking them both back to the task at hand. He lowered her bottom back into the water and she stopped yelling and went back to happily splashing the water.

"She certainly knows what she wants," Ashley said, dribbling a stream of warm water over Casey's shoulders to rinse the soap from her body.

"Admits it and is not afraid to go after it. Unlike another person in this room."

"You surely are not referring to me."

"If the underwear fits…"

"I *do* know what I want, Kyle Blackstone—a successful career. And I *am* going after it."

Only her voice was huskier than it had been a minute before, and her breathing was quicker. She'd felt something when their hands had touched and their gazes had locked—maybe not the same force he had—but something all the same. There was at least a tiny chink in her armor.

They finished the bath without further incidence, but Kyle wasn't quite ready to give up on the night. He still had a bottle of wine and a couple of steaks. And if Ashley needed to work, well, he could talk beef as well as the next guy. And anything a cowboy could do, he could do better. Except for tending livestock, of course, or roping, or riding horses. But there were no cows or horses in the Prentiss Apartment Building.

LILY STOOD at the worktable, putting the finishing touches on a wall grouping she and Cole had made for the nursery. He'd cut the figures out of wood and she was painting them. A horse, a cowgirl swinging a rope, and a cowboy roping a steer—appropriate for a baby who'd grow up on the Garrett ranch. "I could do a better job of this if my stomach would let me get close enough to the counter so I could get the details right."

Cole stepped behind her and wrapped his arms about her, letting his hands rest on the bulge of her stomach. "If you had a flat stomach, we wouldn't be decorating a nursery."

"I wouldn't have missed this for the world." She dipped the point of her brush in the jar of red paint, blotted away the excess and applied the paint to the cowgirl's lips. "Me, a mother. I still can't believe it—except when I receive a strong kick just below the rib cage."

Cole kissed the back of her neck. "You've come a long way from the FBI forensics center in Dallas."

"I've never regretted the decision to leave there. I loved it at first, but the crimes were too barbaric, too vicious. I'm glad some people can handle the work, but I wasn't meant to. The images were far too haunting when I turned out my light at night."

"You get no argument from me. If you hadn't started Finders Keepers with Dylan, you would have never located me."

"You were pretty lucky at that, Mr. Bishop." She turned and feathered his mouth with kisses.

"Luckiest man in Texas, Mrs. Bishop. Not only did I marry a gorgeous and very sexy woman, but I got adopted by a pretty neat family as well. So, give me the news. What's up with Ashley?"

"Hard to tell." She finished the cowgirl's mouth and deposited the brush in a jar of water. "She's totally engrossed in the baby that was left at her neighbor's door, but I get the feeling it's a little more than that."

"Don't tell me your career-driven sister is interested in the father of the kid. Just last week she gave me her opinion of men and relations! ps in no uncertain terms."

"I know. I've heard the diatribe before," Lily admitted. "The minute you get involved with a man, your life is thrust into chaos."

"That's the lecture. Either they want to hit on her until they get her into bed, or else they want to put a ring on her finger and put an end to her dreams of moving up the ladder of success until she reaches her pie in the sky in New York City."

"And as far as I could tell before today, she was convinced that Kyle Blackstone fell in the first category. But I always suspected she was infatuated with him. No woman talks about a man they're not interested in as much as she talked about Kyle.''

"She never said anything good about him."

"But she never said anything really bad, either. Just that he was cocky, flirtations and arrogant. And she always admitted he was movie star material. When I saw them together today, I picked up some very strong vibes."

"So you finally got to meet the infamous neighbor."

"I did, but he wasn't what I expected."

"You mean he didn't ring your bell?"

She laughed and rolled her hand across her stomach. "I doubt if he could have even found my bell. But he was good-looking. Lean. Athletic. Fabulous smile, though he wasn't doing a lot of that today. But I just have this feeling about him."

"Are you sure it's not your P.I. mind at work?"

"It could be." She washed the paint from her brush as the ideas that had bounced around in her mind all afternoon came into focus. "Someone dropped a baby at his door. He doesn't even know if it's his, yet he has no immediate plans to get DNA testing. That doesn't make a lot of sense to me."

"Did he contact the police?"

"No. He didn't do that, either. He's decided that if it is his daughter, then it has to belong to a woman named Tessa Ortiz. He hasn't been in contact with her for over a year, but now he's determined to find her and get some answers for himself."

"I hope you're not about to tell me that you offered your services in tracking down the woman. You're on leave until after the baby comes. You promised."

"I know. All I did was give him a list of instructions for caring for the baby and my strongest urging to get DNA testing immediately. I can't imagine he wouldn't do that."

"Give the guy a break. He's probably still in shock over finding the baby at his door. Could be he's still in love with this Tessa woman and hopes they can get back together."

"I definitely didn't get that idea." She studied the wooden cowgirl she'd been painting. "And there was another thing. While I was at Ashley's, someone who didn't give their name called and warned her that she should stay away from him. I'm not sure he's the man he purports to be, Cole. So I did a little investigating on my own today."

His understanding look changed to a scowl. He was so protective these days, but she understood why. Actually she loved him for it. It was a side of him she'd never expected to find inside the gruff exterior of the loner she'd first met less than a year ago.

"I only did phone work, Cole. No leg work."

Cole took both of her hands in his. "Have you told Dylan about this?"

"There's nothing to tell. The background check didn't pull up a thing. He has no criminal record, not even any past-due parking fines. He graduated summa cum laude from the University of Texas and was admitted into the law program, where he continued his record of academic excellence. He passed the bar on the first attempt and went to work for Bragg, Cotton & Lerner. He's still with them."

"But you're not satisfied."

"I didn't say that."

"You didn't have to. I know you far too well to rely on words."

"I just don't want to see Ashley get involved with him if it's going to lead to her getting hurt."

"Knowing Ashley the way I do, I imagine it's this Blackstone guy you need to worry about. By the time he falls head over heels in love, she'll get a big ad campaign going and simply write him out of her life. 'Dear John,' or in this case Kyle, 'I sent your saddle home.'''

"No saddle for this man. I don't think there's a shred of cowboy in him."

"Then I guess she'd have to send his briefs home, the legal ones, that is. But if you're worried about him, why don't you ask Ashley to invite him and the baby out to the ranch for the weekend? That way we can see what he's really like and practice having a baby in the house."

"Excellent idea—but I've already told Calley we'd come to Pinto this weekend—unless you have other plans."

"My plans for the weekend are just to be with you. Does this visit have a reason behind it other than to see our friends?"

"You do know me too well. Now that Calley's started working for Dylan and me out of Pinto, I'm itching to see her setup."

"How's Matt doing with the horse ranch Violet Mitchum left him."

"He loves it, and so does Calley."

"Are you sure you feel like such a long drive?"

"I'll be fine, and it'll do us good to get away. Once the baby comes, we'll be sticking close to home for a while."

"You've never heard me complain about staying home." He kissed the back of her neck. "Now, if we're all through talking about Ashley, I say we go to bed. I hear that traveling is not the only thing a man misses out on in the first few weeks after delivery."

"You're on, cowboy."

She smiled as they walked out of the workshop together. It wasn't so long ago that she'd been as set on being a career woman as Ashley was now, though her reasons for doing so were different. Falling in love with Cole had changed everything. This was the same kind of love and happiness she wanted for Ashley.

With the right man, of course. She just wasn't convinced that Kyle Blackstone was that man.

"I SAY WE HAVE one more glass of wine—this time on the balcony," Kyle said as he set the last of their dinner dishes into the sink.

"With all the work I have to do, I shouldn't have even stopped for dinner."

"You know what they say about all work and no play?"

"Hopefully that it gets you promotions and big bonuses."

"No, it turns you into a party pooper. But if you must work, I'll help you. We'll take the wine to the patio and do a little moonlight brainstorming."

"With a little more wine, I'll become giddy."

"Giddy is good for stimulating creativity." Kyle refilled her glass. "It breaks down the inhibitions and enables your muse to take over."

Ashley twirled the red liquid. "I don't know about my muse, but your steaks should have provided some inspiration. They were delicious and cooked to perfection."

"Thank you. Steaks I can handle. Feeding and bathing babies—that's an entirely different story. Actually, a different language." He took her hand and led her to the French doors. "I'm good with words, too, and I definitely owe you a favor for getting Casey to sleep. So come sit with me for a while and hit me with your ideas."

"On one condition."

"Name it."

"You won't start in with your seduction routine. I didn't come over because I have some secret desire to sleep with you. I'm not exactly a frustrated virgin, you know."

"Good. I say let Captain Kirk go where no man's gone before."

"And don't start with your innuendos, either. We're neighbors. Nothing more."

"I'd like to think we're friends."

"I don't know you well enough to be your friend."

"Another reason we need to spend more time together."

It was probably a mistake to stay longer, but she was really hung up on the ad campaign and Kyle did have a very quick mind. It was at least possible that brainstorming with him would jump-start her creative juices. And here she went again, lying to herself about her reasons for wanting to be with Kyle.

Glass in hand, she stepped through the French doors and onto the covered balcony. She breathed deeply, letting the cool night air fill her lungs and clear her head. San Antonio by night. She never tired of the sight, and Kyle's view was even more spectacular than her own. She walked to the edge and peered at the river below them. It cut its narrow and shallow swath through the center of the city, a ribbon of water that carried tourists in brightly colored river taxis and lent a festive air to the open-air restaurants and promenades that bordered its banks.

The Garrett ranch would always be home, a place to go to regroup and be with family. But she liked living in the city, liked the pace and the excitement. Liked the restaurants, museums and shops. She'd known city life was for her from her very first semester at the college in New York City. One day she'd go back to the Big Apple, sit at a big desk in one of the premier advertising firms on Madison Avenue. That's why she had to keep her goals in sight, even when faced with the kind of temptation Kyle offered.

He walked over and stopped at her elbow. "I know I'm not supposed to talk about anything but beef, but you look dazzling in the moonlight."

Awareness sizzled through her. She didn't want to be affected by his nearness, didn't want to react to his words, yet she ached to touch her lips to his. Longed to respond the way any other woman would who'd just spent the biggest part of the evening with a very attractive and attentive man.

Only one kiss would lead to more. One night of intimacy would lead to complications. Especially now that she'd seen him with Casey. Now that she'd watched him cuddle the baby in his arms while he gave her a bottle.

"I have to go," she said, suddenly sure she could never pull this off.

"We just walked out here."

"I know, but I have to go."

"Stay awhile longer, Ashley. Please. Just stay and talk. That's all. I promise." She heard a need in his voice she'd never heard before, a sincerity, a vulnerability. But it was her own feelings that frightened her now, her own needs and weaknesses.

"I can't stay, Kyle. I just can't."

He let go of her and backed away, but the look in his eyes told her that she couldn't have scorned him more had she slapped him across the face. Confused and hurting, she rushed through the living area and out his front door. Escaping like a teenage girl afraid of her first kiss.

Thankfully, he didn't follow her. She wasn't sure she could look him in the eyes and say no again. Her pulse was still racing when she reached her own door. A big white envelope was propped against it with her name printed on the outside in black ink. Hesitantly, she picked it up.

She stuck it under her arm and pulled her key from her pocket. When she started to insert the key, she realized that the door was not completely closed. Anxiety built as she lingered, not willing to step inside when she had no idea if someone was waiting there for her to walk in.

But before she could step away, the door eased open of its own accord. Something brushed against her leg, and instinctively she screamed.

CHAPTER SEVEN

THE CREATURE that had wrapped around her leg took off in a howling ball of fur.

Mikasa. A cat. She'd practically had a heart attack over a cat. Kyle was the first one to reach her, but she was cognizant of other doors opening up and down the hall. She'd probably woken up the whole eighth floor.

"Are you all right?"

"I'm fine. It was just Mrs. Flarrity's cat. I started to push my door open and she ran out." Nothing, yet she was still shaking.

Kyle turned away from her and waved to the people who'd gathered in their robes to see what had prompted her screams. "Everything's under control," he announced. "It was nothing but a cat so you can go back to sleep." He turned back to Ashley. "How did the cat get into your apartment?"

"Apparently I left the door open a crack."

"I can't believe you left your door unlocked."

"It wasn't on purpose. My hands were full of groceries when I went out, and I guess I just didn't pull the door completely shut."

He stooped and picked up the card she'd apparently dropped in all the fuss. "What's this?"

"Someone left it at my door."

He turned the envelope over in his hand and then ripped it open. The card inside was a flowery display with the word *Sweetheart* printed in red across the top. He opened it and read the commercially printed sentiment out loud.

"Loving you has made my life complete." He handed her the card. "He's also added his own note."

"Something equally as syrupy I'm sure." She read the note out loud. "'Keep your love pure. You won't be sorry.'"

"Sounds like a Chinese fortune cookie."

"He's not the most creative cookie maker in the kitchen, but he's persistent."

"How often do you get these notes?"

"I got the first one just before Christmas, and this is about the fifth one."

"Five times in approximately two months."

"Sometimes it's just a note, but a couple of times he left a bouquet of daisies with it. Actually this is the first time he's left anything at my apartment. Usually it's stuck on the windshield of my car in the office parking lot. It could be the same guy who sent the flowers to the office today, though I can't be certain. It doesn't fit his usual pattern."

"And you don't know who he is?"

"Not a clue. His notes sound as if he's some love-struck teenager."

"A kook would have been my assessment. Have you reported this to the cops?"

"Yeah, right. Hey, officer, could you take time out from chasing murderers and drug dealers to read my fan mail? No, it's not threatening. No, it's not lewd or lascivious. Just a secret admirer."

"He's stalking you, Ashley. I don't like it one bit. Tell you what, you go back and stay with Casey a few minutes and I'll check out your place."

"Surely he didn't go inside my apartment."

"You are far too trusting."

"You're starting to sound like my brother."

But she didn't argue with him, mainly because she was relieved he was going inside to look around. Her nerves were still jangled, the result of the earlier adrenaline rush.

Yet this constituted one more entanglement with Kyle, and she knew she had to distance herself from him. She had to stop everything cold turkey while she still could. And she would—right after he checked out her apartment.

"I won't be long," he said, gently shoving her toward his door. "If I see anything that looks suspicious, I'll come and get you."

"But you don't think anyone's in there now, do you?"

"Nothing I can't handle." He smiled, in his usual heart-stopping style that lit up his eyes and dimpled his chin. Her heart did a traitorous flip-flop as she turned her back on him and walked away.

Cold turkey. That was the only thing that could save her.

IRRITATION SKITTERED along Kyle's nerves, like pinpoints of glass being ground into his flesh. He could understand Ashley having a secret admirer. There was plenty to admire, but the way he saw it, skulking around a woman's apartment building and place of employment and leaving notes and flowers sounded more like intimidation than admiration.

He walked through the apartment, looking first to see if anything seemed out of place, then opening closet doors and peering under beds. You couldn't be too careful in cases like this. If the man had found the door ajar or if he'd bumped against it and knocked it ajar while making his delivery, he might have slipped inside. Might have looked through Ashley's personal things without her knowing. A pervert would likely get some kind of sick kick out of such actions.

In fact, Ashley might not have left the door unlocked at all. It wasn't much of a challenge to pick these locks if you had the right tools, and the tools were easy to come by in the city.

But if anything was amiss, Kyle couldn't tell. Ashley's closets were neat and organized, the larger boxes on the bottom of the shelf, the smaller ones on top. A place for everything and everything in its place. Not exactly the way he lived, but it must work for her.

He stopped at the bathroom door. Fluffy towels the color of cafe au lait hung from the towel rack, and a basket filled with lotions and creams sat next to the tub. A white terry robe hung on the back of the door.

Pangs of arousal stirred inside him. There was no way to stand inside this room and not imagine her standing naked under the spray of the shower. No way not to envision her smoothing one of the fragrant lotions over her long, tanned legs, no way not to think of touching her.

He turned and walked toward the door, suddenly feeling as if he were the intruder in her life. He hadn't stalked her, at least not in his mind, but he had looked forward to seeing her at the health club. It was her body that had attracted him first. After all, he was a man. But it had been her easy smile and quick wit that had made him single her out to talk to, no matter how many other women were hanging around.

His goal all along had been to wear down her resistance. Mainly because he knew once he dated her, she'd become like all the others. Dispensable. So far, things weren't working according to plan.

He stopped at the door and gave the apartment one last look. Even if the stalker had been inside earlier, Kyle was certain he wasn't here now. He let himself out, this time making sure the door was locked behind him.

A minute or two later, he stepped inside his own front

door. "Ashley?" There was no answer, but he could see the soft glow of light from the lamp in the bedroom. "All's clear," he said, keeping his voice low so as not to wake Casey, but loud enough so Ashley would hear him and not get spooked again when she saw him standing over the bed.

His worry was wasted. She was curled up in the bed next to Casey, both of them sound asleep. Two dark-haired beauties. One innocent and helpless, looking like a doll on display in a storefront window. The other hauntingly beautiful, impish, seductive. The kind of woman a man could wake up beside every morning and never get tired of the thrill.

Something turned inside him, like the click of a dead bolt in a rusty lock. He felt weak, defenseless, the way he'd felt so many times in his youth. He thought he'd left those fears behind him, conquered them with his law degree, his career, his devil-may-care facade.

But they were still there, just waiting for the right time to surface, to remind him of who he really was. And even if he could magically change into a permanent kind of man, Ashley Garrett wasn't interested. She had her career to keep her warm at night.

He walked to the bed, pulled the covers over Ashley and tucked them under her neck. Hesitating for only an instant, he touched his lips to hers. She squirmed, then curled her knees up to her chest without opening her eyes.

Kyle grabbed a pillow from the other side of the bed and a blanket from the closet before he tiptoed out of the room and down the hall.

Back to the sofa. Again.

THE MOOD IN Ashley's office could be described in one word. *Hectic.* Miss one day of work and every emergency possible popped up. Another one of Murphy's Laws, she was sure.

The shoot yesterday had been in Mark's bivouac. He was the media guy; she was the account exec. The only reason she'd planned to be there at all was because the PR guy who was handling the campaign for the soap company had a tendency to panic and she wanted everything to go smoothly.

It hadn't. The makeup lady had arrived late. The photographer arrived on time, then realized he'd brought the wrong film with him and had to make a trip back to his office. And the actress the PR guy had insisted on using because of her wholesome freckles muffed her lines so badly they had to do a half dozen takes to get a decent one.

And then there was Kyle. Half the women in the office had already been in this morning to ask questions about him. Was she serious about him? Did he have a brother? Basically, was he available?

She looked up as Mark sauntered through the door. He walked over and propped himself on the back edge of her desk. "I said if I ever had another day like yesterday, I was going to quit and find a dishwashing job. This may be the day."

"What now?" she asked, slipping her notes into the appropriate folder.

"Mitchum just assigned me the media direction on the Craven Bakery account."

"What's so bad about that?"

"It means I have to spend time with Ralph Daily, and I'd rather walk on hot coals than work with that whining nitpicker of an account exec."

"He's not that bad."

"Not to you. He practically drools when you walk by. But the last time I worked with him on a project, he complained constantly. He also botched everything up, but to hear him tell it, nothing was ever his fault.''

"So what are you going to do about it?"

"Just what I'm told, unless I come up with a good reason why I can't do it. That's why I'm here."

The comment set off alarms. "Does this have anything to do with me, because it better not. I'm not getting into your problems with Mr. Mitchum or Ralph."

"Not exactly. I just told the boss that you had already asked me to work on the TV and radio ads for the Ranchers Association and that the work would be extensive and extremely time-consuming."

"In my family, we call that a lie."

"A white one, though. The Ranchers Association is a big account, and what with wanting to spend time with the new boyfriend, you could use a little help. I'm good with anything to do with Texas themes. Remember the ad I did for that new boot outlet?"

"You didn't mention a new boyfriend to Mitchum, did you?"

"No, of course not. But he's probably heard by now. A cross between Tom Cruise and Mel Gibson. That's what one of the secretaries said. They're starting a pool on how long you'll keep him around before you dump him. They have a lottery for who gets to go after him then."

She groaned. "To set the record straight, Kyle Blackstone is not my boyfriend."

"My neighbors never come to the office with me."

The irritation swelled inside her until she thought she'd pop like an overfilled balloon. "How do you know that he's my neighbor? You've never been to my apartment."

"Sure I have. I took you home one night last fall when your car was in the shop."

Now she remembered. How could she forget? That was right after Mark had come to work for the firm, before he found out that she did not date co-workers. He'd made an untimely pass. She'd set him firmly in his place.

"But that's not how I know he's your neighbor," Mark added. "You mentioned him one day over coffee in the lounge. He has a one-track mind and a bed to back it up. I think that's how you put it." He grinned and leaned in closer. "So, boyfriend or no, that account is going to be a lot of hard work and Jim Bob McAllister is going to be a royal pain. So how about officially requesting me for all the media work associated with the campaign?"

"Okay. You can be the media man, but I'm running the show. Nothing gets done without my approval."

"Anything you say. And if you want to work on it this weekend, I'm free."

"My plans are up in the air, but I'll let you know. Mr. McAllister's coming in Monday and I'd like to have several ideas sketched out, though I expect them to be in very rough form."

The buzzer on her desk sounded and she punched in the receiver button to pick up her secretary's voice.

"I know you told me to hold your calls, but Kyle Blackstone is on the phone. He says it's an emergency."

Mark produced an I-told-you-so grin. She pointed a finger and directed him out the door. "Put him through, Ellen."

"Ash, this is Kyle."

"What a surprise! What's the latest emergency?"

"Casey won't take her bottle. When I try to put the nipple in her mouth, she spits it out."

"I'm at work, Kyle. I can't believe you called to tell me this."

"I don't want her to starve."

"Are you sure you mixed the formula correctly?"

"If I can try a case in court, I can follow a few simple directions."

Ashley doubted Casey would starve, but what did she know? "I'll call Lily and get back to you."

"I knew you'd come through. And while you have her on the phone, ask her if it's all right if Casey chews on my keys. I think she likes the way they rattle. That was the only thing that would make her stop crying."

"You let her put your dirty keys in her mouth?"

"Just once. She's quick. Then I washed them in soap and water. Oh, yeah, and the good news is the crib came. It doesn't have anything on the mattress, though, just some kind of slick covering."

"You have to put a sheet on it."

"I tried that. The sheet was so big it slipped loose and made a big wrinkled mess in the middle of the crib."

"Not one of your sheets. You have to use a crib sheet. Don't you remember buying some the other day?"

"No, but I'll take your word for it. If we bought them, they have to be around here somewhere."

"Try the hall closet."

"It's a jungle in there."

The buzzer on her desk sounded again. "I have to go, Kyle. I'll call Lily and see what I can do, but you need to start looking for someone to help out with Casey. I can't keep doing this."

"Who would I call?"

Casey started crying in the background and Ellen was at the door signaling to Ashley that she had an important call waiting. "I've got to go, Kyle. I'll try to get in touch with Lily and get back to you. In the meantime, don't call me. I'll call you."

"What if I have an emergency?"

"Okay. You can call, but only if it's a *real* emergency." She hung up the phone and threw up her hands in exasperation. "Who now?" she asked as Ellen pointed to her to take line two.

"Jim Bob McAllister. He is one persistent man."

"Aren't they all?"

But it was Casey who stayed in her mind when she tried to turn her attention back to work. Kyle was doing the best he could, but the baby needed someone to take care of her who knew about babies. She needed her mother.

BY NOON, Ashley had taken three more *emergency* calls from Kyle. He'd lost his list of instructions and couldn't remember how to mix the formula. Then he found the instructions in his shirt pocket, but Casey's bottom looked red and irritated when he changed her and he didn't know what to do about that. The third call was just to tell her that Casey had finally taken three ounces of formula.

In fact, between talking to Kyle and Lily, she'd gotten almost no work done. At this rate, she'd have to work all weekend just to have something to show McAllister on Monday. Maybe she'd drive to the ranch on Saturday and stay until Monday morning. That way she could work without interruptions in a setting that should be more conducive to dreaming up appropriate themes.

Her secretary stepped to her door.

Ashley threw up her hands. "Don't tell me. It's Kyle Blackstone with another emergency."

Ellen smiled and nodded. "Shall I tell him you're in a conference?"

"No, I'll take it. I can't wait to see what kind of problem he'll come up with next. He could be a one-man sitcom."

"And as gorgeous as he is, I wouldn't miss an episode."

"You, too, Brutus."

KYLE SAT ON the edge of his bed watching Casey sleep. An angelic aura surrounded her now, but the morning had been pure chaos. Clearly he was not cut out to be Mr. Mom. If he hadn't had Ashley to call on, he didn't know what he would have done. But he couldn't keep this up for long. Sooner or later Ashley would refuse to take his calls. Probably sooner from the tone of her voice that last time.

Besides, he couldn't stay off work indefinitely. If he didn't find Tessa fast, he'd have to give up the search. But not yet. If the baby was his, Tessa was the mother. If the baby wasn't his, then why had someone left a poor, defenseless baby with a man like him?

He was fast reaching the end of his e. He'd sped down what appeared to be open road , only to meet brutal dead ends. Not one of Tessa's friends or ex-co-workers had any idea where she was living now.

He had to believe the doll in the wicker basket had been left there for a purpose, but if it was supposed to trigger some memory in him, it wasn't working. So, he had a baby in the house that might or might not be his, a gorgeous, sexy woman in his life who didn't really want to be there.

Worse, instead of just making a play for Ashley, he was actually falling for her faster than a man toppling over the top level of seats at a Texas Rangers game. And not to be left out, some lovesick stalker was leaving flowers and notes at Ashley's door and possibly following her around.

Casey stirred in her sleep and managed to get most of a fist into her mouth. "I know. This isn't a bit easier on you. But it looks like you're stuck with me awhile longer. Either that or you get turned over to 'The Authorities.' Believe me, kid, you don't want to go there."

Stretching, he caught a glimpse of himself in the mirror. There were dark whiskers dotting his chin, hair that hadn't been combed, a T-shirt stained with formula. If he hurried he just might get in a shower before the baby woke up. Either that or he could make a few more desperate phone calls.

He opted for the latter. Thumbing through the phone

book, he located the number for Ernie Brooks. He didn't know the man well, but he'd met him a few times in the laundry room. He was a retired FBI agent and it appeared he kept good tabs on what was going on in the building. There was always a chance he'd seen the woman who had been in the building the same night Casey had been left at Kyle's door. If not, he might be aware of some stranger walking the halls with flowers in his hand.

He located the number and punched it in. All he had to lose was the time it took to make a phone call.

The phone rang four times, and he was about to give up when a deep male voice answered.

"Hello."

"Ernie, this is Kyle Blackstone, from the eighth floor. We've talked a few times in the laundry room and in the elevator. I'm the guy who hogs three washing machines."

"Ernie's not here right now. This is Mitch Barnes."

So this must be the man who was staying with Ernie. He'd seen them together a few times. The man was pushing forty, a good three inches taller than Kyle's five feet ten inches. Around two hundred pounds of what appeared to be mostly muscle. Not a man you'd want to tangle with in the dark, except that he did have a slight limp.

"Do you know when Ernie will be back?"

"Not until this evening, but I can give him a message for you if you like."

"Actually, you might be able to help me. I know this sounds strange, but someone left—a surprise package at my door the other night. I need to give the gift back to the donor but I don't know who left it. I was wondering if you saw anyone come into the building Tuesday night with a large laundry hamper on their arm. I think it may have been an Hispanic woman. At any rate, she had dark hair and eyes."

"And she left you a baby."

"How did you know that?"

"Gossip—travels faster than a speeding bullet. I haven't seen anyone who fits that description, though. Is the baby yours?"

"I'm not sure. There was a note with the baby that says I'm the father, but it was the first I'd heard of it. Right now I just want to find the woman who deserted the child."

"I wish I could help. Have you thought of calling in a professional to conduct the search?"

"I hadn't thought I'd need to. If I'm the father, then there's only one woman who could be the mother. I was sure I could track her down with a couple of phone calls. Unfortunately I was mistaken."

"Don't give up. For the sake of the baby, you have to find the mother. If you don't, no one will."

Odd that he was talking to a stranger about this, yet the man's advice paralleled his own feelings. "Do you have any suggestions as to how I'd go about searching for a woman when I have no real leads to follow?"

"There's always a lead somewhere. You just have to search until you find it."

"I'm trying." He stretched his legs in front of him and scratched his whiskered chin. "While I have you on the phone, I have another question."

"Shoot, though if it's about caring for a baby, you're out of luck."

"No, it's about a stalker."

"Is someone stalking you?"

"No. He's after a friend of mine, and I'm not actually sure *stalker* is the right term since the man's only left flowers and notes and hasn't made any threats."

"The threats may come later. A man obsessed walks a thin line."

"You sound as if you're familiar with the practice."

"Just what I've heard Ernie mention. Who's the victim?"

"One of my neighbors on the eighth floor."

"Has she notified the police?"

"Not yet. I just thought I'd ask around and put people on the alert to watch for some stranger coming into the building with small bouquets of flowers."

"If I see anyone who fits that description, I'll give you a call."

"I'd appreciate that. And ask Ernie to do the same."

"You got it. And good luck with the baby."

Kyle gave the man his phone number and thanked him for his advice before he hung up the phone. The man hadn't been any real help, but his words about the notes changing to threats burned across the lining of his stomach. Ashley might be willing to let the creep continue to leave flowers and notes at her door or on her car, but Kyle wasn't. Not if he had to install hidden cameras or stand guard over the area with a shotgun.

Not that he had a shotgun or would know how to use it if he did. But he was damn good with his fists, so bring the filthy coward on.

He stood and headed to the bathroom for a past-due shower. He never made it. Casey had other plans and she announced them at the top of her lungs before the water had time to get hot.

IT WAS AFTER SIX by the time Ashley finally gathered her things and closed her office door behind her. As much as she would have liked to be heading to the gym for a workout session with Bernie, she'd had to cancel again. She had to get some work done.

Too bad. Since Bernie had been overseeing her exercise program, she'd lost an inch in the waist and two through the hips. She was now a perfect size six, which meant she could wear that divine cocktail dress she'd gotten on sale at Neiman Marcus last fall and the snazzy blue suit she'd purchased on her last trip to visit old college chums in New York.

Thoughts of clothes danced in her head like sugar plums in the old Christmas classic. Only in between every pirouette, Kyle Blackstone's face appeared, the same way it had all day. She could imagine the satiny skirt of the cocktail dress swishing around her legs as they danced to a swing band in some cosy nightclub.

His arms would tighten about her waist and pull her close. He'd smell like the outdoors, all fresh and spicy, and his body would be hard and unyielding. Hers would be lithe and agile, and when he held her close, she'd mold herself against him.

By the time she reached her car she was warm and tingly and thoroughly disgusted with herself. She would check on Casey tonight, make sure she was fine, and that was all. Then she'd go immediately to her own apartment, have a light dinner and work on the Ranchers Association campaign.

She was strong. She could do it.

THE MAN STOOD in the shadows and watched as Ashley flounced to her car, her high heels clicking along the pavement, her silky hair bouncing with each step, only to fall back in perfect place about the smooth flesh of her bronzed cheeks.

She was sophisticated and girlish at the same time, serious, yet playful, a combination that drove men crazy. And if he didn't make his move quickly, he was going to lose her.

Anxiety rolled and thundered inside him. He wouldn't give up. Giving up was what losers did, and he wasn't a loser. No matter what anybody thought, he wasn't a loser. He would prove it to all of them.

CHAPTER EIGHT

ASHLEY STEPPED OFF the elevator on the eighth floor, suddenly tired and with serious second thoughts about stopping by Kyle's apartment to check on Casey. If she went straight to her own apartment, she could have soft lights and a glass of cold wine while she unwound in her very comfortable chair. Her space would be quiet and orderly. No emergencies. No surprises. No interruptions.

Kyle's place, on the other hand, was sure to be chaotic. But when she passed his door, she stopped. The door was ajar and she could hear Kyle singing along to one of his country CDs, a little off-key. And the warm and tingly feeling she'd felt in the parking lot at work exploded into a full-blown sizzle. She knocked and waited.

"Come in, if you dare."

She peeked around the edge of the door. "I can come back later if this is a bad time."

"Don't even think about it." He walked out of the kitchen, a glass of water in one hand, Casey riding the opposite hip. He was barefooted, unshaven, dressed in a stained T-shirt and a pair of gym shorts adorned with fuzz from Casey's new baby blanket.

But Casey was smiling at him and clenching her fingers about his nose. He pried her fingers loose and tickled her tummy. She laughed out loud and then poked a thumb into her mouth and rested her head on Kyle's shoulder.

Something tightened in Ashley's chest and she found it difficult to breathe.

"I know I look like something Mikasa dragged in from beneath the stairwell," he said, "but you don't have to stare at me like that."

She kept staring, mesmerized. She'd never seen him look worse. She'd never wanted a man more. The feeling scared her to death. She took a step backward.

"Do I look that bad?"

"No. You look—fine."

"Now you're lying for sure. But lie all you want. Just don't leave, unless you want to hear a grown man cry."

She swallowed hard, determined to get past the moment of weakness. "How would I ever go on living with a tragedy like that on my conscience?" She held out her hands and Casey came to her willingly.

"Look at the fickle little goose," he said. "Sucking up to you after I spent the day taking care of her while you selfishly went about trying to make a living."

"I might have done a better job of it if I hadn't been interrupted six times an hour."

"You exaggerate. I never called more than five times in any sixty-minute period. I kept count. Anything over that, I called Lily direct. In fact we've talked so frequently, we're now best friends. She'll probably ask me to be her baby's godfather."

"More likely she'll change her phone number to keep you from harassing her."

"So that explains that strange message from the phone company the last time I tried to call." He raked a handful of dark hair from his brow. "Care to stay for dinner? I'll cook, that is if I can find a can of something to open."

"Only if you shower and shave first." Not that she was concerned about his appearance, and certainly not that she wanted him to look any better to her than he already did, but the poor guy obviously needed a break. "I promise to take good care of Casey while you get cleaned up."

"Now I know I love you. But I must warn you, it's time for her bottle, and she's perfected the skill of spitting when she burps and aiming it so that it never hits the cloth on your shoulder."

"Oops. Tell you what, I'll go home and change into something a little less expensive first, though I'm sure Casey is too much of a lady to spit milk onto a silk blouse."

He put his hands together in prayer position. "Promise you'll come back."

"As soon as I change."

"While you're at it, consider something comfortable and less confining. That little black thingy you wore the other night would be perfect."

"Don't push your luck."

She backed out the door and hurried to her own apartment, certain that if she had any willpower at all, it had evaporated in the heat of the last few minutes. Last night she'd wanted to kiss Kyle so badly she could taste it. A few minutes ago, she'd had a serious attack of lust just from watching him interact with Casey.

She should be running in the opposite direction at the speed of light. Yet she was humming a Mariah Carey tune while she slipped into a pair of jeans and a bright-yellow T-shirt. Still, she planned to keep things under control until she made up her mind exactly what to do about Kyle.

She'd sleep in her own bed tonight.

IT WAS A FULL two hours later before Ashley and Kyle leaned over the rented crib to tell a bathed and fed Casey good-night. They were making progress, though. Neither Kyle nor Ashley had gotten drenched in the process of bathing her, and this time Ashley had been careful to avoid standing too close to Kyle. And Casey had taken a full six ounces of formula, and hadn't spit up at all.

Now she was all scrunched up, on her side with her

little bottom poked out behind her. Kyle tried to insert a pacifier into her mouth. She spit it out and replaced it with her favorite thumb. A second later, her big eyes closed and the long, wispy lashes curled about her cheeks.

"She looks pretty innocent right now for a baby who had me jumping through hoops today."

"She is innocent, Kyle. Think what it must be like for her, ripped from everything familiar and dropped into a new life with people she doesn't know."

"I have trouble thinking of anything else," he said as they quietly walked from the room. "I've called everyone I know who might have even a clue about where Tessa's living. No one's heard from her since she left San Antonio almost a year ago."

"It's hard to believe she left without telling anyone where she was going, especially her sister."

"You wouldn't think so if you knew Tessa. Her family is a lot different from yours. She has a brother in California she hasn't seen in five or six years. They don't even exchange Christmas cards. Her sister lives right here in San Antonio, but half the time we were together, the two of them weren't on speaking terms."

"What did they argue about?"

"You name it. They both had explosive tempers and their grudges had a long shelf life." He walked to the door that led to the balcony and stared out. "I don't want to give you the wrong impression of Tessa. She has a lot of commendable qualities, and she's extremely intelligent."

"And very pretty, I'm sure."

"That, too."

"I still think she may be in some kind of trouble, maybe even in danger," Ashley insisted, unable to let go of her initial theory. "She may have given up her baby in order to keep her safe. It's the only thing I can imagine that would make a woman give up a baby. I know I couldn't do it.''

"Trouble or not, I can't find her, so I can't help.''

The opening she was waiting for. She pounced on it. "The sensible course of action would be to hire a professional.''

"Like your brother?''

"He's the best in the business.''

"Lily told me the same thing today. She said she'd handle it herself if she wasn't so far along in the pregnancy.''

"What did you tell her?''

"That I'd think about it. The truth is, I'm pretty much convinced Tessa isn't Casey's mother, yet I still feel responsible for the baby. Someone came to me for help, and they must have had their reasons. They said they'd be back for her. Too bad they didn't say when.''

He leaned against the door frame, half in the shadows, half in the glow from the lamp in the living room. The teasing smile he usually wore so well had been replaced with an expression that made him seem older, deeper, more complex. She sensed a seriousness about him that hadn't surfaced before.

He turned to face her and took her hands in his. "I couldn't have taken care of Casey the last two days without your help, Ashley.''

"I'm sure you would have managed.''

"No. Finding out that I might be a father has been an incredible experience. It's not easy to explain, but I feel drawn in two opposite directions. I feel a bond with Casey that can only be explained by our being blood kin. Yet part of me refuses to accept the fact that she could be my child. At times I feel that the life I knew doesn't exist any longer, and that no matter how this turns out, I can't go back to being the man I was.''

This was a different Kyle from the one she was used to.

Less cocky. Far more honest. The feeling that swept through her now was different as well. Almost like an ache, a longing that she had no idea how to fill. And even though the baby was definitely not her child, she had the same bizarre feeling that her life would be different from this point on. Perhaps that was the main reason she was afraid to get involved with Kyle. She liked her life the way it was.

"I guess I'm just overwhelmed," he said. "Casey is totally dependent, and I'm not used to looking out for anyone except myself."

"I'm not sure I could have handled it as well as you have."

"I guess none of us is sure what we'll do until we're put to the test." He placed a hand at the small of her back. "Now, about that dinner I promised you." His tone changed, from serious to light, steering them back into more familiar territory.

But Ashley wasn't quite ready to end the conversation.

"I really think you should call my brother Dylan and talk to him, Kyle."

"Why don't you tell me more about that fabulous brother of yours?" he asked as they stepped back into the living room. "How did he get into such an unusual business?"

"He was an undercover detective on the Dallas Police Department for a while, even managed to infiltrate the ranks of the Texas mafia when J. B. Crowe was still running the show. In fact he was in on Crowe's arrest. And my sister Lily worked in the FBI Forensics Center in Dallas until she decided that was not the life for her."

"So they just gave up their jobs, moved back to Trueblood and started a P.I. business?"

"I think it was the ranch that really brought them home. Anyway, their agency is called Finders Keepers and they specialize in locating missing persons." She gathered Casey's toys as she spoke. "I talked to Dylan today and he's willing to take on the search for Tessa. It's your decision, of course, but you can't go on like this forever."

"I know. I was thinking I could give it a week. If I haven't located Tessa by then, or if someone else hasn't come back to claim Casey, I'll have the DNA testing done, and that will be it. But if Dylan thinks he can find Tessa, I could put off the testing awhile longer."

"I'll leave you his number. You can call him tomorrow and work out the details. Now I say we eat. And you don't even have to strain yourself opening a can. When I went home to change clothes I brought back a container of frozen vegetable soup that Lily sent home with me the last time I was at the ranch—just in case your cupboard and fridge only hold beer and pretzels."

"Wise woman. And by the way, I like your choice of attire." He stood back and gave her the once-over. "Not quite as classy as the black thingy, but you fill out the jeans to perfection. That Bernie obviously knows how to tone a woman."

"They say every person has a talent."

"Yeah? You show me yours and I'll show you mine."

"I think I'll pass on that offer—unless your talent is coming up with a dynamite slogan and concept for the Ranchers Association's big push to improve their image."

"Try me. You just never know what I might come up with."

"You've got yourself a deal."

"Soup first, then work," he countered. "I'm famished."

"THINK BEEF."

"I'm trying, but then I look at you, and the thoughts that come crashing into my mind have nothing to do with a cow." Kyle sat beside Ashley on the sofa. She was hold-

ing a number two pencil and scribbling notes on a legal
pad. He was looking over her shoulder, actually *at* the
shoulder that the wide-necked T-shirt had nearly slipped
off. It was creamy and white and looked more tempting
than any beef he'd ever laid eyes on. He trailed his fingers
from her neck to her arm.

"You're not helping, Kyle. Think slogans."

"Gotcha."

She leaned back and closed her eyes. "I'm picturing
cowboys. Rugged. Manly. A spirit of adventure of and
romance."

"Slogans, right?" He tried. But everything he could
think of had to do with the woman sitting next to him.
Hair a little mussed. Makeup worn off, T-shirt just a wee
bit snug over her breasts now that she'd leaned against the
back cushions of the sofa.

"Cowboys do it with their boots on," he offered, knowing full well that wasn't what she was looking for. Still, a
trace of a smile tugged at her lips.

"I doubt Jim Bob McAllister does. I just hope he does
it on his home range, 'cause the man is not doing *it* on
mine."

So her sense of humor did occasionally slip into her
work. That surprised him, as did a lot of things he'd
learned about Ashley in the last two days. Like the fact
that she had a warm spot in her heart for babies though
she tried hard to pretend it didn't exist. That even the worst
of days brightened the second she walked through the
door.

"The best beef is home beef," she said. "Do you think
McAllister would buy that theory?"

"He might, depending on whose home he was in at the
time. And as long as the home is in Texas."

"Spoken like a true Texan."

"A Texan from Illinois."

Her eyes flew open. "You're a Yankee?"

"I think they call folks like me a damn Yankee."

"What's the difference?"

"We come down here and stay. I even have a Stetson somewhere to prove I'm adjusting to the mores."

"Stetson or not, you are no cowboy, Kyle Blackstone. I doubt you've ever been in a saddle. But being from Illinois does explain your lack of a decent drawl."

"Does a saddle on the back of a mechanical bull count?"

"Please, deliver me." She laughed, a genuine, giddy feminine sound that dipped inside him and triggered all kinds of reactions. All of them treading the dangerous waters of passion. Dangerous because he didn't dare do anything that would send the lady running.

She sipped her wine and stretched her legs in front of her, slipping out of a pair of brown sandals and propping her bare feet on his coffee table.

A fire settled in his belly and sizzled along his nerve endings. He'd been attracted to Ashley from the first time he'd seen her hurrying down the hallway, the heels of her pumps clicking against the polished wood, head high and silky skirt swishing about her thighs.

But what he was feeling now went way beyond attraction, dug a hundred times deeper than the lust he usually felt when he was turned on by a woman. This was a kind of shimmery heat that stuck in his throat and set his insides tumbling as if he were on the down spin of a giant Ferris Wheel.

He snaked his arm about her shoulders. "Beef is where you find it."

"Real beef for real Texans," she whispered, but her voice sounded different, breathless, a little husky.

He met her gaze, and there was no denying the smoky glaze of desire. "When you're hungry, go for the gusto."

But now it was his own voice that dropped so deep it cracked.

"You mean like now?" She scooted closer, her face tipped to meet his, her lips moist and quivering.

"I can't think of any better time."

"Neither can I."

CHAPTER NINE

ASHLEY TOUCHED her lips to his, tentative, whispery soft. His heart pounded against the walls of his chest as he waited, trying not to show how eager he was. If she had any idea how she was affecting him, she might panic and bolt the way she had last night.

She leaned into him and he drew her close, his body pressing against hers as the kiss deepened. He couldn't think, couldn't reason, couldn't do anything but feel. It was a man thing, this losing all control when the woman you ached for kissed you and played with your mind. One part of his body swelled to attention while his brain turned to mush.

Ashley's hands splayed across his back, pulling him closer, and it slowly hit him that she was reeling with the same passion that possessed him, so strong it was as if neither of them could pull away. She parted her lips, darted her tongue inside the chasm of his mouth and then retreated. Blood roared through his body with the force of a tidal wave. This was no ordinary kiss, no amorphous moment in time.

When she pulled away for breath, he winced from the loss. And from the force of her hands pushing against his chest.

"Answer the phone, Kyle."

He tried to pull her close again. She ducked from the circle of his arms. "You have to answer the phone."

The damn phone. He hadn't even heard it. "Let it ring,"

he insisted, trying once more to pull her into his arms. "If it's important, they'll call back."

"No. It could be Tessa. Hurry. Answer it before it wakes Casey. If she gets up now, she may stay up for hours."

He let go of Ashley and scanned the area, his gaze following the direction of the jangling ring. Cordless phones had an uncanny way of disappearing in his apartment.

Finally, he spotted it peeking from beneath the baby blanket he'd tossed on the chair. He dived for it, reaching it and punching the Talk button before the caller gave up and broke the connection. "Kyle Blackstone. Start talking and this had better be good."

"If this is a bad time, I can call back later."

The voice was vaguely familiar. "Who is this?"

"Ernie Brooks, from the fourth floor. My friend Mitch said you called today. Said you were asking about a dark-haired woman, possibly Hispanic, who's been seen in the building."

"Have you seen her?"

"I think so."

Ashley was standing a few feet away, smoothing her clothes and her hair, looking a lot like a woman on her way out—the last thing he wanted to happen. But he couldn't ignore this call. Jumping into action, he moved to the door and blocked her exit. "I can make time to talk about this, Ernie."

"Do you know the woman?"

"I'm not sure. Look, I'm not going to beat around the bush with this. You know part of the story. It seems everyone around here does. Basically, someone left a baby girl at my door with a note that says she's mine. I think this might be the woman who made the delivery."

"I'm not sure it's the same woman, but the one I saw seems to fit the description you gave Mitch. I'd put her at five feet six or seven inches tall, under 120 pounds, wavy shoulder-length hair. Her eyes were dark, and she had really long lashes. Curves in all the right places.''

"You have a great eye for details.''

"A holdover from my working years with the Bureau.''

"So when and where did you see this woman?''

"Actually, I've seen her twice. The first time was Tuesday night. She walked into the building at the same time I did, but she didn't seem to know exactly where she was going. I asked if I could help her, but she said no. A few seconds later she turned around and left. She didn't have a basket or a baby with her at the time, but she looked upset and her eyes were swollen as if she'd been crying.''

Crying. That would fit. Surely a woman about to desert her baby would shed a few tears. It was the secrets he couldn't quite figure out, the way she could just leave the baby without talking to him. Except that he'd made it clear to Tessa that he wouldn't be ready for marriage or a family for many, many years.

"Are you still there, Kyle?''

"Yeah, sorry. When was the second time you saw the woman?''

"Yesterday.''

He swallowed hard. While he'd been revisiting all of Tessa's old haunts, doing everything he could think of to track her down, she might have been in this very building. This close, but still she hadn't knocked on his door and come to him.

But the good news was that if the woman Ernie had seen was Tessa or even the woman who had left the baby, then she was still around. If she'd come to the apartment building twice, she'd likely come again. He'd alert everyone in the building if it came to that, offer a reward if someone would just call him when they saw her.

"I think we're talking about the same woman, Kyle, but

I can't give you any additional information. I didn't see her go into any apartment or see what kind of vehicle she was driving. For all I know she may have come by taxi or even walked in off the street."

"I understand. Just keep your eyes open. Ask your friend Mitch to do the same, if he will. If either of you see her, call me immediately. Try me here first, but I'll give you my pager and my cellular number as well."

"I'll do that."

Kyle gave him the numbers and thanked him again for calling back. He was about to hang up when Ernie stopped him.

"Mitch also mentioned that you're concerned about one of your neighbors who has a man stalking her. Would that be Ashley Garrett?"

"Yeah, but I don't know if *stalking* is the right word. Ashley thinks the situation is harmless, but he's left flowers and notes at her door and on her car when it's parked in the garage at her office. No identifying signature."

At the mention of her name, Ashley stepped closer and her mouth drew into a scowl.

"She needs to be careful, Kyle. If the relationship shows any sign of escalating—any sign at all, she should notify the police. Actually it's probably a good idea to alert them to the situation now, though they won't be able to do anything at this point."

"What kind of sign?"

"Changing his MO—perhaps leaving gifts of a personal nature instead of flowers. Increasing the frequency of the notes and gifts. Calling her on the phone. Making comments that make her think he's watching her."

"You sound as if you have a personal working knowledge of guys like this."

"A lot more than I care to remember. Most of the time

the situation's harmless, but when it's not, it can be—well, just warn her to be careful."

Deadly. That was the word Ernie didn't say. Unsaid, it filled Kyle with an icy dread that he didn't want to reveal to Ashley. "Any other suggestions as to how she should handle this?"

Ernie hesitated. "I wouldn't want to frighten her. Just have her be wary and watch for the signs I mentioned. I know I don't have to tell a connoisseur like you that she's not only a damned good-looking woman, but personable and friendly as well. When she smiles or looks at you with those emerald eyes, men take notice. Even an old codger like me gets a rise in the pulse rate just from being around her."

"So you think this could just be a neighbor or an acquaintance who finds her attractive. Maybe a guy she works with."

"Could be and probably is. But there are more psychos out there than you can shake a stick at. Guys hanging precariously close to the edge can mistake smiles and conversation for genuine attraction. I've seen it happen more than once."

"I'll talk to her."

"Good. If she has any questions, send her to see me. Apartment 408. I'm home most of the time."

"Thanks, Ernie. For everything."

"Sure. And I hope you find the mother of the baby. In the meantime, I'll keep my eyes and ears open. It's the first time I've felt useful in quite a while."

"Thanks."

They said their goodbyes. Kyle turned back to Ashley, but the fire that had blazed inside him a few minutes ago had been doused by a cold spray of double-edged reality involving two women. Casey's mother and Ashley.

One had deserted a baby even though she was so worried about her she sneaked back into the apartment building to check on her. *If* the woman in question was actually the one who'd dropped off the baby. So far he had no real proof of anything.

And then there was the case of Ashley and the flower-toting stalker. A shy guy who was afraid to let her know that he was crazy about her? Or a dangerous psychopath suffering from what he believed to be unrequited love?

She touched her hand to his arm. "Who was on the phone?"

"Ernie Brooks from the fourth floor."

"The retired FBI guy?"

"That's the one. How well do you know him?"

"I see him around the building and occasionally run into him at the coffee shop on the corner. If he's there when I stop in for cappuccino, I join him. He's a nice guy."

"If you go around smiling, batting your eyelashes and having coffee with every nice guy you meet, no wonder one of them is stalking you."

"I don't *bat* my eyelashes. I don't have a stalker, either. You're making a mountain out of a molehill, as my dad would say."

"I'm supposed to. I'm a lawyer. And I'm not trying to magnify the situation. I just think you should be careful. Ernie agrees with me. In fact, he thinks you should notify the police."

"It won't do any good."

"It can't hurt."

"I'll think about it. And I am careful. Right now, I'm also very tired. And since I don't have a plush job like you, I do have to show up at work in the morning."

"I don't have a plush job. Fortunately I have a couple of weeks of unused vacation time." And a case that was going to court next month, but there was no use bringing that into the current negotiations. "You can't leave now," he insisted. "We were in the middle of something when the phone so rudely interrupted us."

"We were in the middle of a mistake."

"And you know what they say about half-done mistakes." He touched his lips to the back of her neck, then nibbled her earlobe. "If you stop before you see them through to their conclusion, they will never come out right."

"Or never have the chance to make you regret them."

She wasn't buying. He'd have to think of a better argument. "I thought you wanted to brainstorm slogans for the Ranchers Association."

"I tried. You were uncooperative."

"I was just getting the hang of it." He nuzzled her shoulders. "I was about to hit you with my best shot."

"That's what I'm afraid of. Something like, Get branded by a cowboy for the poke of your life."

"Not even close." He wrapped both arms around her. "Stay with me tonight, Ashley."

"I can't, Kyle."

"You stayed one night. The world didn't come to an end."

"That was different. We hadn't kissed then. If I stay now, we'll make love and I'm just not ready for that."

"You seemed ready before the phone rang."

"I'm not saying I wouldn't enjoy it. I'm human."

"Then you do admit there's a certain chemistry between us?"

"It would be hard to deny after that kiss."

"Then stay. For tonight. That's all I'm asking."

"You say that now, but that's not how these things work out. If we make love once, we'll do it again. We become intimate, and then we expect certain things of each other. The relationship becomes complicated. Finally one person wants out and there's a bitter breakup."

"You have us breaking up before we even get together. How did you get so cynical so young?"

"From dealing with men and relationships. And I'm not cynical—I merely deal in reality."

"Maybe you were with the wrong men before."

"It's not the relationship or the men. It's the timing. I'm not ready for any kind of commitment."

"Then we'll be perfect for each other. I'm not asking for a permanent relationship and I won't make demands on you."

"Is that what you told Tessa? I want you—until I don't."

"I didn't break up with Tessa, if that's what you're getting at. She broke up with me."

"Why?"

"Because I was honest with her. I told her I wasn't ready for marriage and a family and that I wouldn't be for several years. She opted to move on. It wasn't easy for either of us, but I understood."

"If you parted on such friendly terms, why didn't she come to you, Kyle, and tell you that you had a daughter? Why didn't she give you a chance to do the right thing and share the responsibility for raising the baby even if the two of you didn't decide to get married?"

"So that's what's really bothering you. You think I'm the reason Tessa deserted her baby instead of coming to me and asking for my help."

"It's a reasonable assumption. You were with her for two years. She had plenty of time to get to know you and to learn to trust you."

"Which is why I doubt that Tessa is Casey's mother. I've told you that."

"That's the other thing that doesn't add up, Kyle. You doubt she's yours, yet you keep putting off going in for

DNA testing. You just don't seem like a man who'd take on this kind of responsibility for a child who's not yours."

"Would you like me better if I just threw her to the wolves?"

"The people in Social Services are not wolves, Kyle. They're responsible adults with the resources to do what's best for her."

"I don't have the answers you want, Ashley. I may be way off base, but I'm doing what I think is right for Casey. None of which changes the way I feel about you. I like you—a lot. I want to be with you. Is that so bad?"

"You don't really know me. I just fell into your life along with the baby. You don't know about my dreams, my peeves, my frustrations. You don't even know what I like to do in my spare time, what makes me laugh or cry."

"I know you work too hard. That you don't know much more than I do about tending babies, yet you jumped right in when you found out that Casey was stuck with me. I know you're warm and funny and that you turn me on just by walking into a room."

She tilted her face and met his gaze. "If you're not careful, you're going to give lawyers a good name."

"That still sounds like a goodbye."

"It is, for now. But for the record, you are a hard man to walk away from."

"Is that supposed to bring me some kind of satisfaction when I crawl into bed by myself tonight?"

"Good night, Kyle." She offered a wave of dismissal.

"I'll walk you to your door."

"That's not necessary."

"I know. But I'd like to all the same."

She rose to her tiptoes and kissed him on the mouth, sweet and quick before she pulled away and fit her hand in his. It wasn't the same as taking her to bed with him and making love until the sun came up. But it felt really good. All warm and gooey, like chocolate chip cookies hot from the oven.

It was a feeling he didn't remember ever having before.

ERNIE HUNG UP the phone and went back into the kitchen to find Mitch starting a fresh pot of coffee. "Planning on another sleepless night?"

"I've come to expect them."

"You won't be off work forever, you know. As soon as the torn Achilles tendon heals, they'll reassign you and fly you off to some new part of the country."

"And a new identity." Mitch turned the switch on the coffeemaker and shuffled back to the table, his limp proof that his injury had not healed as quickly as he'd hoped it would. "A new city. A new job. A new me. Only after a while they all run together like cream being stirred into black coffee." He shrugged his shoulders. "I'm not sure it's all worth it anymore, Ernie."

"I'd say you're getting a case of cabin fever. Maybe we should go out tonight, down a couple of beers and see what we're missing."

"We know what we're missing. A lot of cigarette smoke. A bunch of guys like us sitting around wondering how they let everything get away from them."

"Hell's bells, you are down. What brought this on?"

"Too much time to think. When I'm on the job, life just happens. I don't have time to wonder why. Sitting around all day, every day's given me plenty of time to wonder, and I'm not sure my life's going anywhere."

"You're one of the best undercover agents in the business. I should know. I trained you."

"Which means I know how the best criminal minds work. I know how to kill, maim, torment. I've slept in the same room with serial killers and had dinner at the same table with child molesters. Not a lot of great memories to look back on.''

"You apprehended over ninety percent of the offenders you went after. I'd say that's something to be proud of.''

"It means ten percent of the criminals are still walking the street—along with the guilty ones that some judge or jury let off. Or that some misguided parole board let loose so they could go back to what they'd started.''

Ernie fit his fingers into his pocket. No cigarettes. There hadn't been any for years, but times like these he still reached for one. He knew what Mitch was going through, or at least he thought he did. Every man in law enforcement felt this way from time to time. It came from eating a steady diet of all that was bad in the world.

And he was certain that Kyle's situation had gotten to Mitch, as well. "Are you still thinking about trying to track down your father?''

"I'm thinking about it. It's a tough decision to make. I've made it thirty-seven years without knowing who he was. It might be better if I never know.''

"Maybe you need a real change of pace, Mitch. A torn Achilles tendon might keep you from going undercover, but it wouldn't keep you from going under the *covers*.''

Mitch grinned. "You got a woman picked out for me, old pal?''

"No. I'd suggest Ashley Garrett, but I think Kyle Blackstone has his eye on her and he'd be a hard one to beat out.''

"Do you blame him? That woman has it all. Brains, looks, a smile to die for.''

Ernie pulled a couple of mugs from the shelf. "And a stalker, at least it sounds like a stalker to me. Notes and flowers over a two-month period without ever once signing his name. Makes you think of that Dubekki case, doesn't it?''

Mitch made a face. "I try to never think of the Dubekki case."

"I know what you mean. It occasionally gives me nightmares even now. Dubekki started out the same way. A harmless secret admirer. Only as soon as the women would start dating someone else, he'd go berserk. The man had more loose screws than an old jalopy."

"And he left a string of bodies that stretched from California to Florida."

The aroma of coffee wafted into the air. Ernie usually limited himself to three cups a day. Two when he first got up. One at the coffee shop after his morning jog. But the damn stuff smelled so good tonight, he might have one. If it kept him awake, he could always read.

Mitch opened the refrigerator and took out a carton of half and half. "Do you think Kyle has a chance with Ashley Garrett?"

"He'd probably have a better chance if he hadn't just had a baby dropped at his door," Ernie answered. "A woman like her probably isn't overly eager to take on another woman's family. A man's past has a way of catching up with him."

"Not always. Not if he's lucky or if he's smart enough." Mitch picked up the coffeepot. "I guess two clean cups mean you're going to join me."

"Why not? I hate to see a friend drink alone."

Mitch poured the coffee and took his to the table, where he dropped into a chair. He added the milk and stirred slowly. His blue eyes were shadowed and Ernie suspected there was more on his mind than Ashley or the Dubekki case or even his job. He'd thought the same thing ever since Mitch had taken him up on his offer to stay at his place while he recuperated.

But he didn't like to ask too many questions. Mitch would tell him whatever he wanted him to know in his own good time. Still, he'd bet it had something to do with a woman. That's what it usually took to bring a smart, sensitive, good-natured man down to the level where Mitch was wallowing now.

"You ever been in love?" Mitch asked, as if he'd been reading Ernie's mind.

"I'm sixty-seven. I've been in like, love, heat and everything in between. With any luck I'll be there again."

"So how come you never got married?"

"I did. Twice. The first one decided one man wasn't enough for her. The second wife decided she needed all of me. She gave me the ultimatum. Her or the job. It was no contest." He stretched his legs under the table. "What about you? Have you ever met a woman you thought you'd like to wake up beside for the rest of your life?"

Mitch ran his index finger along the rim of his coffee cup, his lips drawn into straight lines that seemed to almost disappear. "Maybe."

"That's sounds mysterious."

"Let's just say I haven't been put to the test as yet. Now, why don't we discuss something besides women, some subject where we might exhibit a little expertise. And I don't mean files from the FBI."

Ernie switched the conversation to baseball, a safe topic that wouldn't put either of them on edge. Mitch's love life, or lack of one, was no concern of his. Still, if he were a betting man, he'd lay odds that there was a woman on Mitch's mind. One he wanted to go after or one he'd let get away.

Mitch finished his coffee, walked to the counter and ran water in his cup before depositing it in the sink. "I think I'll take a walk," he said.

"This time of the night?"

"Actually, I only plan to walk the halls and ride the elevator up to the eighth floor."

"On the trail of a good-looking woman who may have dropped a baby off?" Ernie asked.

"Her, or a man with flowers in his hand."

"Then you can forget walking away from your job, Mitch Barnes. You've got the blood of a lawman running through your veins."

"Yeah, but I'm thinking of searching for a cure."

ASHLEY CHECKED the last frames for the Power Point presentation she had scheduled for four o'clock. Unlike the Ranchers Association project, this one had fallen into place from the very beginning. One of the major department stores in town was looking for a way to increase their share of the high-end clothing market, and she had come up with several terrific key ideas, at least that was the way she saw it. Today she'd find out if the president of the company and his marketing team agreed with her.

"Delia asked me to bring these storyboards to you. She said you needed them for a pitch this afternoon."

She looked up as Mark Beall stuck his head in the door, storyboards in hand. "Thanks." She stood and took them from him, checking the last-minute changes as she did. As usual, Delia had done a fantastic job.

"You must be having a light day if you're serving as Delia's errand boy," she said, turning her gaze back to Mark.

"No. I just stopped in her office to check on an account we're both working on. Now I'm on my way to get one of the writers to work miracles on an ad script that one of my clients provided. The dialogue reads like something from the fifties."

"Will the client let you do the rewrites without their input?"

"Let's hope. As you know, I'm not the best of team players."

"You keep saying that, but I've never found it to be true."

"Working with beautiful women is worth a few concessions."

The comment made her uneasy, and Mark had been throwing out this type of remark with increased frequency over the last couple of weeks. She decided not to let this one ride. "I'm not a woman when I'm on the job, Mark. I'm a genderless advertising executive. I don't expect or want concessions."

"Sorry, Ash, but unless you start coming to work in formless sweats with curlers in your hair, I'm not likely to forget you're a woman. But I'll try to watch the compliments when we're on the job."

On the job was all she had to worry about. She never dated co-workers. It was a long-standing rule that she had no intention of breaking, not even if she'd been attracted to Mark—which she wasn't. He was creative and smart and a good man to have on her side when she had a job to do, but that's as far as it went.

He started out the door, then stopped. "What time do you want to get together this weekend?"

"This weekend?"

"Yeah, don't you remember? You said you wanted to work on the RA campaign. I turned down a date who had two tickets to the Spurs game, so I hope we're still on."

She tamped down a swift surge of guilt. She'd already taken on Kyle's and Casey's problems and she couldn't handle anyone else's. Thinking back over the conversation in question, she tried to remember exactly what had transpired. "You must have misunderstood me, Mark. I remember saying that I appreciated your offer to work, but I don't remember confirming it as a done deal."

Mark walked to her desk and perched on a back corner. "You sound a little stressed. Is Jim Bob McAllister making unreasonable demands? If he is, you need to tell him off.''

"Right. And how long do you think it would take Mr. Clintock to place my head on his chopping block?''

He leaned across the desk in conspiratorial fashion. "So that's what he keeps in that locked file cabinet in his office.''

The buzzer on her desk sounded, but before she had time to respond, Kyle stepped through her door, baby in arms. He was dressed in a business suit and a light-blue shirt and tie that set off his dark-blue eyes. Her heart did a childish flip-flop at the sight of him, and memories of last night's kiss sent heat rushing through her senses.

"I hope we're not interrupting anything?'' he said, his gaze fastened on Mark.

"What are you doing here?'' she stammered, determined not to let him see how his unexpected appearance had affected her.

"Casey missed you. We decided to come and take you to lunch.''

"Cute baby,'' Mark commented, not budging from his spot by her desk.

Ashley clamped her hands into fists. "Thank you for the storyboards, Mark, and good luck with your script changes.''

"I'll handle it.'' He glared at Kyle as he walked out.

"Friendly guy.''

"He usually is.''

"He hid the trait well just now. At least he did once I walked through the door. He seemed to be plenty friendly before that.''

"Something tells me you didn't come here to talk about the friendliness of my co-workers.''

"No. Casey decided that since the day was so gorgeous,

we should come and take you to lunch on the River Walk.''

"You should have called, Kyle. I don't have time for lunch. I'm giving a pitch at four."

"A pitch?"

"A presentation. I show the client what I have in mind for them and hope they buy it."

"Oh, that kind of pitch. Don't worry. I'll get you back long before four."

"I have a million things to do before that."

He perched on the back edge of her desk. "You have to have food. We'll just walk down to the River Walk and eat al fresco."

Casey let out one of her squeals of delight and reached for a colorful paperwcight on Ashley's desk.

"See, she insists you go with us. Now what could you positively have to do that's more important than making her happy?"

"The paperweight would make her happy."

But Ashley had to admit that she was just a tad hungry. And it was a beautiful day, and Casey was looking so adorable, and— "Okay, Kyle. A very quick lunch."

The buzzer sounded as they started out the door, but now that she'd decided to go to lunch with Kyle and Casey, she was eager to be on her way. She touched the button on the intercom.

"I'm going out for lunch, Ellen. Take messages and tell the caller I'll get back to them this afternoon if it's an emergency or first thing Monday morning if it isn't."

"It's your sister Lily and she says it's important."

"Okay. Put her through."

She picked up the receiver. "What's up, Lily?"

"Don't get upset with me, but I did a background check on Kyle Blackstone."

"Why would you?"

"I had a few concerns about a woman dropping off a baby at his door instead of visiting him in person and asking for help."

Ashley wanted to protest, to tell Lily she had no right to check out her friends as if they were common criminals. Only the concerns that Lily had were the same ones that had been lingering on the edge of her awareness ever since Casey had appeared on the scene. "Did you find out anything?"

"A little. That's why I called."

A dead weight settled in Ashley's chest. She hated to hear what was coming next, yet only a fool would turn her back on the facts. "Kyle and Casey are here now," she said.

"Should I call back later?"

"No." She turned and stared at Kyle. He'd picked up the colorful paperweight and was holding it up so that Casey could see it better. Man and child. Maybe father and daughter. They made a very appealing picture. Ashley let her gaze drop to her desk. "No need to wait, Lily. There's no time like the present."

CHAPTER TEN

THE BABY KICKED hard and Lily patted her stomach through the heavy denim fabric of her maternity skirt. She'd hesitated to call Ashley with the news she'd just learned, but if Ashley was going to let an innocent baby draw her into a relationship with a man she'd been avoiding for months, she deserved to know at least as much as Lily knew about the man in question.

"I'm waiting, Lily. Say whatever it is you have to tell me."

"Can Kyle hear your end of the conversation?"

"Clear as a bell."

"But you don't have me on the speaker?"

"You're entirely confidential."

Lily took a deep breath and plunged ahead. "I conducted a garden variety background check."

"And...?"

"Everything checked out fine. No arrest records. No bankruptcies, not even an unpaid traffic fine."

"Let's skip to the *but*. I'm sure there is one or you wouldn't have called."

Ashley's tone was singed with irritation. Lily wasn't sure if it was caused by her prying or by Kyle's visit to Ashley's office. Or maybe Ashley had passed the stage of wanting honesty where Kyle was concerned.

"Frankly, I had planned to give up the search at that point."

"But something drove you on."

"Not me, but my assistant. I forgot to inform her of my intent to abort. That's when she discovered that Kyle Blackstone only came into existence two years ago."

"I'm not following you."

"He changed his name—legally, the summer after he graduated from law school and accepted his current position."

"And that's bad?"

"Not necessarily. People can change their name for a variety of reasons," she explained. "Most of them harmless."

"You must not believe that's true this time."

Lily took a deep breath. If this turned out to be nothing, she'd feel like a real heel. Kyle might be the perfect man for Ashley, and here she was dripping poison into the relationship's bloodstream. Nonetheless, his refusal to have immediate DNA testing worried her, especially when combined with his hesitancy to call the authorities and have them begin a search for Tessa Ortiz. Separately, nothing seemed important. Added together, it made him look like a man who had something to hide.

"I'm still here, Lily."

"Okay, I'll put this as simply as I can. Frequently people change their name because they're running from their past or they want to keep someone from finding them. I don't know if that's the case with Kyle, but I just think you should be cautious. Don't rush into *anything*."

"*Anything?*"

"Okay, don't rush into a relationship."

"You know my views on that."

"I know what you've told me a thousand times, but Kyle's a handsome, sexy man. And you're going to fall one day. It's just a matter of time."

"You'll be third-grade room mother for your kid by then. Now, take care of yourself and forget about me. I'm in no danger of falling into anything except fatigue brought on by attempts to work miracles for the Ranchers Association."

"Are you still planning to drive down tomorrow?"

"I'll be there, but not before noon. I have to take my car in for an oil change in the morning. The things a woman does when she doesn't have a man in her life."

"In that case, I may miss you altogether. Cole and I are leaving to drive to Pinto about eight."

"Tell Matt and Calley hello for me."

"I'll do that, and I hope you're not angry about the background check. I only did it because I care about you."

"I know. I'm not mad, though I do wish you'd ask before you start doing things for my own good. I'm all grown up, and I can take care of myself. Now, go take a nice long nap. And tell Dylan and Dad I'll see them tomorrow afternoon."

They said their goodbyes and Lily hung up the phone, not nearly as convinced as Ashley that her little sister could resist the charms of Kyle Blackstone. She'd seen them together. Knew that even before Casey had arrived on the scene, Ashley had been infatuated with the man, even though she might not have admitted it to herself.

Now that Lily had met him, she could understand the attraction. The man reeked of charisma. And that was before he smiled.

CASEY LET OUT a high-pitched squeal and swung her arms in the air.

"I think that means she wants a chip," Kyle joked from his seat across the narrow table from Ashley. "I'd go easy on the salsa though. It might clash with the formula she had a little earlier."

Casey squealed again and made a series of chirping noises.

"There was definitely no mention of chips in that outburst," Ashley assured Kyle.

"I suppose you understand squeals and baby babble."

"Certainly. She asked if I'd report you to the Humane Society for suggesting she eat a substance unsuitable for human consumption."

Casey squirmed and Ashley adjusted her hold on the little darling while Kyle dipped a chip into the bowl of salsa that sat between them. Only instead of poking the dripping chip into his own mouth, he reached across the table and fed it to her. She opened her mouth before a stream of salsa splashed to the table or the front of her blouse.

The action was playful, yet when his fingers brushed her lips, they awakened a stirring of desire that sent Ashley reeling. She felt the blush redden her cheeks and was glad Lily couldn't see her now.

The waitress showed up about that time with their order. Chicken fajitas, guacamole and an order of refried beans. Ashley turned her full attention to the food. It was much safer than interacting with Kyle.

"Do you want me to take Casey?" he asked as she spread the napkin on her lap. "It's difficult to eat and entertain her at the same time, and I'd hate for you to get a stain on that suit."

"I can manage. I'm not really hungry anyway."

"What's wrong?"

"Nothing." Nothing except that the man sitting across from her that she knew so little about had turned her life upside down in the last few days. She'd let him, of course. Let him worm his way into her routine, eat up the time she needed for work. Now she was even having lunch with him and Casey in the middle of a workday. Worse, she'd practically dissolved into a swoon right at the table from just the brush of his fingers against her lips.

"You don't seem yourself. If that McAllister guy is coming on to you again, I'll be glad to punch the jerk in the nose for you."

"You'll do nothing of the sort. He's a very important client."

"He's a dirty old man in cowboy boots."

"Fifty is not old. My father's sixty-one and he's not old."

"McAllister's not old when compared to your father. I rest my point." He filled a soft flour tortilla with strips of sizzling chicken and peppers and set it on her plate. "You didn't get another flower delivery, did you?"

She shook her head. "No flowers. No cards."

"Just Mark Beall hanging over your desk. I wouldn't be surprised if he's the secret admirer."

"You're being ridiculous, Kyle. Mark knows I don't date co-workers."

"Like that would stop a guy from trying. He's nuts about you. I could tell that from the way he was leering at you when I walked in on the two of you."

"He doesn't leer, and he has a lot more right to be in my office than you do. He *works* there and that's what I should be doing."

"So that's it. You're angry because I dropped in unexpectedly today? I thought women were supposed to like surprises from the men in their lives. I know I heard that somewhere."

"Probably in a commercial I wrote. And the surprise in the ad was diamonds, not lunch. Besides, you know how important my job is to me."

He flashed her a smile, one that parted his lips, showed his front teeth and sent her pulse spiraling. "You kiss mighty good for a woman married to her job."

"I didn't say I wasn't talented."

Kyle filled his own tortilla and began eating, taking big

bites and chewing as if he were ravenous. Apparently his concern for her disposition did not affect his appetite. But then, why should it? He needed help with the baby; she came running. He popped in and invited her to lunch; she dropped everything and joined him. He kissed her; she melted. Well, actually she'd kissed him, but the result was the same.

The whole situation irritated her and she decided to hit him with Lily's findings head-on, see what kind of explanation he offered. "That was my sister Lily who called while you were in the office."

"I gathered as much. How's she doing?"

"Fine, but she had a question about you."

"Is she still concerned that I haven't had DNA testing?"

"Actually she wanted to know your full name."

"Finally, a question I can answer. Kyle Evan Blackstone." He took a long drag on his iced tea. "Has a nice manly ring to it, don't you think?"

"Is that why you *chose* it?"

He arched an eyebrow. "Does this conversation have a point?"

"Lily was wondering why you'd changed your name."

"Interesting." He cocked his head at an angle and stared at her. "Does your family investigate every man you date, or do I rate special treatment?"

"It's not like that."

"So what is it like?"

He was irritated and with good reason. He'd given them no reason to go digging into his past, to make assumptions when they had no real evidence. "I'm sorry, Kyle. Lily was worried about my getting involved with a man who'd had a baby left at his doorstep, but she had no right checking into your past. And you definitely don't owe me any explanations."

"Apology accepted. I don't know what kind of ideas

are floating around in Lily's mind, but you can assure her that I'm not an escaped criminal and I have nothing to hide.''

"I'll tell her."

"I know what's bothering you and Lily, but I just plain don't like the idea of using a blood test to find out that I'm a father.''

"It's dependable.''

"It's cold. A man has expectations about that kind of thing.''

"You had expectations about being told you were a father?''

"Sure. I imagined coming home one day in the far distant future and having the woman I love tell me that she's pregnant. We'd hug and talk about names and get all sloppy with sentiment. You know, one of those Kodak moments. What about you? Don't you have any plans for having children?''

"I haven't given it that much thought.''

"But you do want children?''

"I guess.'' The talk put her on edge. She'd always said she wanted children one day, but marriage and motherhood had loomed so far in the future they seemed almost like another life. "The food is wonderful,'' she said, changing the subject. "I don't know why I've never come here before.''

"Probably because you have to leave your work and walk out the office door to get here.''

They finished the meal in near silence while Casey drifted off to sleep in the circle of Ashley's left arm. She checked her watch. "I wish I didn't have to wake her, but I have to get back to the office. I have a full afternoon of work before I do the presentation at four.''

He grimaced. "I hate to hear that.''

"I don't mind working.''

"Mind? You love it. But I need to ask a favor and it would be a lot more likely you'd say yes if you weren't bogged down in work."

"I feel for you. I really do. But whatever you're about to ask, the answer is no. I can't possibly miss any more work."

"Please, Ashley. I wouldn't ask if this wasn't an emergency."

"Your whole life is an emergency, Kyle."

"I know, but not like the next two hours. I have to go into the office and take a deposition for a case that goes to trial soon. The man lives out of town and this is the only time he can make it in."

"Take Casey with you."

"I can't. My boss would fire me on the spot."

"I'm not the only woman you know, Kyle. Call one of the women from the health club. Try the one you were with the night I discovered Casey in the basket. She was obviously smitten by you."

"Smitten? Do people still use that word?"

"Then she was panting and drooling all over your neck and shirt. Is that better?"

"Sounds good to me. But I wouldn't dare call her for this. You're the only woman I'd trust with taking care of Casey." He pointed to the sleeping child. "Look at her, perfectly content in your arms."

"There's bound to be at least a dozen day-care centers just in the downtown area. Call one of them."

"I called *all* of them. Most have a six-month waiting list, and they laughed out loud when I asked about walk-in status."

"You only need one, Kyle. Surely you could find one day-care center that would take Casey for the afternoon."

"I did, not six blocks from here. Three babies no older than Casey caged in their baby beds crying. No one even bothered to go to them and see what was wrong. I told the woman in charge what I thought of their baby care practices and marched out. Actually, they ordered me out, but I was leaving anyway.''

The thought of strangers ignoring Casey's cries carved away a thick slice of the resolve Ashley had mustered a minute ago. She didn't want her in a place like that either, but that didn't mean he could dump the baby on her.

"Today is out of the question, Kyle. The presentation is important and I have a boss, too, you know.''

"Please, Ashley. Just this once. I'll be back long before four.''

"It's ten before one now, and I still have some fine-tuning to do on my pitch.''

"You can put Casey in her chair while you work. Or lay her on her blanket. They're both in the car. As long as she can see you, she'll be fine.''

"Until she gets hungry or her diaper needs changing.''

"Pleassse.''

"Why can't you take her with you, Kyle? You have an office.''

"I told you why. I have to take a deposition. I'll be back in plenty of time for you to dazzle them with your brilliance.''

A couple of hours tending Casey and she'd be the talk of the office for months to come. Ashley Garrett, confirmed career woman, changing diapers on company time.

"Just this once,'' he begged. "Name your price.''

"There is no price steep enough for what you're asking. Besides, you don't keep your word. My grout's still dirty.''

"Forget the dirty grout. I'll replace the floor. Hell, I'll replace the kitchen. Just two hours. I wouldn't ask if it wasn't extremely important.''

She knew she'd be sorry, but he was desperate. And

begging. "If you're not back by four o'clock, I'll kill you."

"I'll load the gun." He jumped up, raced around the corner of the table and kissed her, full on the mouth, right in front of everyone.

And once his lips touched hers, she forgot all the reasons why she was not supposed to be getting involved.

ASHLEY LOOKED AT her watch again. Three-fifteen. In exactly forty-five minutes, she was expected to be wowing her audience with ways to attract buyers to designer fashions. And Kyle was nowhere in sight. He hadn't even called to report he was on the way or stuck in traffic or attacked by a gang of marauders.

All of which would be better for him than facing her ire if he didn't show up.

But she had to admit that things had gone far better than she'd anticipated. All the women in the office had oohed and aahed over Casey for the first half hour, passing her from one to the other shamelessly, especially since none of the big bosses had returned from lunch.

But when the fun had worn off for Casey, she'd begun to whine and fuss, not happy with anything Ashley had tried until she'd finally fallen asleep. Now she was sleeping in her baby seat, her little head resting against the side. The picture of sweetness and innocence.

Delia walked into the room with a stack of booklets still warm from the printer. "Everything's in order."

"Great. I don't know what I would have done without you this afternoon."

"No problem. The next time the art department's in a tight spot, I'll come looking for you."

"A lot of good that would do you. You've seen my drawings."

"Well, the first time we need someone to draw horses

that look like pigeons, I'll give you a call. What else can I do for you, little substitute mom?''

''To start with, don't call me that. If you really want to help, you could take those booklets to the conference room and spread them out on the table, one in front of every chair.''

''What about the storyboards?''

''Ellen already has those in place.''

Delia crossed the room and stood over Casey, staring down at her sleeping form. Casey squirmed and cried out in her sleep. ''She's so cute, Ashley. No wonder you're attached to her.''

''I'm not attached.''

''Have you always suffered from this type of delusions about yourself?''

''Really. I'm not attached. I'm just helping out a desperate neighbor.''

''A neighbor who looks like Kyle Blackstone. We should all be so lucky.''

''Don't tell him that. If his head gets any bigger, he'll have to buy two hats and sew them together just to cover it.''

''Vain or not, I'd let him set his boots under my bed any night of the week.''

''If he doesn't make it back here in the next ten minutes, he'll be sleeping in the morgue.''

Casey stretched and started to wail, a shrill cry that seemed different from any Ashley had heard before. Dropping her pen to the desk, she ran over and stooped down beside the baby. She screamed all the louder and kicked the blanket from her legs.

''What's wrong with her?'' Delia asked, stepping closer.

''I don't know. She usually wakes up happy.'' Ashley picked her up and rocked her in her arms. Instead of quieting, Casey kept sobbing, and big tears rolled down her fat red cheeks.

"It's all right, sweetie. Ashley's here and you're fine."

"She looks awful red," Delia said. "I don't remember her being that color when you came back from lunch."

Ashley studied Casey's face and decided Delia was right. She held Casey against her chest and rested her cheek on the baby's forehead. "She's hot. I think she has a fever."

Delia put the back of her arm to the baby's forehead. "Oh, Ashley. She's burning up. The poor darling is sick."

"But she was fine at lunch."

"Babies can get sick fast. My niece does that. One minute she's playing, the next her fever is shooting up like Mr. Clintock's blood pressure when we lose an account."

Panic rolled in Ashley's stomach. Casey looked so pitiful, and she wouldn't stop crying. "What do I do? I can't bear to see her like this."

Delia shook her head. "Does she have a pediatrician?"

"I'm sure she must, but I don't have any idea who it would be."

Casey's cries grew weaker, but her face was still blood-red, and her eyes had a watery glaze to them. She was sick, really sick. At this point, Ashley didn't feel much better. Her insides were quivering and her heart had turned itself inside out. "I'm taking her to an emergency room. I don't know a lot about babies, but a high fever can't be good."

"You have a pitch to give."

"Right. A pitch." She'd forgotten it for a minute, but even if Kyle walked in the door right now and took Casey to the hospital himself, she'd never be able to stand in front of a group of executives and say anything that made sense. Not when she was so worried about Casey, she couldn't think straight.

"Mr. Clintock's going to kill me, but I can't give the pitch. Not now. I'll have Ellen call and try to reach the people before they get here. If not, they'll just have to understand. Would you try to explain to Mr. Clintock that I have no choice. He can assert his power and rake me over the coals later."

"The man has kids himself. He'll understand."

"Yeah, right. And I'll understand the theory of relativity when described in Portuguese." Ashley gathered Casey's things and stuffed them into the diaper bag.

"What should I tell Kyle when he shows up?"

"If he ever gets here, tell him to meet me at the emergency room at Methodist Children's Hospital on Floyd Curl."

Delia followed her out the door. "Call as soon as you know something, Ashley."

"I will."

Casey lay against her shoulder, deathly still and quiet now, though her body still shook occasionally from the powerful sobs that had possessed her a few minutes earlier. Ashley knew people were staring as she rushed down the hall, but she didn't stop to offer an explanation. Running out on her job to tend a sick baby. She'd never live this down. But right now, she couldn't care less. All that mattered was Casey and that she be all right.

KYLE SWERVED INTO the first available parking space and jumped from his car. Five until four. He'd never planned to cut it this close, but some idiot had rammed his car into a signpost on McCullough, and traffic had backed up for blocks before the tow truck cleared the scene. Still, if the elevator wasn't hung up somewhere, he could make it in time for Ashley to begin her presentation.

It was four o'clock exactly when he stepped inside the waiting room for the offices of Clintock, Mitchum and

O'Connell. The first person he saw was Delia. She rushed toward him with a look of doom plastered on her face.

"Do I dare step inside," he asked, "or is Ashley waiting to greet me with a two-by-four upside the head?"

"She's not here, Kyle."

"Where is she?"

"At Methodist Children's Hospital. You need to get there as fast as you can."

His chest squeezed shut, forcing the air from his lungs. A million questions darted through his mind, but all he could get out was one word. "Casey."

Delia laid a hand on his shoulder. "You're white as a sheet. Don't go passing out. Ashley and Casey need you."

"What happened?"

He listened to Delia as long as he could. Something about fever and crying and rushing to the emergency room. When he could stand it no longer, he backed through the door and took off running down the stairs. Ten flights, but it was better than standing and waiting for the elevator.

Someone had trusted a helpless baby into his care and he'd let them down. He was still the same old loser he'd always been. Choosing a new name hadn't changed that. Neither had a law degree, fancy suits and an expensive sports car.

He could pretend all he wanted. Laugh and flirt and play the big shot. But when it came down to the bare ugly truth, he was still Kevin Black from the redbrick building behind the tall black fence.

CHAPTER ELEVEN

ASHLEY STOPPED in midstep and spun around as the door to the emergency waiting room swung open and Kyle rushed inside. He saw her at once and crossed the floor in an instant. He looked as scared as she felt, and her insides quaked all over again.

"What happened?"

"I don't know exactly. Casey played for a while, but then she got fussy. I walked her and played with her, but nothing made her happy. Finally, she fell asleep, and I thought she was just whining because she was tired. When she woke up, her little body was burning with fever." She blurted out what little she knew, suddenly feeling a suffocating wave of guilt, as if this were somehow her fault. "I should have realized she was sick sooner."

"Don't blame yourself. I'm the one who should have been there. She's my responsibility and I palmed her off on you when I knew how busy you were." Kyle opened his arms and Ashley stepped inside, forgetting her anger over his being late.

Tears stung the backs of her eyelids, but this time she didn't try to stop them from falling. A sick baby. Fever. An emergency room. She was so far out of her element she might as well have been off on a mission with Captain Kirk and Mr. Spock. "I just hope she's all right," she muttered between her sniffling.

Kyle stroked her cheeks with the back of his thumb, catching her tears. "Where's Casey now?"

"A nurse took her. I wanted to stay with her, but the nurse said I was too upset, that I should wait here until they'd finished the tests. I just went back to the desk and asked, and they said the doctor was with her now."

Kyle led her to a chair, then took the one beside her. He exhaled sharply, then buried his head in his hands. For a minute she thought he might be fighting tears as well, but when he looked up, his eyes were dry, clear, stone cold.

"This has gone on too long."

"What are you talking about?"

"The waiting, the not knowing whether or not I'm Casey's father. If I'm the father, I'll have to find a way to cope. If not, I'll turn her over to the authorities just as you and Lily said I should do all along. Desert her the second time, this time to people who'll have no reason to care about her. Might as well drop her in a black hole somewhere."

"You won't be deserting her if she's not yours to desert. Besides, I'm sure they'll find a very good home for her."

"And I'm sure the Cowboys are going to win the Super Bowl this year."

"Does this mean you've given up on finding Tessa?"

"It means I'm not sure I want to find her after this. I've had Casey in my care for less than a week and I could never just stick her in a basket and abandon her. Dump her on someone who knows nothing about her. No medical records. No doctor's name. For all we know this might happen all the time. Casey might have some serious medical problem that I've neglected from sheer ignorance."

"I never thought of that." And now that he'd brought it up, it sent new worries crashing through her system, worries she couldn't deal with right now. "Don't jump to conclusions, Kyle. We'll just wait and hear what the ER doctor says."

"Like we have another choice. I hate to admit it now, but my first thought the night you found Casey was that leaving her on my doorstep was some kind of cruel prank. The second was, please don't let this be my baby." He ran a hand along his neck, stretching the kinks from it as he massaged. "Now, whether she's mine or not, I just want what's best for her."

Ashley laid a hand on his thigh. "*'Love me.'* That's what the note said, Kyle. I think her mother must love her, and that's why you have to at least find Tessa Ortiz and see if she's the mother. You can't give up."

"I didn't give up. I failed."

That was one and the same as far as Ashley was concerned. If Tessa was out there, someone had to know where she was, and she could be found—if the right man was looking for her.

"I thought you were the one arguing that I should have the DNA testing."

"I still think you should. But if she's your daughter, then you also have to find her mother."

"Mrs. Garrett." She jumped at the sound of her name, or at least almost her name.

A young man in a white coat walked toward her, a stethoscope dangling from his neck. "I'm Doctor Jenkins and I've just finished checking out the test results on your daughter."

Kyle leaped to his feet. "Is she all right?"

"She will be, Mr. Garrett. She has a viral infection. There's not a lot we can do for that except let it run its course, but we've given her medication to keep the fever in check. The good thing is she's basically a healthy baby and she'll be fine before you know it."

Relief washed over Ashley, leaving her weak. She leaned against Kyle and he circled her waist with his arm. She'd expected him to bluster at the mistake in name, but he was so intent on hearing what the doctor had to say, *Mr. Garrett* didn't seem to register.

"How long will it take for the infection to run its course?" he asked.

"It could take as little as twenty-four hours, but it'll probably hang on awhile longer."

Kyle dropped his hand from Ashley's waist. "Will we be able to take her home with us?"

"I'd like to keep her here another hour or two, make certain that the fever doesn't shoot back up on us. Also, we've given her liquids through an IV and I'd like her to stay with us until she wets her diaper. We'll make sure she's not dehydrated, but it's likely you'll be home by bedtime."

"It sounds like you've covered all the bases."

"I try to, but since you don't have a local pediatrician, I'd like you to give the nurse on duty here a call in the morning. If Casey's still battling fever or seems as lifeless as she did when you brought her in today, I'd like to see her again. If she's doing fine, then you won't have to make a return visit."

Still Ashley worried. "What if she gets worse during the night?"

"You know the way here, Mrs. Garrett. And someone's always on call."

"When can we see her?" Kyle asked.

"Follow me. I'll take you to her room. At least one of you should stay with her until she's ready to leave ER."

"I'll be right here." Kyle turned to Ashley, the familiar gleam back in his eyes. "Are you ready, Mrs. Garrett?"

ASHLEY FOLLOWED the doctor down the hall, her nose stinging from the odor of antiseptic and cleansers. Poor baby. The little darling was probably scared to death, feeling as if she'd been deserted all over again.

Ashley found out differently the second she stopped at the door of the cubbyhole that the doctor had graciously referred to as a room. An auburn-haired nurse was rocking Casey and talking to her in a mixture of baby talk and hospital jargon. Casey might not understand the words, but she grasped the concept of attention perfectly. Her big brown eyes peered from beneath her long lashes and she was looking right at the nurse as if she were vitally interested in every syllable.

She turned her gaze to them as soon as they stepped into the room but didn't become animated the way she usually did when Kyle walked into her line of vision.

He waved his fingers at her as he stopped beside the rocking chair. "Looks as if you found a friend," he said, bending over to trail a finger across her sweet baby cheek.

The nurse looked up at Kyle, and Ashley noticed the spark of interest that he always elicited from women the first time they saw him. Not quite a drool. More of a silent *wow*. And, as always, Kyle laid on the charm. He smiled broadly as he reached down to take Casey from the woman's arms. "This is not the kind of treatment I got the last time I showed up in ER."

"You probably went to the wrong ER. Or maybe you weren't as vocal in your demands as your daughter is. She lets us know anytime we do something she doesn't like."

"That's my girl." He cradled the baby in his arms and turned back to Ashley. "How does she look to you now?"

"Much better. Not nearly as red, but she still seems a little listless."

"She's a sick little girl," the nurse said, "though high fever in a child this age is not as significant as it is in an adult. Still, the first time it happens, parents always panic."

"I was no exception," Ashley agreed. "But then you know that. You saw me when I brought her in."

"You did the right thing." The nurse stayed a minute

longer, mostly to ogle Kyle, then left them alone with Casey. Kyle stared at the baby in his arms for long seconds, then touched his hand to her forehead as if he were assuring himself her fever had gone down to at least near normal.

"I promised you a new kitchen for this afternoon's favor. I guess I owe you a house now, Mrs. Garrett."

"You'll be lucky to afford the cleanser for the grout after you pay this hospital bill, Mr. Garrett."

He closed his eyes, made a face and muttered a mild curse. "I never even thought about that. I'm surprised they took you without a policy to cover expenses."

"I gave them my VISA."

"That explains the Mrs. Garrett."

"Not entirely. The minute I walked in they started asking questions. Was I the parent or legal guardian? Who is her regular pediatrician? Has she had previous illnesses? I wasn't taking any chances on their not treating her, so I opted for a series of white lies. I told them s' was my daughter, and gave my dad's address in Trueblood to explain why we don't have a local pediatrician."

"You told them you were Casey's mother! You, the confirmed bachelorette. I'd have paid a week's wages to see that performance, that is if I didn't need the money for the bill."

"At that point I would have told them I was the father and made them believe me, if that's what it took to get help."

"I knew you were worried when Delia told me you rushed off without giving your pitch."

"You would have to remind me of that. Mr. Clintock's probably filling out my termination papers as we speak, the dear."

Kyle stared at her, concern drawing his brows closer together. "He wouldn't really do that, would he?"

"No, but he'll greet me Monday morning with one of those moving lectures on handling job responsibilities. And he's not going to understand how a baby I'm not even kin to kept me from doing what he's paying me to do. Never mind that I've handled more accounts than anyone in the office over the last twelve months or the fact that I work twice as many hours as some of his employees."

"Would it help if I talked to him?"

"Oh, yeah. I can see his face now when I announce that my neighbor, the lawyer, is going to speak on my behalf."

"I am an extremely competent lawyer. I could probably get you a bonus for all those overtime hours."

"Or get me a nice spot in the unemployment line."

"Hey, that might work out well. Are you interested in a job as nanny?"

"This is not funny, Kyle."

"So who's laughing. Definitely not me."

"At least Casey's better. Things could be worse."

"Her health is definitely most important," he agreed, "but let's pray things don't get worse. If they do, I might be the one looking for a job."

"Why? Didn't you take the man's testimony?"

"I did, but then my boss wanted to talk to me about some of the discoveries, and I told him I couldn't stay. He was not a happy camper."

"Did you tell him about Casey?"

"No. I thought I'd wait until after the DNA test results come in, which is another reason I can't keep putting it off."

Still, she heard the hesitancy in his voice and was bothered by it. DNA testing was simple and gave quick and incontestable results. Why would he be so reluctant to have it done?

Lily's words of caution darted through her mind. *A man who changed his name might have something to hide.* Ashley found it hard to believe that Kyle harbored deep, dark secrets from his past, but then what could she really know about a man who'd been no more than a neighbor before this week?

"She's already falling asleep," Kyle said, breaking into her thoughts. "Guess I'm not as fascinating as the nurse was."

Ashley walked over so that she could see for herself. Sure enough, Casey's eyes were closed tight and the thumb on her left hand was securely lodged between her lips.

She looked peaceful now, but the sounds of her cries still echoed in Ashley's brain, bounced around and collided with the feelings of sheer panic that had sent Ashley driving like a madman to Methodist Children's Hospital. Delia had said she was attached to Casey. Ashley had denied it, but there was no denying it now.

An attachment. The word seemed far too weak for the depth of emotions that had turned her inside out this afternoon when she'd realized Casey was so sick.

She'd denied the attachment to Casey. Was she doing the same where Kyle was concerned? Pretending the attraction was merely physical when it went much deeper? Was she falling in love with Kyle Blackstone?

No, she couldn't be. She had her plans and goals and he wasn't part of them. Suddenly she felt the need to escape, to get out of the room, to go somewhere she wouldn't look up and see Kyle.

"I need to go and call Delia. I told her I'd let her know as soon as I found out something about Casey's condition."

He waited until she got to the door before he spoke. "Thanks, Ashley. For everything. And in case Delia doesn't tell you, I was back at your office for four o'clock. Barely, but I made it."

She nodded, not trusting her voice to say more.

IT WAS NEARLY nine o'clock by the time Kyle pulled into the apartment parking garage with Ashley following close behind. He left the first vacant spot for her, and she pulled into the space, carefully avoiding the black van that extended at least six inches over the yellow line.

She slid her fingers along the button that unlocked the backdoor, then pushed the driver's door open and stepped onto the concrete. The overhead light nearest her had burned out, leaving her in an isolated pocket of gray shadows. It didn't matter. Kyle would be back to help her with the baby in a matter of seconds.

Casey had slept all the way home, but now that the car had stopped, she started to fuss. Ashley opened the backdoor and went to work on the dratted catch on the baby seat. She'd already lost one fingernail to the mechanism.

"It's okay, sweetie. You're all through with doctors and nurses. We're home now."

"My, you are the maternal one."

She spun around at the sound of the male voice, familiar but not Kyle's.

"Mark Beall, what are you doing here?"

"Saving your beautiful ass."

"What do you mean?"

"Your pal Jim Bob came by to see you today. He left a file for you to look over before your meeting with him on Monday. I decided I'd do the chivalrous thing and drop it off for you." He poked a manila folder into her hand. "I looked over it. It's not *all* bad."

"Thanks."

Kyle picked that moment to arrive, his arms filled with the diaper bag and the various other paraphernalia that went everywhere that Casey went. "You never know who you'll run into in dark parking garages," he said, shifting the gear so that he could extend a hand.

Mark offered his as well, but she couldn't help but notice a spark of tension between the two of them. "Mark brought me a file that I needed from the office," she said, hoping to defuse the situation.

"After-hours courier service. Nice work if you can get it."

"Anything for my partner here." Mark put a hand to her shoulder.

"It will save me a trip to the office," she said, moving from beneath his arm. "Do you want to come in for coffee or something?"

"No, actually I just had a cup. A friend of mine lives a couple of blocks from here. We hit a movie after work, then grabbed a sandwich and an espresso at that shop on the corner. I knew I was coming this way. That's why I brought the file along. Ellen said she'd called and left a message on your home phone, but I thought I'd save you a trip back to the office."

"Mighty thoughtful of you," Kyle said. "Were you just going to stand around in the parking garage until Ashley got home?"

"No, I was going to leave it at her door. As luck would have it, I ran into Ashley first."

Ashley bent over and lifted Casey from her car seat.

Mark stretched his neck for a peek at her. "Is she all right now?"

"She will be. And thanks for the file. I may find time to look at it tonight."

"Glad to do it. You owe me lunch, though."

"Name the day."

They said a quick goodbye and Mark left.

Kyle followed Ashley inside the building. "'You owe me lunch, though,'" he mimicked, doing a perfect imitation of Mark's Texas drawl.

"Give the guy a break. He was doing me a favor."

"He was hoping to find you alone and that you'd invite him in. I know men like that."

"You *are* a man like that."

"That's why I know what they're thinking. I've told you before, I wouldn't be a bit surprised if he's the one bringing you flowers."

She waved the file at him as she boarded the elevator. "No flowers. Just work. I should get on it now."

He leaned in close and nuzzled the back of her neck as the elevator ascended. "I have a better idea."

"I'm sure you do. But you have a baby to take care of."

She stepped off the elevator, then stopped dead still. A man was standing at her door. His back was to them but she could see a huge bouquet of flowers in his hand. Her secret admirer was about to lose his anonymity.

CHAPTER TWELVE

"WHAT'S WRONG?" Kyle asked, stepping around her. "Did you drop something?"

"There's a man at my door," she whispered. "Holding a bouquet of flowers."

"Your secret admirer. Caught in the act." Kyle's words were clipped, as if he were trying to bite back a burst of anger. If so, he failed miserably. He fished in his pocket for his keys, then held them out to her, the point of a silver one extended. "Take Casey into my apartment. I'll take care of this."

"You certainly will not. You may be Casey's caretaker, but you're not mine."

At that moment her guest turned around, saw them and nonchalantly motioned them over.

"Ernie Brooks?" The name came out in unison, neither of them able to believe that the retired FBI agent from the fourth floor had been the person delivering notes and flowers to her door for the past two months. Especially after he'd seemed so concerned about her safety.

Kyle strode toward him. "Care to explain this, Ernie?"

"Hey. Simmer down. You've got this all wrong. I'm not the deliveryman. I just happened to find the evidence. And you're not going to like what I found this time." Ernie held up a brown envelope, then handed it to Kyle. "Take a look at this."

Ashley took the flowers while Kyle peeked inside the envelope. The bouquet was much larger than usual, a mixture of daisies and daffodils and baby's breath. "The man must work for a florist," she said, "or else he has a lot of money to waste."

"I think it's time to alert the police if you haven't done it already," Ernie said, shuffling and burying his hands in his pockets.

"Have you got a minute?" Kyle said. "I'd like to talk to you about this, but I have to get Casey to bed first. She's had a rough day."

"Lead the way."

It angered Ashley that Kyle and Ernie were making decisions as if she weren't standing there with them, as if this problem didn't concern her and only her. "Kyle can put Casey to bed, and you can talk about this with me," she insisted. "This has nothing to do with Kyle."

Kyle slapped the brown envelope against the wall. "I'm not trying to usurp your authority, Ashley, and I'm not suggesting you aren't capable. But this has moved from nice to nasty and something's got to be done about it."

She stared at the envelope. "What kind of sick note did he leave this time?"

"It's not the note that worries me." Kyle touched a hand to the small of her back and nudged her toward his apartment. "He left a pair of ladies' panties. Likely yours."

Kyle took the key from her hand and unlocked his door just as Mrs. Flarrity's door creaked open. The woman stuck her head outside, her mass of frizzled red hair balled around her slender face. Kyle and Ernie walked inside. Ashley paused.

"I heard voices. Is something wrong?"

"Not a thing, Mrs. Flarrity." Mikasa squeezed between Mrs. Flarrity's leg and the door and slunk over to Ashley, purring demurely as she curled around Ashley's ankle, waiting to be petted.

"Sorry, Mikasa. I have my hands full. You'll have to wait until later for your stroking."

Mrs. Flarrity stuck her hands on her ample hips. "This must be the busiest floor in the building tonight."

Ashley stepped closer. "Did you see someone out here earlier?"

"No, but I heard them. Someone banged on your door for a good five minutes. If I hadn't been soaking in the tub, I'd have come out here and told them you weren't deaf. If you'd been at home you'd have opened the door long before that."

"What time was that?"

"I'd say a half hour ago. Were you expecting company?"

"No, but there was a package at my door. I was hoping you'd seen the person who left it."

"No. I haven't seen any strangers. Just that man who's been staying with Ernie Brooks, the one with the limp. He walks the halls sometimes. Early in the morning. Late at night. He's out at all hours."

She was talking about Mitch, but he was not the stranger Ashley was concerned about. "If you do see someone leaving a note or flowers at my door, I'd appreciate it if you'd notice what he looks like and let me know."

"I will. Kyle Blackstone already asked me to keep an eye on your place. But then I don't really trust him, either. He's too good-looking for his own good and has too many lady friends. My third husband was like that. Every time I turned around, he was out catting around. That's why I got rid of him and got me a real cat, one who stays home at night." She reached down and picked up Mikasa.

Ashley shifted Casey so that her arm didn't go completely numb on her.

Mrs. Flarrity reached over and pulled the blanket down a tad so that she could get a glimpse of the sleeping infant.

"She's a cute baby, and I see our good neighbor's got you taking care of her. Is it his or is he just keeping her for somebody?"

"I'm not sure."

The woman squinted and wrinkled her brow. "He's not married, you know."

"I know."

"But he's got his share of girl friends. So don't you go falling for him."

"No, I'm not."

She shot Ashley a look that indicated she didn't believe her. "If you're half smart, you'll march in there and give him back his baby. If it's his, he should take care of it." And apparently that was all Mrs. Flarrity had to say. She shut the door without a good-night.

Ashley walked through the open door of Kyle's apartment. He and Ernie Brooks were deep in conversation. Kyle held a note in his hand. Ernie held a pair of silky red panties in his, panties that looked a lot like a pair she'd thought she must have left in one of the washers or dryers in the apartment laundry room.

"I'll be back as soon as I put Casey to bed," she said, walking past the two men.

"I'll help you." Kyle jumped to his feet and followed her to the spare room where he'd put the crib.

Casey barely squirmed when Ashley put her down, just curled up and stuck her thumb in her mouth. Ashley touched her hand to Casey's forehead. "A little warm, but nothing like it was this afternoon."

"When she wakes up, I guess I'll learn to use the baby thermometer Lily had me buy." Kyle leaned over the crib and kissed Casey on the top of her head. "Sleep tight, sweetie. You were a real trouper today." He put a hand around Ashley's waist. "And so were you," he whispered, his mouth so close to her ear that she felt the warmth of his breath on her neck. He took her hand and led her to the door. "We better get back to Ernie and the latest gift from your psycho admirer."

"And my dad's worried that I'm never going to have a real boyfriend."

"This is not a joking matter, Ashley. Ernie's ex-FBI and he thinks the fact that the man had a pair of your undies is serious."

Her skin crawled at the thought of some creep handling and doing who knew what else with *her* red panties. "Believe me, Kyle, I'm not joking."

ASHLEY SAT on the couch next to Kyle. Ernie took the overstuffed chair in the corner of the room. As soon as they were all settled, he handed her the underwear. "Do you recognize these?"

"They're mine. I just don't know how this person, whoever he is, could have gotten his hands on them."

Ernie leaned forward. "The stalker could be a friend, maybe someone who's been inside your apartment."

"No men have been in my apartment except Kyle, and that's only happened in the last day or two."

"Have you had any break-ins?"

"No."

"She left her door unlocked the other night while she was helping me with Casey," Kyle said. "I checked the apartment after that and nothing appeared to be out of place, but I wouldn't have had any way of knowing if he'd just taken a pair of undies from her bureau."

"The panties were missing before that night. I didn't think anything about it. I just assumed I'd left them in the laundry room. I've done that before."

"The man could have found them there," Ernie said. "He might have been watching you and took them when you weren't looking."

The mere thought made the hairs on her neck stand on end and sent a frigid tremor creeping up her spine.

Ernie drummed his fingers against the arm of Kyle's chair. "Have you noticed anything else missing over the last two months?"

"Nothing but a pair of silver earrings. I may have misplaced them or lost them while I was exercising or while trying on clothes at the mall."

Ernie crossed a foot over his knee. In the light of the lamp he looked younger, more virile than he did in the coffee shop in the bright light of day. A nice guy, one who hadn't seemed hard enough to be FBI material. Tonight, however, he looked the part. His face was like a shield, hard and muscular. His eyes seemed to be carved of granite, and when he looked at her, she felt as if he could see her fears, her weaknesses.

"He not only leaves flowers and gifts at her house," Kyle explained. "He leaves them at her office as well, and on her windshield in the office parking lot. He seems to be everywhere."

"He does now." She picked up one of the green denim throw pillows from Kyle's couch and buried a fist in it. "Before this week, it wasn't a big deal. Every week or two, I'd find a bouquet of flowers on my windshield with a nice little note. It seemed so harmless, almost sweet. Now it's like a constant barrage."

"Has something significant happened that might have triggered the change in intensity?"

"Not with me. Nothing except that the more I become entangled in Kyle's life, the nuttier the fruitcake admirer of mine becomes. I guess it's always like that. When trouble rains, it pours."

"The correlation may be a lot more significant than that."

"What do you mean?"

"I think he may be reacting to what he sees as your growing relationship with Kyle." Ernie picked up the brown envelope, stuck his hand inside and came out with a card.

Her hands trembled as she took the note. Fatigue, anger, aggravation. The fusion of emotions had her so shaken she could barely function. "Shall I read it out loud?"

"Only if you want to," Kyle said. "We both read it while you were talking to Mrs. Flarrity."

She opened the card and read to herself as a cold numbness settled inside her, chilling her to the bone.

Ashley, we are meant to be together. The love we'll share will be pure, but you must not let anyone come between us. No one. Do not defile our love or destroy what fate has meant to be. That's why I'm returning this piece of clothing. I've slept with it under my pillow so that I would feel close to you, but now I want you to wear them so you'll feel close to me. Already you love me, though you don't realize it yet. I see it in your eyes when we talk. I will reveal myself to you soon, and when I do, you will know that I am your one true love.

The words rocked through her brain, and she tried to imagine who might have written them. There was no man in her life. Surely she hadn't given any one reason to believe she cared for them. She talked to everyone, tried to be pleasant. No, she flirted. It was her way. It made people feel good, but she'd never believed her actions would fuel this kind of bizarre reaction.

"I have no idea who wrote this," she said. "It's—"

"It's sick." Ernie finished her sentence for her. "And that's what worries me."

"I'm sure I haven't given anyone reason to feel this way."

Ernie smiled. It reached his eyes but did little to soften the hard lines and crevices set in his face. "You didn't do anything. Men like this live in a world of their own making. They confuse reality with delusion. He's become obsessed."

Kyle grunted. "Sounds more like he's *possessed* to me."

She shrunk against the back of the couch. "So what do I do now?"

"Go to the police. Tell them everything. Most of all, you need to be very careful. Avoid isolated areas. Go to the laundry room with a friend. Have the night watchman walk you from your car to your room when you come home by yourself late at night."

"In other words, I give this man control over my life."

"Just until he's caught."

She exhaled sharply and wrapped her arms about her chest. Kyle put an arm around her shoulders. "I'll be here anytime you want me. I can take you to work and drive you home."

"And my friend Mitch and I will both keep our eyes and ears open. Nothing like having your own FBI agent in the building, not that the agency claims me anymore, but I still remember all the tricks."

"I appreciate that."

Ernie stood and stepped toward the door. "I'm going to get back down to my place and leave you two alone, but you need to follow through on contacting the police."

"I will. I'm going to my dad's ranch tomorrow. I need a quiet place to get some work done, but I'll call them first thing Monday morning."

Ernie stuck his faded baseball cap back on his head. "In the meantime, give some more thought to anyone who's asked you out or seems to be hanging around whenever he gets the chance. If the police know who they're looking for, they have a lot better chance of finding him. They might even find that he has a record. Kooks like this one frequently do, though it might be for minor stuff. They can go along fairly normal for years, then all of a sudden go into overload. Almost like they blow a gasket.''

Kyle walked to the door with Ernie, and the two of them stood in the hall talking for a few more minutes. Ashley was certain that her red panties and her stalker were the topic of their conversation, but she'd heard enough for one night.

She stretched and walked back to the door of the make-shift nursery. She needed to hear Casey's rhythmic breathing, needed to see her little thumb tucked securely inside her mouth.

She heard Kyle's footsteps behind her. A second later she felt his arms around her waist and he pulled her close. His arms were stiff and she could feel the tension that knotted his body.

"At least Casey is sleeping peacefully," he said. "That's one of the advantages of being too young to know when your world has been turned upside down."

"I envy her that." Ashley turned to face Kyle. "Now we better get out of here before she wakes up and decides to do some world turning of her own."

When they reached the living room, she picked up her purse and the file Mark had brought her and started toward the door.

Kyle grabbed her arm. "Where do you think you're going?"

"Home."

"Just like that?"

"It's where I live. I go there every night, usually long before this time."

"You don't have to go at all. You can stay here. I'll pour you a glass of wine and make you dinner."

"Canned soup?"

"I can do pizza. It's one of my best dishes. And I can have it ready in forty minutes."

"Forty minutes or the next one's free."

"Oh, so you have that same recipe."

"On my speed dial. You don't need me now, Kyle. Casey's asleep, and we both need to get some rest, too."

He pulled her into the circle of his arms. "It's been a long, hard day on all of us, but that's not why I want you to stay." His voice was husky now, the earlier anger replaced by a seductive tremor that sent her pulse rate spiraling.

"Why do you want me to stay, Kyle?"

"I don't know. I really don't know, but I do."

And then his lips were on hers. She knew she should push away, that if she didn't turn and walk out the door, she might never leave, but her body overrode her mind. The need was palpable, a rush of heat and breathless energy that consumed her.

It had been months since she'd been with a man, but the feelings that shook her now were the result of more than abstinence. It was Kyle that she wanted. Not the Kyle she'd known before this week, but Kyle, the man who held Casey in his arms as if she were some precious treasure that might break if he held her too tightly.

Kyle the man who tended a tiny, helpless baby when she was ill. The man who'd rushed to the hospital in pure panic. The man who'd sat beside her tonight while Ernie Brooks had told her how sick he thought her secret admirer had become.

She threw herself into the kiss, releasing the emotion she'd held in check all day. Her fingers tangled in his hair, and she felt the hardness of him pressing against her. It would be so easy to stay tonight, to make love with him. Easy tonight, but what about tomorrow and the string of tomorrows after that? She pulled away.

"Did I do something wrong?"

"No, it's just me. I really can't get involved with you, Kyle. It won't work. It never does."

"We're already involved, Ashley. And how can you know whether or not it will work if you're too afraid of your feelings to even give us a chance?"

"My life is already too complicated. My job is demanding. My career is important to me. I have a stalker. And you have a baby here that may or may not be yours."

"I can't argue any of that. But it's fine with me that you have a job that you love. I have one, too, and I don't want to have to constantly explain to someone why I have to work late some nights and bring home work some weekends. And as for your stalker, I'm not going to rest anyway until the damn lunatic is caught. And that leaves Casey. At this point, I have no answers for that. I don't know if she's mine."

"You don't know because you won't go in for testing. It's a simple process. Lily told me how it works. They don't even have to draw blood anymore. They can swab the insides of your cheeks and gather enough substance to see if you and Casey have matching DNA."

"It's not the test I'm worried about, Ashley."

"Then what is it? Are you afraid to face the truth, afraid to accept the responsibility for her? Because if that's the case, you're doing it already and you're doing a great job in spite of your lack of experience. You'll be a great father."

"I doubt that."

"Why do you doubt it? I've seen you with her and I don't doubt it."

He let go of her and walked away, his shoulders

drooped. He pushed open the French doors and stepped onto the balcony. She followed him. If he had answers, she'd like to hear them. But when she reached his side, it was only the look of defeat she saw on his face.

"I don't know anything about families, Ashley. I don't know what fathers do or how they do it."

"You know as much as other men. You were part of a family."

"No, *you're* part of a family. I hear you talk about your sister and your brother and I know that you have something I'll never have. And when you talk of your dad and going to the ranch, I try to imagine what going home would be like. I can't."

He was baring his soul and she could hear the pain in his voice. She'd pushed him too hard, demanded too much. "You don't have to tell me this, Kyle."

"I think maybe I do. If you're afraid to get involved with me now, you may as well know the whole truth. Then you'll be glad you're on your way out of my life and not on your way in."

"It can't be that bad."

"Try this. My mother walked off and left me in the house alone when I was two years old. A neighbor found me. I was eating dry cereal. I'd managed to push a chair to the counter and climb up so that I could get that little bit of food."

"Didn't your mother come back for you?"

"No. They found her body in the car about a mile from our apartment, dead from an overdose. Of course, I didn't learn that until years later."

"Who raised you?"

"The *authorities*. They bounced me around from one foster home to another. They weren't all bad. They just weren't mine.

"But you're so well-adjusted, so outgoing."

"I worked hard to get here, and I'll keep working hard. But it won't change who and what I am. So it's probably as good a time as any for you to run home. I'll even walk you to your door. And my offer still stands. If you need me for a ride to work or for anything else, all you have to do is call. No strings. No demands."

The *authorities*. No wonder he hated to call them. It was all so clear now. He thought he was doing the same thing to Casey that had been done to him when he was only two and scared, hungry and alone.

"I guess that explains why you've hesitated to have the DNA testing done."

"I just wanted to give the mother, whoever she is, a chance to come back and reclaim her baby. If Casey really is mine, I'll take care of her—somehow. But if the DNA testing proves she's not mine, I'll be legally bound to report it immediately. Then I'll be forced to hand her over to some stranger who doesn't know her from Adam."

"Why didn't you tell me this before?"

"I've spent my life trying to get past those years, past the hurt and pain of never belonging. I saw no reason to toss it right into the middle of anything that might develop between us. Besides, I really thought I'd put it behind me until Casey appeared at my door."

So that's why he had changed his name. He was trying to close a door on a past that was too painful to remember. It was probably a wise decision. Ashley, on the other hand, had been about to make a very big mistake.

She turned and walked back into the apartment. She shed her shoes first, kicking them to the corner of the room. The blouse came next. She unbuttoned it and slipped it over her arms, dropping it to the couch. She was unzipping her skirt when Kyle turned and saw her.

"What the hell are you doing?"

"You invited me to spend the night. I always sleep in the nude."

CHAPTER THIRTEEN

KYLE STARED AT Ashley, her perfect form outlined in the moonlight, a silky slip the color of her flesh clinging to every curve. He ached to take her in his arms and make love with her. But not if this was what it seemed.

"Is this a sympathy act, Ashley?"

"Is that what you think?"

"It has all the markings. I bare my soul, tell you about my unfortunate past, and all of a sudden you decide it's time we make love."

Her hands flew to her hips, and her eyes flashed green fire. "You know you're really starting to get on my nerves, Kyle Blackstone. First you want me. Then you get some crazy notion that I'd actually make love to a man just because he had a rotten childhood. If I did that, I'd be busy every night of the year, going to bed with half the men who cross my path."

"So you tell me. What's the sudden attraction when you were so adamant a minute ago that you wanted no part of me?"

"Oh, I wanted you, Kyle Blackstone. I've wanted you from the moment I first laid eyes on you at the health club. Every time we exchanged an innuendo, I wanted to touch you, to kiss you, to make love to you like you've never had it before." She walked over and began unbuttoning his shirt.

Something wild and rampant exploded inside him. But still he needed to know the full score. Dealing with his past always did that to him, exposed his vulnerability, dissolved the self-confidence he'd gained through all the tough years of getting his law degree and making something of the kid who nobody wanted.

"If you wanted me before, you sure hid it well."

"I am good, aren't I?" Her hands slid under his shirt and her fingers tangled in the hairs on his chest. "I even kept from admitting it to myself."

"Are you that afraid of getting involved?"

"Yes. I'm still afraid, but right now I want you too much not to give us a chance." She touched her mouth to his chest.

The scent of her washed over him, perfume and soap and sweet-smelling shampoo. Intoxicating, or maybe it was her touch that was affecting his mind, driving him wild. Reason flew from his mind. He'd dreamed of this for weeks, dreamed of making love with the beautiful Ashley Garrett.

For all he knew, he might be dreaming now. If he was, he hoped he never woke up. She loosened his belt, then tugged at the catch on his jeans, letting her thumbs sizzle across his naked stomach. He moaned as her fingers made contact with his erection.

He slipped his hands beneath the narrow straps of her slip and bra and pulled them over her shoulders. Her breasts spilled out, perfect, pert, the pinkish nipples standing erect. His insides quivered, then tightened painfully.

"Undress me all the way, Kyle. Slow, so I can soak in the feelings."

"I'm not sure I can go slow, but I'll try." He peeled the slip down her body, inch by inch, until it glided past her hips and fell to her feet. She braced herself with her hands on his shoulders as she stepped out of it and kicked it out of the way.

The panty hose were the real challenge, and his rough

thumbs snagged and pulled at the delicate mesh. He knelt and tugged them from her feet. She was naked now. Standing so close her breasts brushed against his chest. The blood rushed through his body like Niagara Falls and his breath came in sharp, painful gasps.

"You're beautiful, Ashley. Soft in all the right places."

"And hot in all the right places."

She rose to her tiptoes and pressed her lips to his, and the minute she did, his fragile grasp on control vanished. The hunger took over, raw and unbridled, and he couldn't get enough of her. He kissed her mouth, the curve of her neck, the swell of her breasts. And all the while her hands were roaming his body, burning across his flesh, touching and teasing until he thought he might lose it completely.

He picked her up and carried her to his bed. But instead of lying down, she got on her knees and tore the remaining clothes from his body. When he stood naked, she stretched out on the sheet, her hair fanning the pillow, her body glistening like gold in the dim glow of light that wafted down the hall.

"Do you have protection?" she murmured.

"Now you ask." He opened the drawer by the bed and pulled out a small silver package. "Fortunately, I do. I'd have a tough time going to the drugstore to…" His words became lost in a moan as she stroked the hardness of him. Shaking from desire, he climbed onto the bed and pulled her down beside him.

He wanted to touch her, stroke her, find every place that made her writhe in pleasure, but he simply couldn't. Not this time. So he rose up and fit himself inside her.

She was pliant, slick, heated, and she wrapped her legs around him, rocking him to her. He thrust inside her, over and over, a dance he'd done before, but this was the first time it had seared to his very soul. A moment later she moaned in pleasure and he rode the crest all the way to the top.

Never had it been like this, and he knew that if he lived to be a hundred, nothing would ever compare with the thrill of making love with Ashley Garrett for the very first time.

ASHLEY RUBBED HER EYES with the heels of her hands and stretched, sliding her limbs across the smooth sheets. It must be morning. The sun was up. She stared for a moment getting her bearings. Ohmigosh! She was in Kyle's bed.

Memories stirred, and the sweet warmth of satisfaction curled like whipped cream inside her. She'd made love to Kyle not once, but twice last night. The first time had been so heated, so driven it had been over almost before she had convinced herself it was really happening.

The second time had been slow and thorough, and she'd savored every sensual sensation. She had been so ready. In fact, once she'd made up her mind to do it, she hadn't experienced a second's hesitation. Even better, there were no regrets this morning, at least not about making love with Kyle.

The smell of frying bacon and fresh-brewed coffee drifted down the hallway. Obviously he was cooking breakfast. She considered going to the kitchen to help, but decided against it. She felt positively decadent lying here, and besides, she'd gotten up at four in the morning and given Casey a bottle.

The viral infection had her off her regular feeding schedule, but Ashley hadn't minded the loss of sleep. Casey had been hungry and fever free and she'd fallen asleep in Ashley's arms as soon as she'd finished the bottle. Kyle hadn't even budged when she'd crawled back into bed beside him. Still, it had been nice to snuggle next to a warm body, especially after the red panty ordeal of the night before.

"Hey, you did wake up." Kyle stepped through the doorway balancing a tray of food and coffee.

She glanced around the room, but didn't see a clock. "What time is it?"

"Ten before nine."

"You're kidding. I never sleep this late."

"It's the bed. You should probably sleep in it every night." He set the laden tray on the bedside table and leaned over for a kiss.

"I haven't brushed my teeth."

He kissed her anyway. A real kiss. Long and wet. The kind Ashley could have spent a day getting into, if she'd had a day.

"Where's your clock?"

"On the dresser, behind that stack of magazines. If I keep it by the bed, it's too tempting to roll over and press the snooze button. But once my feet hit the floor I can make it all the way to the coffeepot without having to open my eyes."

"Such talent."

"Are we still talking about my sleepwalking?"

"That's the only area I've seen where you couldn't use a little improvement," she teased. He lunged for her, but she ducked and scooted past him. "I think we should check out breakfast before it gets cold.

"Oooh. Breakfast burritos." She lifted the edge of one of the flour tortillas and peeked at the ingredients. "Bacon, eggs, cheese and salsa. Someone went shopping."

"Casey and I went to the market yesterday morning. She wowed all the clerks. A couple of them offered to take her off my hands."

"You do need a sitter."

"Not yet. I still have vacation time, though it's killing my boss for me to actually take it."

She picked up a mug of coffee and put it to her lips. It was strong and black.

"If you need cream and sugar, I can get it."

She waved him off. "This is fine."

"See. I knew we were compatible." He picked up his own burrito and took a giant bite.

She did the same, holding the napkin under her mouth to catch the dripping salsa. "This is good."

"I'm glad you approve. Actually, you've now officially tasted all three of the dishes I can cook. Steak, canned soup and burritos."

"Throw in a pizza every now and then and I can live on that." The conversation died as they both indulged in the rest of the breakfast. It was best to eat fast if you wanted the food hot. Casey could wake up at any time and demand attention.

Ashley chewed and swallowed, then washed it all down with a sip of coffee. "I've been thinking about what you said yesterday, you know, about giving up the search for Tessa."

"I'm considering it. I've never really believed she was Casey's mother. And if Tessa's not the mother, then the only clue I have is a dark-haired, possibly Hispanic, woman who's been seen in the building. And we can't even be sure she's the one who abandoned the baby.

"If you can't find the woman, Kyle, give Dylan a chance."

"I guess it wouldn't hurt to call him."

"I'm going to the ranch for the weekend. Why don't you and Casey come with me? She seemed to be feeling a lot better when I fed her at four, and Lily and Cole are out of town this weekend so we don't have to worry about Casey sharing her infection with the mother-to-be. You can talk to Dylan in person."

"And what will your family say if you bring a new lover with a baby to visit?"

She fit herself into his arms. "They'd say plenty. That's why I'm taking a *neighbor* and a mystery baby to visit."

"Separate bedrooms?"

"Absolutely. Unless you'd like to wake up to one of my dad's shotguns in your face."

"Separate bedrooms," he agreed, but now that she was in his arms, he was making the most of it. He trailed kisses down her neck.

"I'll call them and tell them you and Casey are coming with me," she said.

"Good." He cupped his hands under her breasts and massaged the nipples with his thumbs.

"I have errands to run before we leave for the ranch."

He murmured something she couldn't make out and splayed his hand across her middle.

"I have to dress and put on makeup, so don't get anything up you can't handle without me."

"Too late."

His fingers strummed her, bringing her to life. So, who needed makeup?

"COULD YOU HAND me that slat by your elbow."

Dylan picked up the piece of freshly sawed pine, blew off a layer of sawdust and handed it to his dad. "Nothing like procrastination."

"Who's procrastinating?"

"From the size of Lily, I'd say you are. She looks like she could deliver any day to me, and this cradle needs a lot more work before it's ready for your new granddaughter."

"The cradle will be ready. The baby's not due yet."

"When Lily went to the doctor this week, he said the baby might come early. She said he didn't seem too worried. Apparently he feels the baby has developed enough now that an early birth wouldn't be too risky."

"I think it'll be awhile yet. She felt well enough to ride to Pinto with Cole this weekend."

"That's only because Lily couldn't wait to see what Calley's office setup is like. You know how Lily loves to give advice."

"Mostly to you," his dad reminded him. "The same way you're always cautioning Ashley about life in the big city."

"Yeah and Ashley doesn't listen any better than I do."

Dylan watched as his father fit the pieces of the crib together like a jigsaw puzzle. His hands showed the signs of Texas sun and years of ranching, but they were still steady. He looked good for his age, in spite of the fact that his once blond hair had turned almost completely gray. Dylan only hoped he held up so well.

William put down his staple gun and nudged his glasses back up his nose. "Aggravating things are always in the way," he muttered. "A man's eyes ought to last as long as the rest of him."

"What do you expect? You're about twenty years past the age most men start wearing glasses for reading and close work."

"I'm not most men."

And that was a fact. William Garrett was a man in a million, at least that's what Dylan's mother used to say about him before she died. William and Elizabeth, lovers right up until the end. His dad loved her even now. He'd had her buried under her favorite tree in the family plot right on the ranch. Dylan had seen him at the grave site when he thought no one was around, stooped down talking to her as if she could still hear him.

"So what do you think about your sister bringing a guy home for the weekend?" William asked, without looking up. "And not just a guy but a fellow with a baby that may or may not be his."

"She claims he's just a friend."

"Maybe so. Maybe not. All I know is she hasn't brought a man home with her since she graduated from college." He slid one of the side slats into the notch he'd made for it and then stepped back to admire his work. "What do you know about this Kyle Blackstone?"

"No more than what Lily's already told the both of us. He lives across the hall from Ashley, and he's a member at the same health club where she works out." Actually, Lily had given him a little more information but had asked that he keep the fact that Kyle had changed his name under his hat until they found out the whole story. "Besides, it's too soon—she barely knows him. I don't think there's any romance in the stars for my career-minded little sister."

"I wouldn't go betting your share of the ranch on that, son. Just because you're still pining over a woman you've known for years doesn't mean it's like that for everyone. I knew your mother was the woman for me the first time I laid eyes on her. It was the same for her."

Dylan let the comment ride. He knew his dad had always suspected he was in love with his best friend's wife, but he'd never admitted it. And his dad definitely didn't know what was going on now. Sebastian Cooper was running in dangerous circles, and if Dylan's suspicions were on target, he was operating a money-laundering operation for the mob.

Sebastian Cooper and Julie Matthews, his two best friends all through college. He'd loved Julie even then, so much he hadn't been able to even think of other women, but she'd chosen Sebastian to be her husband. Now she was paying for that mistake, and so was he. She was the one who'd initially found out about Sebastian's mob connections. Found out and gone on the run with her then unborn son. Sebastian still pretended to believe she'd been killed or kidnapped in a car-jacking. He'd even hired Dylan to find her.

In fact, Dylan was the only one who knew where Julie and her son really were. He'd inadvertently found her and Thomas in Cactus Creek when he'd gone there on another case just before Christmas. He'd do whatever it took to keep her safe. He knew Sebastian suspected his wife was still alive and would harm her if he ever found her.

"You're off in the twilight zone again," his dad said.

"Yeah, it's a case I'm working on. Another woman who chose the wrong man to marry. But this time everything is going to work out."

"You sound awfully sure of that fact."

"As sure as I've ever been about anything." It was the only thing that kept him going.

"Well, you handle that. I'm going to hang it up here and go get cleaned up before Ashley and her new beau arrive."

"He's not a beau."

"We'll see."

And even through the glasses, Dylan didn't miss the twinkle in his dad's blue eyes.

ASHLEY FINISHED her last errand at exactly eleven-thirty, one hour before she was supposed to meet Kyle for the trip to Trueblood, Texas and the Garrett ranch. Not enough time left to get any work done and too much to waste.

But an hour was just enough time to get some exercise. She stopped at a red light and reached for her cellular phone, punching in the number of the health club. If Bernie was there, she'd see if he had time for a personal session.

The light had changed back to green by the time the receptionist answered and she was six blocks farther before Bernie made it the phone.

"Hi, Bernie, this is Ashley Garrett. I hate to call on such short notice, but I have about forty-five minutes to spare and I was wondering if you had time to fit me in?"

He hesitated. "I'm perusing my appointment book, but I don't have an opening until four this afternoon. Saturday's a busy day."

"That's okay, I'll just come in and work out on the machines. And I am sorry about the cancellations. They couldn't be helped."

"No pain. No gain."

Ashley finished the conversation with a promise to call soon for an appointment. She decided to bypass the health club altogether. She'd wait and take a long, brisk walk at the ranch, clear her mind and concentrate on the ad campaign in the presence of cattle and hay and barbed wire. And if that wasn't enough exercise, well, there were other things she and Kyle could do. As long as no one saw her sneak into his room.

Her cellular phone rang a block before she reached her apartment building. "Hello."

"Ashley. I thought I might catch you in the car. I tried your home phone and no one answered."

"What's up, Delia?"

"I kept thinking last night about the flowers and notes you've been getting."

"Me, too. It's taken a turn for the worse. I'll fill you in Monday."

"I think I know who's responsible."

CHAPTER FOURTEEN

ASHLEY'S HAND tightened on the wheel, though she had no real faith that Delia knew her weird admirer's identity. "Tell me who you think is behind the daisy deluge, but please don't say Mark Beall. I hear that enough from Kyle and I know he's mistaken."

"You're not going to believe my candidate, either. I couldn't believe it at first myself, but then I looked at the total picture and it's crystal clear."

"Am I supposed to guess or are you going to tell me?" she asked, trying to jar Delia out of her dramatic mode.

"Okay, are you sitting down?"

"I always sit down when I'm behind the wheel of my car."

"I think your secret admirer is Mr. Clintock."

"Mr. Clintock, as in my boss and part owner of the firm?"

"I know it sounds strange, but everyone knows you're his pet. Only I believe it's more than that. He wants your body and he's afraid to admit it. You know, because of company harassment policies."

"Did you lace your cornflakes with an illegal substance this morning?"

"Just hear me out. He always takes his coffee break at the same time you do."

"So do half the people in the agency."

"He assigned you the big corner office when Martha Yates quit to be a full-time mom."

"I had seniority."

"And I've seen him stand at the door and watch you walk down the hall."

"Big deal. *Every* guy in that office watches *every* woman walk down the hall. I think it's in their job description."

"Make light of it if you want, but he was furious when you left with the baby yesterday, and he almost never gets mad at you."

"Only every time I do something he doesn't like. If you're going to work for Clintock, Mitchum and O'Connell, you'll have to give a hundred and ten percent," she mocked in her best Clintock imitation.

"I think it was because he's jealous of Kyle, Ashley. When you left yesterday, he asked me what your relationship was with the father of the baby that you were tending."

"So that's it. He asked about Kyle and you decided it was because he wants my body. Face it, Delia. Mr. Clintock is not the kind to give cards or flowers, secretive or otherwise."

"I still think I could be right. Ever since his wife left him, he's been moody and grouchy. The only employee he's halfway nice to is you."

"My accounts have significantly increased his bottom line. That's the reason he's nice."

"Still, it could be him. The man is a little strange. You can't deny that. If he did like you, he sure wouldn't want to just up and tell you he wants to wash his dirty socks in the same load as yours."

"What a sickening thought. Are you sure you're not coming down with something?"

"At least consider the possibility that it could be him. He knows where you live. Your address is in your personnel files."

"Get some rest, Delia. You're obviously working too hard."

"There's one more thing."

"He drinks coffee from the same pot?"

"No, I heard this a week or so ago, but it just now hit that this could be important. His secretary heard him talking to Mr. McAllister, and she said that when McAllister requested that you be named to head up the advertising for the Ranchers Association, Mr. Clintock said that was a very wise choice. He emphasized that you were one of his top account executives."

"Wait a minute. Did you say that McAllister specifically requested me?"

"That's the way I heard it."

"No one ever told me that."

"Maybe Mr. Clintock wanted you to think it was all his idea."

Or else Jim Bob McAllister did. He'd probably planned to try his hand at seducing her before she'd even known she had the job. The man was a first-class jerk, and that was the only thing about him that was first-class.

But jerk was it. He was a powerful rancher and oil rich as well. He could no doubt have any number of women at his beck and call and probably did. She couldn't see him stealing her panties from the apartment laundry room. And in spite of Delia's opinion to the contrary, Mr. Clintock was not even in the running.

But someone out there was sick enough to sleep with her panties under his pillow. Who? And what had she done to attract such a weirdo?

She pushed the thoughts from her mind. She had a whole weekend in front of her and she wasn't going to let the psycho spoil it for her. Jerk or not, she had to give Jim Bob McAllister a campaign to knock his socks off. And then there was Kyle.

She missed him already. Casey, too. It would be a great weekend.

"WELCOME TO Trueblood, Texas." Kyle read the sign as Ashley sped past it. "There must be a story behind that name, some macho cowboy in a shoot-out that spilled everybody's blood. A lesser known version of the legendary one at O.K. Corral."

"Men! You always assume that anything of importance happened because of some guy. There's a story behind the town, but that's not it."

He craned his neck for a look at the town before it disappeared from sight. He'd passed through here before, but he'd never paid any attention to the landmarks or the name. Of course, that was before he knew that Ashley Garrett was from Trueblood. "So what's the story?"

"The town was named after Isabella Trueblood Carter. History, or maybe legend, has it that she and her husband took in over twenty orphaned children after the deadly post-WWI influenza epidemic. When she realized that her husband couldn't care for them if she died, she started the Trueblood Foundation, named after her parents, to find parents for all the kids."

"That sounds like the plot for a TV movie of the week. Did she succeed?"

"Her foundation is said to have brought together dozens of families. Aunts, uncles and cousins came from all over the country to collect orphaned kin. So, when she died, the townspeople changed the name of the town from Carmelita to Trueblood."

"Sounds like a good omen to me."

"Look to your right," she said, pointing in that direction. "That's Isabella's Bar, the hottest spot in town."

"I can tell. They even have a satellite dish."

"And *three* pool tables."

"Uptown." He gave a thumbs-up.

"I thought so when I was growing up."

"So your parents let you hang out at the local bar and pool hall, did they?"

"Let me? My dad taught me to play. Back then there was a hamburger joint in the front half. After a burger, my dad and I would go to the back for a quick game. But only if it was early, before the real drinkers showed up. My mom pretended she never liked the idea, but that was just to tease my dad."

"Your parents must have gotten along well together?"

"They were lovers. Still held hands up until she died six years ago."

"That must have been hard on him."

"It was hard on all of us. I still miss her at times. I'm sure he misses her every day. Sometimes I think it's been hardest on my brother Dylan, though. He wasn't here when she passed away and he's never really forgiven himself. He still leaves lilies on her grave on a regular basis. That was her favorite flower and how my sister got her name."

"And Dylan's never been married?"

"No. He hasn't dated all that much. I've only known him to be close to one woman, and they're just friends."

"Who's the woman?"

"Her name's Julie. She's his best friend's wife, only she disappeared last year and no one's seen her since. Sebastian—that's his friend—hired Dylan to search for her, but as far as I know he hasn't turned up any leads. All they ever found of her was her car."

"Do they suspect foul play?"

"That's one of the unanswered questions. The police seem to think it was a car-jacking and that she was likely killed. But her body's never been found, and I'm sure that neither Sebastian nor Dylan will give up looking for her until it is."

"So, do both Dylan and Lily live on the ranch?"

"They do, but Lily and Cole built their own home. A terrific house. I'll give you a tour while we're at the ranch. In fact Lily would kill me if I didn't. She's so proud of the place."

"Still, your father must be one terrific guy to have two of his children move back home to be with him."

"Oh, he is. You'll find that out for yourself. But I think the real draw for Dylan and Lily is the ranch. It's a way of life that gets in some people's blood, as addictive as any drug. At least that's what my dad says."

"Obviously you never became addicted."

"Just the opposite. I went to school in New York and I became addicted to the Big Apple. Not the buildings particularly, and definitely not the winters, but the excitement, the pace of life, the feeling that something big is always about to happen. It's the place to be if you're a mover and a shaker in the advertising world. I expect to be there one day, in an office on Madison Avenue, a corner one with a window, twice as big as the one I have now."

Her whole demeanor changed with the topic, and he had the feeling she might break into a chorus of "New York, New York" at any moment. When she'd been talking about the ranch, she seemed calmer, on a steady keel. But just the mention of New York and she seemed to glow. He became aroused just watching her. Aroused and nervous at the same time.

"How much farther to the ranch?" he asked.

"Not ten minutes. You're not worried about meeting my family, are you?"

"No more than I'd be at meeting a third world firing squad."

"Come on, Kyle. You'll like them and they'll like you."

"Sure, until they figure out that I'm sleeping with you."

"They won't. How could they?"

A million ways. The way he'd look at her. The way she'd smile at him. A knowing glance that would pass between them. "Are you going to tell them about your stalker?" he asked, eager to change the subject.

"I wish you wouldn't use that word. It sounds so sinister."

"It is sinister. What term would you prefer?"

"An uninvited flower-bearing pervert."

"I'm sure that term would make your family feel a whole lot better about the situation."

"I'm not going to tell them."

"Why not? Your brother's an ex-cop. He can give you advice. He might even have friends on the San Antonio force you can talk to, especially since he's in the P.I. business. And your sister Lily is ex-FBI."

"She worked in the forensics lab. Besides, Lily is the reason I don't want to say anything yet."

"Because she's pregnant?"

"It seems a good reason to me. If I say anything to anyone, it will get back to her and she'll get all upset. She'll want me to commute to work from the ranch until the guy's caught, and when I refuse, she'll be put out with me. Dylan and Dad will start in on me, too. It's tough being the baby of the family."

"I'll just bet. Kind of like it's tough being a princess."

"I'm sorry. I'm sure it's much tougher having no family at all."

"I'll reserve judgment on that until I've spent the weekend with yours."

And that would be any minute. He could see the gate for the Double G up ahead. This would be a lot easier under other circumstances. Like if he knew whether or not Casey was his daughter. Or if he and Ashley had been together long enough to work out a few details of their relationship. Actually, one night of making love probably didn't qualify as a relationship, but the way he felt about her definitely did.

He couldn't see himself married or anything like that. But the great thing about Ashley was that she was no more the marrying kind than he was. Just two people who were dynamite together. The future would take care of itself.

He turned and stared at her profile. Perky breasts beneath a red sweater. Adorable nose. Pink, kissable lips. His body hardened and he wondered if it was going to be this way every time he looked at her from now on.

She pulled her red Lexus to a stop in front of the ranch gates.

"Shucks, ma'am, want me to get that gate for you? Then I'll mosey on up to the corral and get your horse saddled up for you."

She gave him a shove. "The gate operates automatically and you'd better stick with the city attorney image. You couldn't even fool the cows with that imitation of a cowboy."

But the only imitation he was worried about was playing the part of nonintimate friend and neighbor, when all he could think of was making love with Ashley again. In a pasture, in the hay, under her dad's roof. Anywhere that Ashley was would be perfect for him.

ASHLEY USED HER FOOT to keep the porch swing in motion while she belted out a Britney Spears tune. The hound that usually followed her dad everywhere had taken up residence on the top step. He wagged his tail and stared at her and Casey while he kept his eye on a couple of ducks that had wandered over from the pond. Not that he'd hurt the ducks, but he liked to play the role of protector and it didn't take a lot of energy to protect them from harmless fowl.

Casey joined in the song, adding a couple of well-placed

smacks of her lips and some mewing sounds. "So you like to get down a little. I thought you might. That song's got a lot more rhythm than 'Old McDonald Had a Farm.' But we could go out and see the horses on Old Will Garrett's ranch, if you like."

Casey puckered her sweet baby lips and started to fuss.

"Okay, no horses, but we do have to spend some time talking about beef cattle, or I won't have a job. How about a talking cow? Or one who sends e-mail? Or a baby dressed like a cowboy? Or a bull and cow making eyes at one another? Or Mr. McAllister getting kicked by a cow? That would work for me."

She'd looked over his file of ideas. They amounted to a couple of random thoughts and a poem he'd cut from a magazine. And, just for good measure, he threw in some pictures of his ranch. None of which did a thing for her creative processes. Neither had coming to the Double G, though she'd hoped it would stir her muse into action.

The screen door swung open and her dad stepped onto the porch, two glasses of lemonade in hand. It was late February, but the afternoon temperatures had climbed into the low seventies. Amazing, since a cold front was supposed to drop the temperatures into the midforties by morning. There was no accounting for South Texas weather.

"You look maternal." Her father tilted his head at an angle and studied her. "It looks good on you."

"Thanks—I think."

He took a seat in the porch rocker. "Dylan and Kyle have been in the Finders Keepers office a long time. I figure Dylan will know everything there is to know about Kyle and the woman he thinks might be Casey's mother before long."

"I told him Dylan would be thorough."

"Kyle seems like a nice guy, but I'm from the old

school. It's hard for me to imagine how a man and a woman could be close enough to have a child together and then lose touch completely in little over a year.''

''That's because you were lucky enough to fall in love once and stay in love.''

He grinned broadly. ''I recommend it.''

''Don't get any ideas, Dad. Just because I brought a guy home for the weekend and I'm sitting out here with a baby in my arms doesn't mean you should start planning a wedding.''

''Who said anything about a wedding?''

''You didn't have to say it. I can read your mind and the twinkle in your eyes.''

''I reckon I can wait until you're ready, especially since your sister is giving me a grandchild any day now.''

''And you need some practice. Do you want to hold Casey?''

''It's been a long time since I held one that size.''

''It's not that hard to hold her. It's the bathing and feeding and changing poopy diapers that's the challenge.''

He closed his eyes and grimaced. ''Now it's starting to come back to me.''

She stood, walked over and handed the baby to him. Casey puckered up again, as if she might start bawling, but he tickled her tummy, and she gave him a second chance. A second later he had her smiling.

His dog walked over and lay at his feet, no doubt making sure he wasn't being replaced. A baby. A weathered, white-haired rancher and a dog. She made a picture frame of her hands and centered the threesome as ideas rushed through her mind. Timelessness. The concept would require some work, but at least it had promise. She walked over and hugged her dad.

''What was that for?''

''Beef, as timeless as Texas. And for being you.''

KYLE DRUMMED HIS fingers on the top of the pine desk. "So you think I should only extend the search to Tessa Ortiz?"

"It's a lot more manageable than trying to find some phantom woman whom you know nothing about."

"And if we find Tessa and she's not the mother?"

"I can continue the search for the mystery woman, but if the baby's not yours, you'll have to give a full report to the authorities. You're legally and morally obligated. At that point, it's really up to them."

"I just hate to see her placed in a foster home."

"Sometimes it's a lot safer and healthier than the one the biological mother would have provided. And under these circumstances, it's possible they'd eventually allow Casey to be adopted. There are a lot of good families out there who'd love to make a place for her in their homes and hearts."

"You're probably right. She just seems so innocent and helpless. I can't bear to think she might grow up unloved."

"If she's yours, you can make sure that doesn't happen. Only the DNA testing will tell you that."

"Or finding Tessa. I'd like to give that a try first."

"Then I'll be happy to take the case. Don't count on any immediate results, though. It sounds as if you've covered the local bases."

"Just go ahead and give it your best shot. I'd pretty much made up my mind to give this another week. I'll extend that an extra week. If you don't find Tessa by then, I'll take Casey and go in for DNA testing. If she's mine, I'll probably want you to keep looking for Tessa. If not, we'll reassess the situation then, but I'll have to go back to work at that point."

"You've waited this long for the testing, I guess a dozen

or so more days won't hurt, but I wouldn't put it off any longer than that. You know more about legal hassles than I do, but it looks to me as if holding on to a baby that's not yours could be opening up a giant can of legal worms."

Kyle nodded. "Just let me know if you find out anything. You have my card."

Dylan assured him he would and waited until Kyle had walked away before slapping his hands behind his neck, leaning back in his swivel chair and propping his feet on his desk. Kyle Blackstone seemed like a nice guy, a little too cocky occasionally, but Dylan had been accused of that a few times himself. The guy needed help, and Dylan hoped he could come through for him. Not only for the man, but for the baby. And for Ashley. He had a feeling she was a lot more involved with this guy than she was letting on. Life was full of complications.

Kyle had a baby, only he didn't know if it was his. His ex-friend Sebastian had a baby he didn't know existed. The emergency beeper at his waist vibrated. Julie. She was the only one with that number. Something must be wrong or she'd have never contacted him. His hands shook as he dialed the number.

She answered the phone with just his name. "Dylan."

As always the voice reached deep inside him and wrapped around his heart. "Is something wrong?"

"I had a nightmare last night. I can't get it out of my mind."

Relief washed over him, leaving him weak. "It's only a bad dream, Julie. It can't hurt you."

"It was so real." Her voice cracked on the words. "Sebastian was here. He held a knife to my throat and told me he was going to kill me."

Her pain tore him apart. He wished he was there to hold her in his arms. He wished Sebastian had never been born.

He wished the world was different, but it wasn't. "He can't find you, Julie. No one knows you're in Cactus Creek. In fact he's in the Waco area right now looking for you there."

"How do you know that?"

"He called and asked me to go with him. I told him I couldn't, that Lily was about to deliver anytime, and I wanted to be here for the birth. It was a lie, but I just didn't want to spend the weekend with him, didn't want to pretend to be his friend when I'm so close to nailing him to the wall."

"He's going to find me here, Dylan. I know that he is. Waco's even closer to Cactus Creek than San Antonio is. He's going to kill me and take Thomas. My arms still ache from trying to hold on to him as Sebastian ripped him from me. I know it was a nightmare, but it seemed so real." She started to sob, and every muscle in Dylan's body tightened, screwing him into hard knots.

"Okay, Julie. There's a safe house in Boot Hill. I'm going to move you there. Just don't cry. Please, don't cry any more."

"I'll try. I can't let him have Thomas. I can't let my son grow up with a criminal for a father."

"He won't. As soon as I have enough evidence to put Sebastian away, I'll go to Zach Logan. He was my boss when I was working undercover inside the mob. He's still on top of things there, and he'll make sure Sebastian goes to jail."

"Thanks, Dylan. And hurry. Please hurry."

His insides were knocking around like trucks in a demolition derby by the time he hung up the phone. He was sure her fears were unfounded. It was only a nightmare, not a premonition. But he'd take no chances, not with the life of the woman he loved. And not with her child.

Knowing what he knew, he'd put nothing past Sebastian. The man he used to call his friend. It was a loss as bitter as bile, as permanent as death.

He hoped for much better for Ashley and Kyle and for little Casey.

THE MAN WALKED through the marketplace, past the band playing loud Mexican music, the women swaying in their tight jeans, past the people lined up to eat at La Margarita's. The smell of onions and peppers was nauseating to him tonight, and the sound of women's laughter and high-pitched voices crashed inside his head like cymbals.

Ashley Garrett was sleeping with Kyle Blackstone. He was certain of that now. Sleeping with him and tending to his bastard child. She had defiled herself and cheapened their love.

He felt betrayed, dirty, debased. She would pay. She'd be real sorry. But it would be too late.

Billions of lights exploded in his brain as he realized what he'd have to do.

No, he couldn't do that to Ashley. He'd go to her and give her one more chance. Just one. After that, it would all be over.

CHAPTER FIFTEEN

"RACE YOU to the corral." Ashley jumped from the bottom step and took off running, her boots kicking up dust along the well-worn path.

Kyle raced behind her. He felt amazingly free with no baby in his arms. Casey had already captivated William Garrett and he'd graciously volunteered to watch her while Ashley and Kyle took a late-afternoon horseback ride so she could show him parts of the ranch not accessible by road.

He caught up to her just as she reached the gate of the corral. Throwing his arms around her waist, he pulled her to him. "I'm not so out of shape I'd let a girl beat me."

She threw back her head. Her hair bounced around her cheeks and her eyes danced mischievously. "I'm not a girl. I'm a woman. I'd have thought you'd noticed by now."

"Why don't you refresh my memory?" He trailed a finger down her neck and outlined the rise of her breasts. "Or are there wranglers inside?" he asked, tilting his head toward the tack room.

"Yes. Several of them, all hiding and hoping we'll give them a show." She cupped her hands around his buttocks and squeezed. "Should we?"

"I love it when you talk dirty to me."

She kissed him on the mouth, a heart-stopping kind of kiss and then pushed away. He followed her through the gate. "Only three horses," he said. "From the way you talked, I expected dozens."

"There are dozens on the ranch. My dad loves horses, but they run free most of the time, or at least as free as they can be inside a horse pasture. These are likely the ones that were ridden today or were brought up to be ridden. The mahogany bay is mine. Isn't he a beauty?"

The bay pranced their way, head high as if he knew Ashley had a treat for him. She didn't disappoint him. She scratched his nose and fed him chunks of apple from her hand, purring sweet nothings into his big ears while she did.

"Hello, Eclipse. Have you missed me? I've missed you."

He neighed appreciatively and nuzzled her hair.

"Eclipse?"

"There was a partial eclipse the day I got him. It seemed fitting. Besides, he's the most spirited gelding at the Double G. He should have a name that represents something extraordinary."

"And which horse did you have in mind for me to ride?"

"Killer's a good choice. Or maybe Bucker over there?"

"I don't think so. Do you have one named Treat-Tenderfoot-Nicely?"

"You wimp. You do ride, don't you?"

"About as often as check I into a hospital."

"Hopefully the two aren't related."

"Only that I've done both of them exactly twice in my life."

"You're kidding, right? I thought everyone in Texas rode horses."

"But I didn't grow up in Texas, remember? I didn't ride until I started college, and then it was only because I fell for this blonde who was on the equestrian team."

"That figures. Did she dump you when she found out you couldn't ride?"

"No, but the horse did." He rubbed his backside. "Ah, yes, I remember it well. After that I spent a lot of time with a coed majoring in physical therapy, getting massages to ease my sore and bruised muscles, not to mention my pride."

"And let me guess, you liked the new blonde even better."

"Absolutely not. How fickle do you think I am? The physical therapy major was a redhead."

She ran her hands up his back, tapping her fingers along his spine. "Just wait until you have one of my massages. You'll forget there ever was a redhead."

"I already have." He turned and took both of her hands in his. "You do know I'm crazy about you?"

She looked away. He'd made her nervous, though he couldn't imagine why. Surely after the way they'd made love last night, she had to know he cared for her.

"Did I say something wrong?"

"No. I feel the same way about you. It's just so sudden that it frightens me a little."

"That's good to know, because it scares me to death. I like to play it cool, but I can't look at you without wanting to touch you. If I touch you, I want to kiss you. And if I kiss you..."

"Don't talk. Just kiss me now, Kyle." She wrapped her hands around his neck and touched his lips with hers. The embers inside him blazed into a full-blown fire. The hunger was overwhelming, the passion consuming.

When she finally pulled away, his lips were numb, the rest of him aching with a need he couldn't begin to fight. She led him into the tack room, and he followed without question. He doubted he'd get his aroused body on a horse at this point, but if Ashley wanted to ride, he'd give it his best shot.

The tack room was dark, with only a rectangle of light

in front of the open door. He scanned the area as his eyes adjusted to the dimness, taking in the array of saddles and bridles and reins. Surely she didn't expect him to know what to do with this stuff. He rested his hand on a saddle horn. "You'll have to help me here. What do you need?"

"You. I need you, Kyle." Her voice was breathy, seductive, silken threads that bound his lungs and stole his breath away.

He turned and saw her, perched on a bed of hay, one boot already off. Her green eyes were smoky with desire, her lips moist, her hands trembling as she tugged off the remaining boot. His throat grew so dry he couldn't swallow, and images stuck in his mind, surreal, as if time had stopped so they could become embedded into his brain.

The odors of leather and horseflesh, the neighing of a horse, a spider spinning a web above the doorway. Life. Simple, but potent. Ordinary, yet he felt as if he'd entered a realm of miracles.

He knelt beside her, knowing that this was different from last night, different from every other time he'd been with a woman. It wasn't the place or the time, or even the fact that they were at her family's ranch. But it was different. He was different and he didn't know why.

"Why are you looking at me like that?" she asked.

"Because you're beautiful. Because you take my breath away."

She pulled him down beside her and he took her in his arms. This time he undressed her slowly, though he needed help with the jeans. "Are these painted on?" he teased, "or were you melted and poured into them?"

"Don't tell me you're complaining."

"Only asking for a little help." She wiggled and pushed them over her hips. He tugged them the rest of the way off, his hands brushing her hips. "You look good in the jeans, but you look fantastic out of them."

When she was totally naked, she started on him, unbuttoning his shirt first and moving steadily down his body. His belt, his jeans, and finally his boxer shorts.

"What, no Spiderman pictures on your shorts?"

"I'm a *Mission Impossible* kind of guy."

"Looks possible to me."

She took his mouth with hers, kissing, nibbling, then parrying with her tongue as her body melded against his. His need for her was hard and heavy, but she forced him to take it slow and easy this time, to let his fingers learn all the places that made her writhe in pleasure. To let his mouth memorize the soft swell of her breasts, the pebbled flesh of her nipples, the smooth lines of her belly. To possess the moist triangle of heat and passionate energy that would make them one. She cried out over and over, and every time she did, he felt as if he'd conquered the world.

"I want you inside me, Kyle. I want all of you."

He raised himself on top of her and entered her slowly, thrusting inside, steadily building to a crescendo that seemed to split him in half until she rocked him home.

Neither of them said anything for long minutes after the climax had come and gone. They just held each other in the late-afternoon sun and let their bodies bask in the afterglow of a kind of lovemaking Kyle had never even known existed.

He almost whispered the words *I love you.* But he'd never said them before—not to anyone—and they wouldn't form on his lips. He wasn't really sure what love was like, but he'd always imagined it would feel warm and wonderful and totally right—the way he felt right now.

MONDAY, MARCH 4. Ashley noted the page on her calendar just before she turned it, readying her desk for Tuesday morning. The past week had to be the quickest one on record. It had been nine days since she and Kyle had

visited the Double G and he had made the decision to give
Dylan until this coming Friday to locate Tessa Ortiz.

Now there were only four days left, and Dylan had nothing concrete to report. It was the week's one disappoint-
ment

In every other way, it had been perfect. She'd spent
every evening and all day Sunday with Kyle and Casey.
She'd spent every night in his bed. Still in the honeymoon
phase, she kept reminding herself. Nothing could stay this
wonderful forever. They were intoxicated with each other,
couldn't even pass in the hall without touching.

And the lovemaking had been beyond anything she'd
ever imagined. Wild, yet tender. Savage in its intensity.
Evocative in its emotion. And no place in the apartment
had been left out. The bedroom. The living room. The
kitchen table. She still had a bruise on her behind from
that. And even the balcony. Actually, twice on the balcony
with the music drifting up from a party below them.

But the most amazing thing of all had been the way
Ashley had bonded with Casey. She'd never thought of
herself as having any maternal tendencies. She still was a
long way from being ready to take on a family of her own,
but Casey was so cuddly and sweet and she made the
cutest little cooing noises when she took her bottle. Every
night but one, she'd fallen asleep in Ashley's arms. Best
of all, the viral infection that had sent her fever soaring
had worn off completely in two days, leaving Casey in her
usual happy mood.

All in all, it had definitely been a week she'd never
forget, but she knew it was harder on Kyle. He was constantly torn, wondering if the baby was actually his daughter, afraid of having the sole responsibility of raising her
and at the same time hating the thought of her growing up
the way he had. He saw her future tangled with his own

past, and nothing Ashley could say seemed to alleviate his fears.

Kyle was not the man she'd thought him to be before she'd really gotten to know him. He was still incredibly sexy, witty and seductive. But he went a lot deeper than that. And, best of all, he seemed perfectly happy with her just the way she was. He didn't complain about her work schedule or her independence. And she didn't feel that his self-esteem was all wrapped up in being the boss in their relationship.

A vacuum cleaner hummed in the next room. She glanced at the clock over her door. Ten minutes before seven. If she didn't scoot out of here fast, she'd miss Casey's bathtime, and watching her splash and kick in the water was always a highlight of the day.

She shuffled through a file, pulled out a couple of pages of notes and tucked them into her briefcase. She had the strange feeling that someone was watching her. When she looked up, Mr. Clintock was standing in her doorway.

"You really shouldn't work late every night, Ashley. That young man you're dating is going to feel neglected."

"I'm packing my briefcase to leave. One more minute and you'd have missed me."

Delia's idea that he might be the man who'd delivered the flowers and stolen her underwear flitted across her mind. But she was sure Delia was wrong.

Besides, there had been no sign of her perverted stalker, as Kyle called him, since the night Ernie Brooks had found the flowers and red panties at her door. It was probably all a sick prank anyway, or someone getting back at her for some perceived slight. People were so moody these days.

"I won't keep you," he said. "I just wanted to tell you that Jim Bob McAllister called this afternoon."

"He's called me every day this week."

"He does like to keep on top of things, to the point of being obsessive. Today he just wanted to talk about you."

"Not complaining, I hope. He seemed pleased after our meeting last Monday and he hasn't found any major fault with anything I've discussed with him this week."

"He is pleased. In fact he's downright excited. I'm going to be honest and tell you that I didn't think you could handle him, but you've proven me wrong. He thinks you're the greatest thing since happy hour."

"He said that?"

"Not in those exact words, but the idea's the same. He's a hard man to please, and apparently you're doing that."

She beamed, inside and out. She'd spent countless hours working on the campaign, but apparently her efforts were paying off.

Her boss tugged at his tie and loosened the top button on his shirt. "As timeless as Texas. The concept should work on lots of levels. I'm looking forward to sitting in on your official presentation Friday. So don't pull anything like you did the other week. No baby emergencies, not with the Ranchers Association. This account is too important to us."

A compliment followed by a reprimand. So like Mr. Clintock. Definitely not stalker material. He had no hidden agenda. He let it all hang out.

"I'll be there, Mr. Clintock, with a presentation that will knock Jim Bob's socks off. Yours, too."

"Good."

"Just for the record, I rescheduled the meeting I missed. We held it Tuesday morning and it was a huge success. There was not one complaint about the cancelation or the project."

"And success is what this firm is about. I want to keep it that way."

He hung around a minute longer, trying to make small

talk, a feat he could never quite pull off with his employees. When he left, she collected a couple of folders, slid them into her briefcase and walked to her door, down the hall and out of her office. She'd almost made it to her car when her cellular phone rang. She grabbed it from her handbag and punched the Talk button, noticing as she did that the parking area was all but empty. Warily looking around her, she fitted the miniature phone to her ear. "I'm on my way, Kyle."

"Sorry, Ashley, but this isn't Kyle."

"Cole. What's up? Is Lily all right?"

"They're coming."

"They who?"

"The labor pains. We're going to have a baby."

She squealed at the top of her lungs, not that there was anyone to hear. "I'll meet you at the hospital. Tell Lily I'll be there. Ohmigosh, Cole, this is so exciting. I'm going to be an aunt. Lily is going to be a mother. You're going to be a father. Does she need anything? Is she in much pain? Make her hurry." She blabbered on until he cut her off.

But she blew her horn and hollered at a pedestrian as she exited the parking garage. "The baby's coming. I'm going to be an aunt."

KYLE STRETCHED OUT in one of the uncomfortable waiting room chairs. Ernie Brooks had been in the apartment when Ashley had called with the news that Lily had gone into labor and he'd offered to come and sit with Casey after Kyle had gotten her to bed.

Ashley crossed her legs and swung her foot. "Are you sure Casey's all right with Ernie?"

Kyle reached in his pocket and pulled out his cellular phone. "You can call him if you're worried, but he has my number and I told him to call if he needed anything at all.''

"I'm just thinking she might wake up, and if we're not there, she might be afraid.''

Dylan laid a hand on Ashley's shoulder. "Okay, tell me what you did with my sister when you confiscated her body? You know the goal-driven young professional who thinks children are best when they're somewhere else.''

She made a face at him. "We'll talk about this in a couple of weeks, after Lily's baby has you wrapped around her little finger.''

"Not me. I'm staying clear of her until she's housebroken. But I do wish she'd hurry up and make her premier appearance. I have to work tomorrow.''

William put down the magazine he'd been absently thumbing through. "If you want, I'll stick my head in and tell Lily we'd appreciate a little consideration out here.''

"You do,'' Dylan said, "and Cole might drag you in to coach the breathing.''

Kyle listened to the good-natured kidding and felt the old ache stirring inside him. As a young boy, he'd pretended he didn't care that he wasn't part of any family, but deep inside, he'd always known differently. As he grew older, he'd seen so many dysfunctional families, he'd decided that maybe he really was the lucky one. But the Garretts were different. Lily's baby would be a very lucky kid.

The judgment was still out on Casey. He was as uncomfortable leaving her tonight as Ashley was. But if Dylan didn't track down her mother soon, he'd be forced to turn her over to strangers altogether. He had no rights at all unless she was his daughter.

The door to the waiting room opened and Cole stuck his head inside, grinning like a kid with a three-dip ice-cream cone. "It's a girl! I'm a dad.'' His voice cracked and his eyes grew downright drippy as the three Garretts ganged up on him and buried him in hugs.

"Can we see her?"

"Is she healthy?"

"Does she look like Lily?"

The questions popped out like kernels of corn over a hot fire.

"Yes to all questions. You can see Miss Elizabeth Reilly Bishop as soon as she's cleaned up. You can see Lily now. I'd suggest you hurry. If you don't, she's going to crawl out of that bed and come looking for you. She's dying to share the good news."

Kyle stayed behind while the others rushed to visit the new mother. He wasn't part of the family—yet.

KYLE WAS STILL stretched out in his chair, watching *Frasier* reruns on the waiting room TV when Dylan returned. "You should have come in with us. Lily asked about you."

"It seemed like a time for family."

"It is a big moment when your twin sister gives birth for the very first time, especially when she'd sworn off men for good before she met Cole and reconsidered."

"I didn't realize you and Lily were twins."

"It's not the sort of thing that comes up in normal conversation."

"I guess not, but the two of you must be very close."

"Not as close as we were growing up, but at times like this, I realize how much she means to me." Dylan shuffled and ran his hands deep in his pockets.

Kyle pulled in his legs and sat up straight. "Why do I have the feeling there's something else on your mind?"

"I have news. I was just waiting until we were alone to break it to you."

"You found Tessa, didn't you?"

"I did."

"Where is she?"

"In Scotland, working for an American oil company."

Kyle's muscles tightened, and something hard and cold settled in his stomach. "And the verdict is?"

"She's not Casey's mother."

He felt hollow inside, empty, numb, everything but surprised. "So why did she just disappear?"

"I have a contact person in Aberdeen. He talked to her today and she told him she'd become depressed after the two of you broke up. She decided she needed a complete change in her life. So when she was offered this position, she saw it as a chance to start fresh."

"I'm not surprised. We were careful, always used protection."

"Well, now I'd suggest you go ahead with the DNA testing."

"There's not a lot of reason to at this point. I was in a relationship with Tessa during the time Casey would have been conceived. Contrary to popular opinion, I'm a real straight guy when I'm involved with a woman. I don't sleep around."

"Good. In that case I won't have to kill you."

Kyle expected he was only half joking. He was sure they all knew Ashley was spending her nights in his apartment.

"Now why don't you go in and see the newest addition to the Garrett household. We can talk about this later."

"Thanks, Dylan. Ashley was right. You really are good at what you do."

DYLAN WATCHED Kyle walk away. He couldn't help liking the man and he was convinced Ashley did, too, though he didn't think any man could rein her in at this point. But if Kyle was willing to give it a try, more power to him.

As for Dylan, all he needed to be happy was Julie. And

for the first time since he'd met her and fallen hopelessly in love, things were falling into place. Sebastian had made one mistake too many. A little more evidence and Dylan could put him away for good. And then Julie and her son could come home.

It couldn't happen soon enough, but he could wait.

In the meantime, he had his work. And he had a new niece. Life wasn't great yet, but it was getting better all the time, unless... No. He had to believe Julie would be safe once Sebastian was behind bars.

DAMN. This was ridiculous, Kyle told himself as he stood just outside the closed door of Lily's room. He should be relieved Casey wasn't his child, not feeling as if someone had just ripped his heart out. His career was just getting off the ground. This was not the time for him to be saddled with a baby. He didn't even have a wife.

The lecture did nothing to ease his pain. He could philosophize all he wanted but it didn't change the fact that the past week had been the happiest of his life. It was the first time he'd ever felt like part of a family, the first time he'd ever cared more about other people than he did himself.

He'd have to give up Casey, but not Ashley. He had the perfect solution. He just had to make sure the timing was right when he hit her with his plan.

CHAPTER SIXTEEN

"AND THAT'S THE STORY," Ashley said. She'd just filled Delia in on the details of the birth of Elizabeth Reilly Bishop and on Dylan's findings. "It was an eventful night."

"It's hard to understand a woman like Tessa."

"I told you. She's not the baby's mother."

"No, but she did just walk out of Kyle Blackstone's life. If it had been me, you'd have had to pull me away with a team of wild horses, or at the very least a couple of linebackers."

"Apparently she thought it was time to move on. I admire her for having the guts to do it. Look how many women we know just in this office who date guys long after the flame has turned stone-cold."

"I know, but we're talking about Kyle Blackstone here. The guy is gorgeous, likes babies, is gorgeous, has a good-paying position, is gorgeous, cooks, is gorgeous...."

"Hey, I get the point—and the feeling that you're trying to tell me something."

"I just hope that now that Casey's out of the picture, you're not going to crawl back into your plastic bubble that only work can penetrate."

"I was never in a bubble. I was busy, that's all."

"That's what I said. And you're avoiding my question."

"You didn't ask one." She put up her hand. "And don't, because I'm not sure what will happen at this point. I like Kyle a lot, maybe more than like him. If this was ten years from now, he might be the guy I'd be ready to settle down with.''

"But not now?"

"I'm not ready for permanence, but I don't think Kyle is either. He's on his way up with his firm and he seems to understand where I'm coming from. It's just that…''

"It's just you're afraid that if you get involved with him, it will complicate your life.''

Ashley exhaled sharply. "It always does. Everything starts out great, then it changes.''

"Boy, are you jaded.''

"I'm not jaded. I wish people would quit saying that. I'm just—in touch with my feelings.''

"That's a nineties term, and we're in the new millennium now. You know what I think, Ashley Garrett?''

"Is there any way short of a meteor crashing into the building and killing us all that would keep you from telling me?''

"Not even then. I think you're just afraid of your own emotions. You thrive on challenges in your job, but when it comes to anything personal, you take the easy way out. That's why the minute you start to care about a guy, you find some reason to run like crazy. Only this time, you could be making a big mistake.''

"Thank you, and I'm glad I'm not paying for your astute observations.''

"Just mark my words, you need to get over it. Take emotional risks. You might lose, but you just might walk away with happily-ever-after.''

"Is that all?''

"No, here's the first storyboard for your pitch to the Ranchers Association. We should have the other two ready by the end of the day tomorrow.''

Ashley looked over the storyboard. "The colors are great. You did a terrific job, as always.''

"That's what I'm here for, to make you account execs look good."

"Glad you know that." She set the board on the floor, carefully leaning it against the side of her desk.

Delia walked to the door, then stopped and turned back to Ashley. "Give Casey a goodbye hug for me."

"I'll do that."

One for Delia and a hundred for Ashley. A woman from Social Services was coming to pick the baby up in the morning. Something burned at the back of Ashley's lids. She blinked, but still a tear escaped and ran down her cheek. She pulled a tissue from the box on her desk and wiped it away. This was absolutely ludicrous. Kyle was doing the best thing for the little darling.

She turned to her computer and started typing in the outline of her pitch to McAllister as another tear started down her cheek.

KYLE SCAVENGED in the drawer for a clean spoon to stir the red sauce that had already bubbled over the side of the pan. The smell of burned sauce. That should make a great aphrodisiac. Tonight might prove to be the most important night of his life, and he wanted everything to go perfectly. So far, it held all the earmarks of a disaster.

He'd spent the morning at the clinic, having what was supposed to be a simple lab procedure. The DNA testing was originally scheduled for Friday, but he'd canceled it since there was no reason to go through with it. If the baby wasn't Tessa's, it wasn't his.

But the social worker handling the case had requested he have it done, so he'd taken Casey in for what they called a buccal swab. The procedure had been simple, a gentle swabbing of the inside of their cheeks. Casey hadn't even fussed.

What the technologist hadn't mentioned when setting up

the appointment was that they were going to be kept waiting for almost an hour before they were actually swabbed.

But that was only the beginning of his big day. On the way back to the apartment, he'd had to stop off at the market for groceries so that he could cook Ashley this wonderful meal of burned red sauce. Then he'd rushed home, fed Casey, tramped to the laundry room carrying her, her dirty clothes and her usual paraphernalia. He couldn't very well send her off forever with dirty clothes—in case it came to that.

Then came the crème de la crème of the day. In the middle of the rinse cycle—cool water for delicates, something new he'd learned from Mrs. Flarrity—Casey had decided to fill her diaper with runny, gross-smelling poop that leaked out from the edges of her diaper. Fortunately, Ernie's friend Mitch arrived on the scene at the same time and offered to finish Kyle's laundry and bring the clean clothes to him.

Now cute little sleepers, soft knit rompers and a couple of dainty dresses with ruffled bloomers were scattered over the couch waiting for Kyle to have time to fold them. Which might be never, since Casey had decided not to take an afternoon nap. Every time he tried to put her down, she fussed.

Casey. She'd turned his free-wheeling bachelor days into havoc. And still he couldn't stand to think that this would be her last day in his life.

Her last day. Unless—

No, he wasn't going to get his hopes up on that score.

The phone rang. It was here somewhere. He could hear it. He started throwing clothes and papers around. On the fifth ring, he yanked it from under the edge of the couch.

"Babies Are Us."

"Could I speak with Mr. Blackstone?"

"I'm Mr. Blackstone."

"This is Leah Carlisle. I'm calling with the results of the paternity testing."

"They told me it would be tomorrow at the earliest before you called."

"No, the results are in, and I thought you'd like to hear them."

She thought wrong, but he listened anyway. When he hung up the phone, he walked over, picked up Casey and hugged her tightly. The ball was now solidly in Ashley's court.

MITCH BARNES PACED the apartment he shared with Ernie Brooks. No matter how he tried, he couldn't get Kyle Blackstone off his mind. He'd noticed the man around the apartment building before this month, thought of him as little more than a young playboy.

Now all of a sudden the guy was distraught over having to give up a baby someone had just dropped at his doorstep—a baby that wasn't even his. Only if the baby wasn't his, why had someone said that it was? Had they left the baby at the wrong door, or had they been trying to fool Kyle into believing it was his? For whatever reason, it took quite a man to take in a deserted baby and care for it. He wondered if he would have been able to handle the situation nearly as well.

It could just as easily have been him that found the surprise package at his door. He knew a dark-haired beauty. Knew the way her slim hips swayed when she walked. Knew the way her eyes danced, the feel of her in his arms and the touch of her lips on his. Knew what it was like to make love to her over and over and still ache for more.

He pushed the tormenting memories aside. It had been only one night in Rio, a Mardi Gras celebration. Nothing more. It was just that he was feeling a little sorry for himself tonight. Once he was back on the job, he'd probably be fine.

Right now he needed to concentrate on Ashley Garrett's stalker situation. He had an idea the man was a lot more dangerous than Ashley wanted to believe. He showed all the signs of being seriously unstable, and if he wasn't stopped, this could turn really ugly, even deadly.

And Ashley Garrett was much too nice a lady to become a corpse.

IT'S NOW OR NEVER, Kyle decided, filling two goblets with an expensive cabernet sauvignon, purchased especially for the occasion. Casey was asleep. The spaghetti—which hadn't turned out half-bad—had been eaten, along with a salad and hot buttered bread, and the dishwasher was cranking merrily along.

So where was the confidence he usually felt in dealing with women?

Vanished. Instead, he could almost feel the awkwardness of adolescence invade his body. The kid from nowhere, the one who didn't have the right clothes, the right social skills. The kid who didn't have a car at all, not even one he could borrow from his old man. The same kind of life he might be about to hand to Casey.

Ashley seemed confident that Casey's mother would show up eventually and claim her. And if she didn't, the consensus of everyone who knew about the situation was that some young couple would eagerly take her into their home as foster parents and give her loving care until it was established whether or not she could be legally offered for adoption.

Only Kyle knew the story from the other side, and no matter what anyone said, he felt as if he were sacrificing Casey, an innocent baby who had nothing to do with the fact that she'd been deserted by the woman who should have loved her more than anything else in the world.

He took a deep breath, exhaled slowly, then picked up the two glasses of wine and walked into the living room. The lights were low, the fire was spitting and crackling in the fireplace, and a new CD of movie love songs was playing in the background. But there was no Ashley.

He set the glasses on the coffee table and walked to the door of the nursery. Ashley stood beside the crib. She didn't look up when he came in, though he was certain she heard his footsteps.

"She's sleeping peacefully," Ashley whispered as he stepped behind her and wrapped his arms about her waist. She pulled the lightweight blanket over Casey, tucking it around her, though they both knew she would kick it off again in no time.

"Do you think she'll miss us?" she said as they left the nursery and walked back to the living room.

"I'm sure of it, especially you. I know how I'd feel if you walked out of my life."

"You'd feel so distraught, you'd have to call one of your groupies from the health club to help you make it through the night," she teased.

"Do you think you'd be that easy to replace?"

"No, but you'd manage."

"Maybe, but I don't want to find out." He picked up the glasses of wine and placed one in her right hand.

"What shall we drink to?"

"We could always drink to beef," he said. "I hear it's as timeless as Texas."

"We'll drink to that when the campaign breaks in May. Tonight should be about Casey. May she always be loved." She clinked her glass against his.

"I'll drink to that."

"What time is the social worker coming to pick her up?"

"Ten-thirty. Unless"

"Unless what?"

He dropped to the easy chair and tugged her down into his lap. "Unless we change their mind for them."

She stared at him from beneath her long lashes. "Why would we do that?"

He summoned what little courage he could find. "Because I told them that we live together and that we might want to be Casey's foster parents until her mother shows up to care for her."

She stiffened and bounded from his lap. "You told them what?"

"Don't get bent out of shape. It was just an idea. I didn't lock us into anything."

"How could you do this, Kyle? How could you start planning my life for me without any consideration for what I want?"

"Look, I know I should have talked to you first, but it just hit me while I was on the phone with the social worker this afternoon. We can do it. We just have to hire someone to watch Casey during the day while we're at work. At night, we'll be here with her, the same way we've been for the last two weeks."

Ashley stared at him, absolutely stunned to hear these words coming out of his mouth. "You thought I'd just give up all my dreams and move in with you to be a live-in baby-sitter?"

"Not just a baby-sitter." He stood up and tried to take her in his arms.

She jerked away, suddenly feeling as if the whole world were falling in on top of her. It was painful to breathe, difficult to swallow.

"This isn't just about Casey, Ashley. It's about us. We're dynamite together. I don't have to tell you that."

She put her hands over her ears like one of the three monkeys whose statues were in every gift store. "I can't handle this, Kyle. Not living together. Not the responsibility for a baby. Probably not even the day-to-day problems of a man-woman relationship."

"You've been doing it."

"For two weeks, not indefinitely. I have to go, Kyle. I'll talk to you tomorrow, but right now I have to go."

He followed her to the door. He was talking, something about forgetting about living together, but she couldn't hear him over the alarms screaming in her mind. She crossed the hall to her own apartment.

A ridiculous bunch of daisies sat in front of her door with a note attached. She picked up the envelope, pulled out the note and shredded it into tiny pieces, then dropped them to the hall floor. Tears were blinding her now, and her stomach felt as if she'd swallowed rat poison. She kicked the daises as hard as she could and sent them flying down the hall like a floppy ball.

A minute later she fell facedown on her couch, a mass of body-racking sobs. She hurt as if someone had kicked her in the chest the way she had kicked the flowers. She didn't even want to think about why.

ASHLEY STRETCHED and her arms flailed off the couch. She forced her eyes open, then closed them again as the first rays of sun filtered through the linen drapes in blinding brightness. She must have eventually fallen asleep, though the last time she'd looked at the clock, it had been ten past three in the morning.

A pain shot up her back as she managed to get her legs over the side of the couch and plant her feet in the carpet. The couch was fine for sitting but definitely not for sleeping. She stumbled to the bathroom and stood in front of the mirror, staring at the dark blotches of mascara that ran from her eyes all the way down her cheeks.

"Too bad it's not Halloween. You'd be ready to go haunting," she said to her reflection. She opened a jar of cleansing cream, buried her fingers in it and dabbed the creamy concoction onto her face. The streaks of black disappeared as she tissued off the cream, but the telltale bags under her eyes continued to bulge. Delia would have a field day with questions.

Too bad Ashley wouldn't have any answers.

She bent over and clutched her stomach, thinking for a minute she was going to be sick, but the feeling passed and she went to the kitchen to start a pot of coffee.

Kyle was probably standing in his own kitchen right now, barefooted and bare chested, hair tousled, his jeans unbuttoned and riding low on his hips.

Her insides quaked, and her muscles went limp. She liked him—liked him way too much. But she couldn't just walk away from her own life. If he really understood her, he'd never ask her to. If he knew her, he'd know she could never give him what he wanted.

So, she'd get dressed, go to her office and somehow make it through the day.

NUMB. That was the only word to describe Kyle's feelings. He'd run the gamut last night. Anger. Hurt. Total disillusionment. He'd walked the floor, drunk bourbon and then switched to coffee when he realized he'd never be able to take care of Casey if she woke in the night and needed him. He hadn't slept at all, had never even undressed and gone to bed, which was just as well, since Casey had gotten up with the sun.

He pushed open the French doors and stepped onto the balcony. It was 10:20. Casey's bag was packed. Her formula and bottles, her clothes, her favorite toys. She was fed, bathed and already down for her morning nap, ready to go whenever Mrs. Cynthia Gavin arrived for her.

It would all be over soon. Just two weeks in his life. Casey had appeared one night, and now she was going to the authorities he should have called in the first place. Ashley was just another woman. He'd forget her like he had all the rest. Life would go on, and he'd be no different than he'd been before. And he was the biggest damn liar in the state of Texas.

CYNTHIA GAVIN WALKED down the hall of the eighth floor of the Prentiss Building, struggling to pull up her drooping panty hose without reaching under her skirt. Deciding it was an impossible task, she let them droop and knocked at the door of apartment 804.

Mornings like this, she hated being a social worker for Social Services. There would be miles of red tape and none of it would likely bring them any closer to finding the mother of this abandoned baby.

It was unfortunate Kyle Blackstone wasn't the father of the baby. He seemed like such a nice man on the phone and good father figures were difficult to come by in the world of abandoned babies.

She shuffled her feet and pushed her glasses up the bridge of her nose. She'd talked to Mr. Blackstone before she'd left the office and he'd said he was here and waiting, so why wasn't he coming to the door? Unless, of course, the doorbell wasn't working. She banged on the door this time. Still no answer, though a door across the hall creaked open and a middle-aged woman peered through the crack a second before pulling it shut again.

Cynthia turned the doorknob and the door eased open. "Mr. Blackstone? Are you in there?" She peeked inside. The French doors were open and a young man with very nice shoulders and a pretty spectacular backside was standing near the railing of the balcony. The sound of a jackhammer on the street below them cracked in her ears. No wonder the man couldn't hear her knock.

She walked toward him. "Mr. Blackstone."

He spun around, a look of surprise on his face.

She stuck out her hand. "I'm Cynthia Gavin. I knocked but you didn't hear me, and since the door was unlocked, I took the liberty of letting myself in."

"I didn't realize I'd left it unlocked, but with all of this noise, I guess it's a good thing I did. Kyle Blackstone," he said, taking her hand in his.

A nice warm handshake and he looked her square in the eye when he talked to her. She liked that in a man. Too bad his girlfriend hadn't wanted to become a foster parent. She glanced around. "May I see the baby?"

"Sure. She's asleep. She always takes a nap about this time. She usually wakes up around seven, takes a bottle, then she plays for a while. She likes to lie on the floor and play with the toys hanging from her floor gym. She's active. Strong, too. I wrote it all down for you."

"That's good. Knowing her routine will help."

"Just follow me. Her crib's in my guest room. Her bag, too. All packed and ready to go."

"I'm sorry it worked out the way it did. I have the feeling you would have made an excellent father."

He ignored her comment and led the way down the hall. She was only a step behind him when she saw the blood drain from his face and the muscles in his neck tighten into protruding cords. "What's wrong, Mr. Blackstone?"

"The crib—it's empty."

CHAPTER SEVENTEEN

ASHLEY MADE IT back home in record time. She'd swerved from one lane to another, honked her horn more times than she had since she'd bought the Lexus nearly a year ago, and run under a traffic light just as it changed from yellow to red. Her breath was coming in short, choppy gulps by the time she knocked on Kyle's door.

He swung it open and stared at her.

"Ernie Brooks called and told me what happened," she said, though he hadn't asked for an explanation. "I came as soon as I heard."

"I didn't think Clintock, Mitchum and O'Connell could operate without you."

"I might deserve that, Kyle, but save it until this is over. Please." She fought to keep her voice steady.

"You're right. I'm sorry. Come on in."

She touched his arm as she stepped around him. He didn't pull away, but neither did he take her in his arms or meet her gaze.

"I don't understand how this could happen, Kyle. How could Casey just disappear?"

"Apparently I left the front door unlocked when I picked up the paper this morning and someone just walked in and kidnapped her."

Ashley massaged a spot at each temple, trying to make sense of what he was saying. "No one would just walk into your apartment and take a baby. Not in the Prentiss Building."

"But they did. I put her down for her nap and walked out on the balcony. I couldn't have been out there ten minutes before the social worker showed up."

"But surely you would have heard someone if they'd walked in the door."

"They're doing repairs on the sidewalk that runs by the river. I didn't even hear Mrs. Gavin until she was almost on the balcony with me."

He paced the room, his muscles drawn so tight she could see the bulges through his cotton shirt. "The police are combing the apartment, knocking on every door to ask if anyone saw anything. I wanted to go with them, but they insisted I stay here in case someone tries to call."

She walked to the kitchen to start a fresh pot of coffee. The cool water spilled over her hands as she filled the pot with it. Water and grounds. Enough for six cups. She went through the motions while her mind struggled to accept the fact that someone had just walked into Kyle's apartment and taken Casey.

Dropped at his door, then stolen from her crib two weeks later. Dropped off and then taken back. That was it. She raced back to the living room. "It has to be Casey's mother who took her, Kyle. She must have found out somehow that you were turning her over to the authorities and she rescued her before you could."

"I thought about that, but she didn't take the doll."

"What does that have to do with anything?"

"The porcelain doll that she left in the laundry basket. I had it lying on top of the suitcase, but whoever took Casey just knocked the doll to the floor and took the bag."

"Maybe she couldn't carry everything."

"She left almost nothing the night she deserted her baby. Nothing but that damn doll. If it was that important, she would have taken it with her when she came back for her daughter."

She longed to go to him and crawl into his arms. She wanted to feel his strength wrap around her, wanted to offer the comfort of her touch, but it was clear he hadn't forgiven her outburst last night.

"Do you want me to leave, Kyle?"

Finally, he looked up and met her gaze. "I never *wanted* you to go. You walked out on me, remember."

He was hurt as well as angry. The proof was in his voice and the shrug of his shoulders. "You took me by surprise last night and I overreacted."

"Would your response have been any different if I hadn't surprised you?"

The question was fair, and she wouldn't lie to him. "Probably not, but I would have handled it better. Nothing's changed about the way I feel about you and Casey. I care about both of you."

"It's not your fault." He dropped to the sofa. "I was in one place. You were in another." He raked his fingers through his hair, brushing it straight back from his forehead. "If I hadn't let my past and the way I was raised affect my judgment, I'd have had the DNA testing done immediately. It would never have come down to this."

She eased to the couch beside him and placed a hand on his shoulder. "You tried to help an innocent baby. You can't take that and turn it into something bad, Kyle. Besides, Casey's with her mother. I believe that. I *have* to believe that."

"I hope you're right. Ernie doesn't necessarily agree with that theory, though."

"Ernie's retired FBI, Kyle. He's bound to think of all the worst scenarios. But there's never been any trouble in this building. It's one of the safest complexes in town. I know. Dylan checked out the crime stats before he and Dad moved me in."

"How can you say we've never had trouble in this

building when some kook has been leaving flowers and notes and even your own underwear at your door?''

And the man had returned last night. She wouldn't mention that to Kyle. He had enough on his mind right now. Still, he was hanging in there. He was like her dad in lots of ways. Dependable, a caregiver.

Last night she'd been sure that walking away from Kyle was the only real option she had. Walk away and forget the way they'd been together. Now she knew that she might walk away, but forgetting would be impossible.

"I made some coffee," she said. "Would you like a cup?"

"I'd love some."

She started to the kitchen, but before she reached it, Mitch Barnes walked through the door, a large brown envelope tucked under his arm.

He tossed the envelope onto the coffee table. "I found this at your door, Ashley. There were no flowers this time, just the note. You need to read it."

The look on his face and the edge to his voice told her that he already had.

She shook her head and backed away. "No, I don't want to read any more notes from that man, whoever he is."

"You have no choice. The man has Casey."

Her breath caught and her heart slammed into her chest. "You have to be mistaken, Mitch. Casey's with her mother."

Kyle snatched the envelope from the table, opened it and pulled out a printed note on a plain sheet of paper. He read out loud as the truth of Mitch's claim hammered its way into Ashley's brain.

"I warned you to stay away from Kyle Blackstone, but you wouldn't listen. Last night I gave you one last chance. I begged you not to let a cheap womanizer ruin your life and defile your body. Instead you tore my note to shreds and left it and the destroyed flowers for me to find. This time you went too far.

I have the baby that you and Kyle Blackstone have been using to play house. If you want her, you'll have to come and get her. I'll let you know the place and time.

Ashley fell to the couch beside him as he read. But this time he wrapped an arm about her shoulders and held her as bitter tears burned her eyelids and rolled down her cheeks.

She wasn't sure how long she stayed in Kyle's arms before she got up and walked toward the door. "I need to go to my apartment so that I'll be there when the man calls."

"I'm going with you, Ashley. Mitch, you find the investigating officer and send him to Ashley's apartment. I'll keep the note."

Kyle's voice was authoritative. She was glad someone was in control because she certainly wasn't.

Kyle took her hand and led her to her apartment. "We have to sit down and talk about this, Ashley. We have to find some way to identify this man. It's someone you know. We just have to figure out who."

But she had been trying to do that for more than two months with no success. She couldn't imagine how today would be any different.

ASHLEY WALKED through her apartment like a zombie the same way she'd been doing for the last three days. Forty-eight hours, and the horrible monster who'd taken Casey had still made no contact with them. No one had said it, but she knew that the longer Casey was missing, the less chance they had of finding her at all. The police were still insisting that they keep the kidnapping quiet. She'd called her office and told them she had the flu. She asked that they cancel all her appointments. She was in no shape to work.

Ernie and Kyle were in the kitchen, going over tiny bits of information, trying to see some pattern they hadn't seen in the last three days. The police were conducting the official investigation, but that didn't stop Ernie and Kyle from working on this every waking hour. And more often than not, Dylan was with them. He was downtown now, calling on favors from detective friends and running checks on the name of every man she could think of that she'd come in contact with over the last six months.

"Are you hungry?" Kyle asked when she stepped into the kitchen doorway. "Mitch brought some ham-and-cheese sandwiches by a few minutes ago. And I made a fresh pot of coffee."

"I can't eat. My stomach feels as if I just did a thousand stomach crunches."

Kyle put down his pencil, rubbed his eyes and stretched. "You know, that's not such a bad idea. You could probably use some exercise."

"You don't think worrying qualifies?"

"I'm certain it doesn't. Why don't you go to the health club and work out? You could call Bernie and get in one of your personal sessions. He's probably not busy in the middle of a weekday."

"No. I don't want to be away from the phone."

"You don't have to be. Take your cellular phone with you and transfer your home calls to that number. If you hear anything, you can call me on my cell phone."

Ernie shook his head and swallowed a bite of sandwich. "I don't think it's a good idea for Ashley to go out alone until this guy is arrested."

"She wouldn't have to," Kyle explained. "The health

club is just around the corner. I'll walk her over and meet her there when she's through.''

"In that case, I agree with Kyle. Exercise clears the mind. If you get that blood pumping, you might come up with something you've forgotten.''

"I still don't like the idea of leaving here." But admittedly she was going stir-crazy, sitting and waiting and worrying when there was nothing she could do but go over and over the same stuff for hours on end. Nothing in the man's notes had ever given a hint of who he was.

But a little exercise might help her get some sleep tonight. She'd hardly slept at all over the last two nights and her eyes were beginning to look like burned-out sockets. "Okay, guys. You talked me into it. Just give me a minute to grab my gym bag and I'll get out of your hair."

A COOL MARCH WIND slapped her in the face as they exited the apartment building. It was the first time she'd been outside since Casey had been abducted, other than to step onto her balcony. People passed her on the street. A kid rode by on a bicycle. As impossible as it seemed, outside her apartment, life went on as usual.

Kyle walked beside her, her gym bag slung over his left shoulder. They hadn't talked about their argument the other night, but she was sure it was as much on his mind as it was on hers. He'd been tender and thoughtful throughout the whole ordeal, but the tension from the argument still hung between them, like a thin veil that separated them while giving the illusion that they were close enough to touch.

The desire that had burned inside her last week was smothered under the stress of the situation, but her feelings for him were stronger than ever. Now when she touched him, it was for reassurance and to absorb some of his strength.

Nothing was ever quite as bad when he was around. She liked seeing him in her kitchen over her first cup of coffee in the morning. Liked his walking into her bedroom to tell her good-night. She even liked watching him eat.

In spite of everything, his appetite was ravenous. He could down two whole sandwiches in the time she nibbled on half of one. He was as worried about Casey as she was, but he handled it differently. It was as if he got tougher with the task. No wonder he had fared so well in spite of his background—or maybe he fared so well because of it.

He took her hands in his as they reached the door to the gym. "You have your phone and your workout clothes. Go get 'em, tiger. And leave the worrying to me for the next hour. I'm good at it."

"You're good at a lot of things."

"I'm learning." He smiled, a feeble attempt, but enough to ease the wrinkles in his forehead. "Do you want me to walk in with you?"

"No. I'll be fine."

"Be careful what you tell people. The police think it's best if we keep the kidnapping quiet."

"Don't worry. Even if the police didn't want it kept quiet, I'm not up to going through the details of the abduction. I just want Casey found, Kyle. And safe."

"That's what we all want." He squeezed her hand. "I'll be back to meet you in an hour. If you get ready to leave before that, just give me a call. Don't start out alone under any circumstances."

"Aye, aye, sir."

"I'm serious, Ashley. Ernie doesn't think it's safe and neither do I."

She reached up and kissed him. Just a peck, but it felt good and right. When this was over, she'd have to make decisions, but right now she was just thankful to have him near.

SHE LOOKED straight ahead of her as she walked to her locker and unlocked it, not wanting to risk making eye contact and having to stop and chat with someone she barely knew. Her locker smelled musty and she made a mental note to bring some Lysol spray the next time she came. She kept a set of workout clothes and a pair of shoes in the locker for those days she decided at the last minute to stop in on her way home from work. Today she only took the shoes as she'd brought a pair of running shorts and an oversized T-shirt from home.

Ten minutes into her workout, she spied Bernie in the corner of the room, watching her. She waved, but he either didn't see her or pretended he didn't. He walked over and started talking to a man who was huffing and puffing his way through a stair-climber routine. She finished her set of leg lifts, then left the machine to go and see if Bernie was available for a session. No use to waste all of her Christmas present.

"Hi, Bernie."

"Hello, Ashley."

He scanned the workout area, avoiding eye contact with her. Evidently he was upset that she'd missed so many appointments. She could understand it. She'd be downright irate if someone had blown off appointments with her the way she had with him.

"I'm sorry I haven't been in, but my life's been one catastrophe on top of another."

"Yeah. And I hear you've been helping out Kyle Blackstone with his surprise package."

His comment caught her off guard. "How do you know about that?"

"Are you kidding? It's the talk of the club. His groupies complain about his absence every night, and Alicia has convinced them all that you've taken their place in his heart."

Right. Alicia. She'd forgotten that the woman had been draped all over Kyle's body the night Casey had premiered. ''I have helped him out some, but actually the baby's not his.''

''Whatever.''

''Look, Bernie, I know it's short notice, but I was wondering if you could fit me in today.''

''You mean now?''

''If you could.''

He shook his head. ''I'm booked solid. Call me later, and we'll set up an appointment.''

''I will.''

He wasted no time in scurrying away. Usually she couldn't get rid of him even if she didn't have a session scheduled. Oh, well, if he was still mad, he'd just have to get over it. Or not—she had too much on her mind to worry about him.

After another twenty minutes, she gave it up. A quick stint in the steam room, then she'd shower and call Kyle to meet her. The locker room was totally empty when she stopped to store her shoes and pick up a clean towel from the supply in the corner. She fit her key into the lock, lifted up on the handle and yanked the door open.

Light from the overhead fixtures glinted off something in the front corner of the top shelf. She reached under the edge of the extra gym shorts and her fingers wrapped around the metal heart. It was one of the silver earrings Lily had given her for Christmas. Evidently it had come off one night when she was changing into her workout clothes.

She ran her hand under the shorts again. There was more. She pulled out a bracelet, one of her favorites. She hadn't even realized it was lost. She felt again, this time running her hand all the way to the back before she touched something silky. She retrieved the scrap of material. A pair of bikini panties. Black.

Earring, bracelet and black bikini panties. All items she could have easily lost at the health club, but how had they gotten in her locker?

Her skin felt clammy, as if something damp and gross were sliding over it. She slammed the locker door shut. Had the answers they'd been searching for been here at the health club the whole time? Was it someone from the club who was stalking her, who had taken Casey?

Without thinking, she ran from the locker room and out to the exercise area. Bernie was at the door that opened to the back alley. It was almost always locked, but it was open now and he was going out it.

She ran toward him. "Bernie. Wait. I have to talk to you."

He turned and saw her, then disappeared through the door. Heart pounding like a savage drum, she raced across the floor and pushed through the door after him. The alley was cluttered with Dumpsters and loose trash that had blown in from the street. A stack of boxes piled next to the building had fallen and were scattered across the area like a crude barrier. A black paneled van was parked between her and the corner, snuggled close to the building, barely leaving room for another vehicle to pass.

"Bernie." She called his name as she walked, her gaze scanning the area for any sign of him. She had no idea which way he'd run, but she had to talk to him. He was here all the time. If someone who worked here was stalking her, he'd know it.

Unless *he* was the stalker. Bernie. At her door. Writing her notes and bringing her flowers. Stealing her underwear for some reason she didn't even want to imagine. Her blood ran cold at the thought. She needed to get back inside and call Kyle and the police. They'd know what to do. They could handle this.

She started to turn back, but the stack of boxes to her left moved. A second later, Bernie's hand closed around her arm.

"We're going for a ride, Ashley. Just you and me."

She tried to jerk away, but a flash of stabbing pain stopped her.

"Don't make me use the knife again, Ashley. Next time it won't be a prick and bleeding to death is a slow, horrible way to die."

"What have you done with the baby?"

"She's safe. I have no quarrel with her. She was just a pawn in Kyle Blackstone's seduction games. Dangle a baby and the untouchable Ashley Garrett will jump into your bed."

"It's not like that, Bernie. I don't like Kyle at all. You know that. I just helped for the baby's sake. Please, just take me to Casey and I'll explain everything." She'd play this any way she had to, say whatever he wanted to hear, as long as she had a chance of saving the baby.

He threw her against the side of the van with such force that her brain seemed to rattle inside her head. Before she regained her balance, he was shoving her inside the back of the van. A second later she felt the sting of ropes as he bound her hands behind her back.

He was too strong to fight. She'd have to outsmart him. Outsmart him or wind up dead before she'd ever gotten to really live.

CHAPTER EIGHTEEN

KYLE PICKED UP his cell phone on the first ring. He was expecting Ashley's call, but this time it was Dylan. He could tell from the excitement in Dylan's voice that something was up.

"I ran a check on all the names Ashley gave me and something finally turned up. We could have our man."

"What did you find?"

"Grover Adams. He was arrested and tried in '97 for raping a college girl in Dallas. Found not guilty. In '99, he was arrested in Austin for roughing up a woman he worked with. He got off with a suspended sentence and was ordered to go to counseling for six months.

"The psychiatrist's report to the court states that he's becoming increasingly antisocial with delusions of such significance as to suggest a severe personality disorder that may lead to dangerous acts of aggression particularly against people he thinks have wronged him."

"Meaning he's a firecracker with a short fuse."

"You got it. The report goes on to say other things, but that's the bottom line."

"Grover Adams." Kyle tried to place the name and couldn't. "Is that someone Ashley works with at the ad agency?"

"No, and Grover Adams is his real name. He's going under an alias here. Bernie Thompson."

"Oh, my god! The guy from the health club. Ashley's there now." And he'd encouraged her to go.

"She's probably safe enough inside the health club. Get down there and get her, but don't give anything away. I need to get this information to the police. Hopefully, if this is our guy and he has Casey, they'll be able to trail him and find where he's keeping her."

"Thanks, Dylan. Ashley says you're the best in the business. You've made a believer of me."

"Just pray that baby is safe."

He'd never stopped doing that. Ten seconds later he was out the door and on his way. Bernie. There hadn't been any love lost between the two of them, but he would never have taken the guy for a psycho. He had noticed the way Bernie always seemed to be watching Ashley when she worked out, but that was because he'd usually been watching her, too. Watching her and plotting and scheming ways to get her to go out with him.

And that was before he'd fallen totally and hopelessly in love with her.

ASHLEY SAT IN the back of the paneled van, her hands tied behind her, a choking hand towel from the health club stuffed in her mouth. No way for her to make a scene so that someone passing by would notice. The only windows were in the front and the far back and she couldn't get to any of them.

They were on I-37 south, heading out of the downtown area. He stayed within the speed limit though cars zoomed by them, and he held the wheel with both hands and stared straight ahead, doing nothing to alert the police that he was a dangerous man. Ashley tried to plan, to think how she could escape when he finally stopped the car and opened the door. But first she had to find out where he was holding Casey.

Kyle would be at the health club by now. He'd be worried sick when he found she'd disappeared, but he wouldn't have a clue that she was with Bernie. He'd call Delia to see if she'd heard from her, and Delia would fly into a panic as well.

Her friend's words came back to haunt her in the dank hole of the van, the same way they'd come back to haunt her over and over during the last two days. *You're afraid of your own emotions. When it comes to anything personal, you take the easy way out. The minute you start to care about a guy, you find some reason to run like crazy.*

Bernie checked his rearview mirror as he pulled into the exit lane, then turned it so that he could see her face. "If it hadn't been for Kyle, we would have been together by now. You liked me. I knew it when you dropped the red panties one night as you left the health club. You wanted me to find them."

Her stomach turned inside out. The man was crazy, and she and Casey were both at his mercy. She tried once more to spit the towel from her mouth, but she only choked on the wads of terry cloth that had inched down her throat.

He threw his right arm along the back of the seat next to him, and she could see his hand form a fist and relax, over and over, the huge muscles in his arm bulging.

"I was your secret admirer," he taunted, "and I was very good at it. I stuffed the flowers and cards into a shopping bag, then dropped them at your door or onto the windshield of your car when no one was looking."

He started to laugh, the chilling cackle of a madman. Fear swelled inside her chest and hammered against her temples. She wanted to scream at him to stop laughing, but all she could do was sit and listen and pray that she and Casey got out of this alive.

Finally he stopped laughing. She could see his face in the rearview mirror. It had twisted into a shape as frightening as any Halloween mask she'd ever seen.

She had played right into his delusions without even

knowing it—had started going to him for private sessions. Even if she hadn't gotten involved with Kyle this would have eventually come to a head.

He turned down a street where small, older houses were crowded together and sat close to the road. He turned again, then slowed. "I treated you like a lady, but you went after the big-time attorney with the expensive suits and fancy car. Now you're going to pay. I have to kill you, but if you're very good and don't fight me when we get out of the van, I'll let you say goodbye to the baby."

He swerved into a driveway at the end of a dead-end street. The lot next to the house was overgrown with weeds. The perfect isolated place for a murder.

He stopped the car, came around the back and opened the door. Reaching inside, he stripped the cloth from her mouth and threw a dirty black coat over her shoulders. Now even if a neighbor happened to be looking out the window, they'd never see the ropes that bound her wrists.

"Just slide out, Ashley. Don't try anything or I'll bury the blade of this knife into your spinal cord."

But he planned to kill her anyway, so what difference would it make if he did it here in the driveway, where there was at least a chance someone would see him, or in the house? But she had Casey to think about. As long as Ashley was alive, she had a chance to save herself and an innocent baby who deserved so much better.

"Where's Casey?" Her voice was shaky and strained.

"The baby is inside."

"You left her all alone?"

"She's fine. I come home every few hours and feed her and play with her. I would never hurt a baby. You were just going to toss her away. I saved her."

"How did you know that?"

"Alicia tells me everything. She called Kyle to ask about the baby and he admitted it wasn't his and that he had to give it up. He would have eventually thrown you away, too. But you couldn't see that. I thought you were different, but you're just like the rest of the groupies.''

"Kyle didn't leave his door unlocked that day, did he?''

"No. Unlocking those doors is simple. Insert the right tool and the lock gives. I was even inside your apartment one night.''

He walked beside her, his hand under the flowing coat, the tip of the knife pricking her skin every time she hesitated. He opened the door to the house and pushed her inside. The first thing she heard was Casey, not crying but making the cute little baby noises that used to make Kyle laugh.

"She's in the bedroom. You can see her, but no funny stuff.''

Ashley hurried down the narrow hall. Casey's eyes lit up the second she saw her and she poked her pudgy arms out, wanting Ashley to pick her up.

"Please, Bernie. Untie my hands so that I can hold her.''

"Only for a minute, Ashley. That's all you have. I have to get back to work before they start looking for me.'' He took the knife and cut through the ropes. She stepped to the worn crib and picked up Casey, cuddling the baby against her chest, right over her pounding heart.

"I'm so glad to see you, sweetie. Your friend Bernie is taking good care of you. He's a nice man. He won't hurt you.''

"Your compliments are too late, Ashley.''

But she kept them up, cooing to Casey while she scanned the area, looking for anything that could be used as a weapon. A ceramic lamp sat on a table in the corner of the room. A picture with a glass frame hung on the wall. And an umbrella lay on the floor near the window.

"Okay, you've had your fun, Ashley. Put the baby down now. You've said your goodbyes.''

"You don't want to do this, Bernie. If you stab me they'll find the blood. It's easy to trace. You'll be arrested."

"There will be no blood. All I'm going to do is inject a lethal dose of tranquilizers into your bloodstream. Then I'll dump your body near the apartment building." He pulled a needle from his pocket and waved it in front of her. "We'll all be so sorry that you overdosed, but you have been under a lot of stress."

"What will you do with the baby?"

"I'll leave her somewhere where she'll be found."

She put Casey in her crib and backed slowly toward the lamp, never turning to look at it. Just grab and swing, before the needle plunged into her veins. Bernie stepped toward her, his muscles flexed, the needle in his right hand.

She lunged for the lamp, but he stuck out his foot and tripped her and she went sprawling across the floor, banging her head against the leg of the table.

"Ashley."

She heard Kyle calling her, but she knew he was nowhere around. She hadn't felt the needle, but Bernie must have injected her as she fell. She was already hallucinating.

Only if she was hallucinating, then Bernie was, too. His smug grin had been wiped away, replaced with a look of sheer panic. He pulled out his knife and pointed it toward the door, ready to strike the moment Kyle stepped inside. She sprang into action.

"He has a knife, Kyle."

Bernie turned to silence her, but her hands were already wrapped around the base of the lamp, and before he could stop her, she hammered it home.

Kyle rushed through the door and she stepped over Bernie's body and into his arms. "You're too late," she whispered. "You missed all the fun."

He groaned and rocked her against him, holding her like he might never let her go. "I'll make up for it later."

A big, burly police officer shoved past them, knelt and fastened a pair of handcuffs around Bernie's wrists. "Guess I'll wait until he comes to before I read him his rights."

"Good idea," Dylan said as he stepped through the doorway. Bernie was already squirming and holding his head, sliding back into consciousness.

She looked at him and smiled, but didn't move from Kyle's arms. "No one told me we were having a family reunion. I'd have dressed for the occasion."

"That's my little sister," Dylan told the cop. "You gotta love her."

"That's my woman," Kyle responded. "And I do."

CASEY WAS HOME, fast asleep in the crib in Kyle's spare room. They'd taken turns holding her and playing with her, smothering her with love until she'd fallen asleep in Ashley's arms.

Now the logs on the grate were blazing, the lights were low, and only a circle of red stain remained in the two crystal goblets that rested on the hearth. Ashley lay stretched out on the carpet in front of the fireplace, her head resting on one of the throw pillows from the couch. Kyle lay beside her, propped up on one elbow, his fingers tangling in her hair. A honeyed warmth crept inside her and wrapped around her heart.

"I never thought when this day started that it would end like this," she said.

Kyle traced a path with his index finger, from her earlobe, down her neck and across her shoulder. "All I know is that I've never been as afraid in all my life as I was when I walked in that health club today and couldn't find you. Then when someone said they saw you follow the now infamous Bernie out the backdoor and into the alley, I think my heart may have stopped beating altogether for a couple of seconds.''

''But not for long. You had to be hot on our trail in minutes.''

''Thanks to Dylan. If he hadn't called when he did, or if he hadn't had Bernie's address when I called back, you would have been on your own. Not that it would have mattered. You had the brute on the floor and knocked out cold when we arrived.''

''But he came to in a matter of seconds. I would never have had time to grab Casey and get of there alive before he attacked again. And once you're in his grasp, there is no getting away. The man is strong as an ox.''

''He should be. He works out for hours every day.''

She reached up and pushed a wayward lock of dark hair from his forehead. ''We make quite a team. Garrett and Blackstone. It has a nice ring to it.''

''I've been waiting for the right time to talk to you about that,'' he said, his voice low and enticing. ''I guess this is probably it. I know I handled it poorly the other night when I asked you—''

She touched a finger to his lips. ''You need to hear me out first.''

''You don't know what I'm about to say.''

''But I know what I have to say.'' She turned on her side so that she could face him as she bared her heart and soul for the first time in her adult life. ''I was wrong the other night—wrong about me and wrong about us. Delia nailed it on the head the other day when she said that I'm afraid to deal with my emotions.''

''I don't think you're afraid of anything, Ashley Garrett. Not after seeing you in action today.''

''No, I have been afraid. In spite of the warnings from you, Ernie Brooks and Mitch Barnes, I pretended that my stalker was harmless. As long as I did that, I didn't have to deal with him. Didn't have to deal with fear and the possibility that he was dangerous.''

"That's understandable. You've led a pretty sheltered life. You're the baby of the family and they all adore you. You've never had to deal with sick scum like Bernie.''

"But it's time I grew up, Kyle. It's time I quit running from anything that makes me deal with emotional issues. It's time I quit running from relationships and emotional attachments.''

"Which makes what I planned to say before I was so sweetly interrupted a lot easier.'' He took her hand in his and kissed the tips of her fingers. "You can run, Ashley. You can hide. You can move to New York or London or the North Pole, but I'm not letting you get away from me unless you can convince me that you really don't love me.''

"I couldn't even convince myself of that. So what do we do now?''

"I've thought about my original offer and I don't think it's such a good idea. Not only did it send you into a state of panic, but if we actually went through with it, it might send your dad and Dylan after me with that shotgun you talked about.''

"That cuts down our options.''

"It leaves the best one. I didn't say this right the other night. I made it sound as if I wanted you with me just so that I could keep Casey.''

"Wait! We can keep her, can't we? You said yourself that the woman from Social Services said they could get approval for us to care for her until her mother shows up.''

"She did, and we can, if that's what you want, too.''

"I do. I really do.''

"Great. But that's not why I want you with me.'' He took a deep breath and exhaled slowly. "I love you. I've never said that to a woman before. But I do love you, so much it hurts. So much I can't bear the thought of waking up in the morning to a life that doesn't have you in it.''

"And I love you, more than I ever thought possible.''

He swallowed hard. "So here's the question. Will you marry me?''

The panic hit again, balled in her stomach, squeezed her chest tight. Marry. A ring on her finger. Live with Kyle forever. Bear his children. See him every morning at breakfast. Crawl into bed beside him every night. Love him for the rest of her life.

"I know you have your dreams,'' he said. "I don't want to take them from you. All I'm asking is that you let me share them with you.''

Slowly the panic subsided. The real tragedy would be if she lost her chance at happily-ever-after. "My dreams have changed, Kyle, or maybe they've just come into focus for the first time in my life. The answer is yes.''

"Yes. You said yes? He jumped up and pulled her to her feet. "You're not kidding me, are you? I mean, I know we joke a lot, but this is no time to tease.''

"I'm not kidding. I can't wait to be your wife. Now kiss me quick and seal the deal so that I can call Lily and Dylan and Dad and the whole world.''

He swung her around the room in a frenzied dance, then picked her up and carried her to the bedroom, kissing her senseless as he went.

Her heart exploded with all the emotions she'd kept pent up inside her for so long. Lily and Dylan would have to wait a while longer for the news. But there was plenty of time.

For now and for always, Ashley Garrett was in love.

TRUEBLOOD TEXAS *continues*
next month with
RODEO DADDY
by B. J. Daniels

Chelsea Jensen was ten years wiser now. She hadn't known then that her powerful father had bribed her lover, Jack Shane, to leave her. She hadn't known Jack had been after her money, or that he'd been rustling her father's cattle. She wouldn't have believed it then. And she didn't now. She knew Jack loved her, and she was determined to get him back.

Here's a preview

CHAPTER ONE

"I WANT TO TAKE you up on your offer," Chelsea said, haughty as you please. It appeared at least one of them had gotten her beauty sleep last night.

His offer? Jack rubbed one aching temple as he tried to remember anything she might have taken as an "offer."

"One week in your world."

He stared at her. She had to be kidding. "That wasn't an offer, Chelsea. That—"

"—was a challenge," she corrected. "A challenge to a woman who's never been challenged, who's soft and spoiled and pampered beyond hope."

He winced. Damn but he regretted those words and he knew when he ate them, they'd go down harder than a bite of one of Terri Lyn's casseroles. "Look, about what I said, I'm sorry."

She put her hands on her hips and cocked her head at him.

"I was completely out of line," he said, hoping that would be the end of it—just as he'd hoped that would be the case yesterday.

"So you admit you were wrong about me lasting a week on the rodeo circuit?" she asked.

He narrowed his gaze, alerted by the edge to her voice, and no doubt hesitated just a little too long.

"That's what I thought," she said giving him a smile that chilled him to the bone. "Let's make it a wager."

"Now wait a minute—"

"Not money, since I have too much and you abhor even the thought," she said sarcastically. "I know! If I make a week on the circuit, then you have to admit you were wrong about me—and us." She raised a hand to silence him. "If I don't make the entire week, then I'll admit everything you said about me was dead-on and you'll never see me again. Deal?"

"Hell, no."

She raised a brow as if surprised he wouldn't go along with a deal like that. "You slandered me and now you owe me the right to prove you wrong," she said, that damned determination of hers burning in her eyes. "Unless you intend to go back on your word."

SILHOUETTE *Romance*

Escape to a place where a kiss is still a kiss...
Feel the breathless connection...
Fall in love as though it were
the very first time...
Experience the power of love!

Come to where favorite authors——such as
Diana Palmer, Stella Bagwell,
Marie Ferrarella and many more——
deliver heart-warming romance and genuine
emotion, time after time after time....

Silhouette Romance——
stories straight from the heart!

Silhouette®
Where love comes alive™

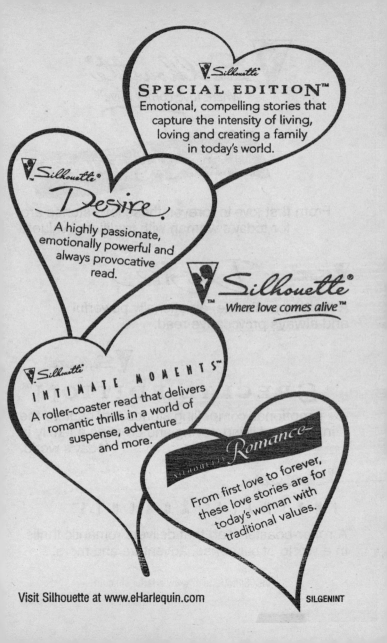

Silhouette

SPECIAL EDITION™
Emotional, compelling stories that capture the intensity of living, loving and creating a family in today's world.

Silhouette®

Desire
A highly passionate, emotionally powerful and always provocative read.

Silhouette®
Where love comes alive™

Silhouette

INTIMATE MOMENTS™
A roller-coaster read that delivers romantic thrills in a world of suspense, adventure and more.

Silhouette Romance
From first love to forever, these love stories are for today's woman with traditional values.

Where love comes alive™

From first love to forever, these love stories are
for today's woman with traditional values.

A highly passionate, emotionally powerful
and always provocative read.

SPECIAL EDITION™

Emotional, compelling stories that capture the
intensity of living, loving and creating a family in
today's world.

Silhouette

INTIMATE MOMENTS™

A roller-coaster read that delivers romantic thrills
in a world of suspense, adventure and more.

Visit Silhouette at www.eHarlequin.com

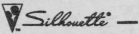

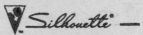